For Irina, who gave more
than she can ever get back

I've been dirt
And I don't care
Cause I'm burning inside
I'm just dreaming this life

— THE STOOGES

A MASQUE OF INFAMY

PROLOGUE

THE NASTY OH-DEAR

The ladies called it the Jackson Home.

"Nobody will be able to find y'all there," they said as we drove through the black part of town. "So you'll be safe."

The silver minivan pulled up to a run-down two-story house on a treeless street among dwellings of similar vintage. We stepped out of the air conditioning and the heat pushed against us like an unruly mob. The sun, directly above in a cloudless sky, beat down without restraint.

At the door, an elderly woman with kind eyes behind a sea of wrinkles greeted us.

"Boys, this is Mrs. Gertie," said Clorise, the one who had done most of the talking so far.

Joey and I mumbled a feeble hello and followed the ladies up a staircase.

"This here's the bedroom," Mrs. Gertie said. "And over yonder, the bathroom." She gestured at the obvious.

Joey and I walked into the bedroom but the ladies stopped short of the doorway.

"We'll check on y'all in a few days," Clorise announced. "So just sit tight and don't make no trouble for Mrs. Gertie, y'hear?"

"Don't worry, guys," the other lady said. Her name was Sandra. She was young and, compared to Clorise, a glamor queen. In the van, I'd watched her apply mascara in the visor mirror and longed to go home with her and watch her put on makeup for the rest of my life. "Everything's going to be alright. You'll look after your brother, won't you, Louis?"

I swore to do my best, though I would have promised her anything so she'd see me as a big man and not some stupid kid.

"Supper's at seven," Mrs. Gertie said. "You'll hear me holler when it's ready."

Joey and I listened to their voices fade down the stairs. Clorise and Sandra thanked the old woman for taking us in on such short notice.

When they picked us up that morning, the ladies had told us about the Jacksons, how they used to have a houseful of foster kids, but since they'd gotten old, the Department of Human Resources only used them for special cases.

Although we were relieved to be the only ones there at the time, when the front door closed with a thud and we were alone in the strange room in a strange house in a strange part of an already strange town, the stark reality of our new surroundings hit us like a Mack truck.

The room was dismal: two beds, a beat-up dresser, a small Zenith on a metal stand and above the TV, a portrait of Jesus.

"What a dump," I said.

"How long do we hafta stay here?" asked Joey.

I stood in front of the small window and looked out at nothing. "Beats me."

"This is a rip-off!"

I couldn't deny Joey's claim that we'd been shafted. The ladies said it was only temporary, but after five minutes in the Jackson Home, we were ready to bail on the whole plan. Besides the general shabbiness, the room smelled like a sewer.

"Did you just fart?" I asked Joey.

"No!"

"Then why does it stink?"

"I dunno. Maybe–"

"Psht!" I sliced the air with my hand. "Go see what's on TV."

Joey turned the knob and a burst of static squelched the silence.

"Fuck, it stinks!" I sat down on a bed and the mattress squealed in revolt. "Seriously, dude, you can tell me. I won't kick your ass for reeking up the place, but damn, own it, at least."

"I didn't do it!" Joey maintained adamantly as he flipped through the channels.

"Then who? It wasn't me." While I was fully aware of the theory that the one who smelt it was usually the one who dealt it, I was not shifting blame.

Joey continued to manipulate the TV. With each click of the dial there was more fuzz. Only three channels came through: *Family Feud*, *Donahue* and *As the World Turns*. Those were our options. But Joey kept switching channels, as if a program that wasn't there before would magically appear.

"Jesus Christ!" I shouted. "Enough already!"

"What do you wanna watch then?"

"Just pick one and get it over with."

"The *Feud*?"

"Survey says, why the fuck not." I was too distracted by the third occupant to care what we watched. I squeezed my nostrils shut. "It stinks like shit," I said, all nasally.

"It's pretty bad," Joey agreed.

"No, I mean it smells like shit. Poop. Crap. Caca. Shit!" I leapt to my feet. "Lemme see your shoes."

Joey lifted up his high-tops. I examined the scuffed and treadworn soles and found what looked like the remnants of gum, but nothing that would cause the offensive odor.

"We gotta do something," I said. "Help me find out where it's coming from."

For the rest of the afternoon, we circled the room and sniffed the air. We looked through the closet, the drawers of the dresser and under the dresser. We searched under the beds and behind the headboards. We lifted up the mattresses and tossed back the blankets and sheets. But nothing. Just lint and dust.

As the day wore on, it seemed like we'd never solve the mystery of the stench.

After a while, we took a break and watched an episode of the *Andy Griffith Show*. During a commercial, Joey went back to the dresser and said, "I think it's coming from around here. Maybe there's a dead rat or something in the... the...uhm, whatchamacallit? You know?"

"You know? You don't know what the fuck you're talking about. We already looked there."

"Well, it's worse here."

Reluctantly, I got up and took a whiff. Joey was right. The smell was more pungent around the dresser. I pulled out the empty drawers, peered behind the dresser and shoved it away from the wall. Just as I'd done before, but still nothing.

"I don't get it." I scratched my head. The stink was like a demonic entity from a horror movie. I stared at the dresser for several minutes and then let out a prolonged *Ooooooo*. "Why didn't I think of this before! Check it out."

I pulled out the drawers again, but this time I lifted them off the runners. There, in the dead space of the dresser, was the source of the foul smell: a pair of shit-stained tighty-whities.

"And we have a winner!" I proclaimed, as if I were Richard Dawson. "Looks like some dirty fucker done pooed his underoos."

"That's so gross." Joey wrinkled up his face. "Who craps their pants?"

"Who craps their pants and hides them in a dresser? That's the real fucking question." I rummaged through our stuff and retrieved a paper sack. "Here, use this."

Joey looked confused. "For what?"

"Don't be stupid. Pick them up with this and get rid of them." I stuck my hand into the sack and demonstrated. "Use it like a glove."

"But why me? I'm the one who figured out where they were."

"Exactly. Finders keepers."

"But... but..." Joey stammered and backed away.

I grabbed his shirt in my fist and glared menacingly. "You know the rules. Do what I say."

"Please don't make me!" Joey whined. He broke free from my clutches and collapsed on the bed in a fetal position.

"Ah, fuck it," I said with palpable disdain. "Be that

way. I gotta do everything myself."

With the sack over my hand, I took a deep breath and reached into the dresser. Carefully, I grabbed the waistband and extracted the underwear.

I held them at arm's length. "What should we do with these?" I asked Joey. "You want them?" I waved the poopy pants in his direction.

Joey screeched and tried to slide down the narrow space between the bed and the wall.

"No! No! No! No! No!"

"Fucking pussy!" I carried the foul undergarment to the bathroom and considered flushing it down the toilet, sack and all, but that would have surely backed up the line. And the garbage can wouldn't do either. So I opened the window and tossed the bag out. I scrubbed my hands with soap until I was sure the taint had been washed away.

Once I'd solved the mystery of the stench, it was Marlboro time. But I didn't have a pack. Didn't even know if smoking was allowed in this place. I kicked myself for not bringing it up with the ladies before they left. Several hours had passed since my last cigarette and the idea that I couldn't smoke only exacerbated my nic fit.

Back in the room, *Matlock* was on TV. I shuffled through the Hefty bag that held our clothes and what few possessions we'd been allowed to take from the house when they picked us up that morning. I had my Black Flag and Metallica tapes, but my Walkman was out of batteries. Besides a few changes of clothes, there was little else. I'd meant to bring a notebook or a magazine, but forgot them in the rush out the door. With nothing better to do, I reclined on the bed and stared at the TV screen. I tried to focus on the show but watched in dismay as every character on the screen seemed to be happily inhaling and exhaling billowy clouds of yen.

"Louis?"

Sometimes, the way Joey said my name really grated my nerves. "Now what?"

"What do you think Dad and Rick are gonna do when they get home?"

"Fuck am I supposed to know?" I snapped. The question had been gnawing at my guts as well, but the nicotine withdrawals were getting worse and I didn't want to think about that stuff. "We got more important things to worry about."

"Like when we're getting outa here?"

"That too."

"What did the ladies say again?"

"They have to talk to a judge or something."

"How long does it take until they talk to the judge?"

"Do I look like a lawyer to you? How am I supposed to know anything you don't? I'm here with you. You're here with me. We know the same shit, which is NOTHING!"

Joey burst into sobs, filtered mournfully through his pillow.

I felt a twinge of remorse. I didn't want to be there either. But I still had faith that everything would work out if we played our cards right.

"Stop fucking worrying so much," I said, my feeble attempt to sound reassuring. "This is only a minor setback. You'll see. We'll be on our way to golden in no time."

PART ONE

Sucks, Alabama

SLAPJACK

We were all over the map, the state of Texas spread out between us on the backseat of the Cadillac Cimarron like a topographical placemat, courtesy of the welcome center outside El Paso. The original plan was to keep track of all the cities and landmarks we passed through on our way from Los Angeles to Alabama, but the barren landscape on either side of the highway offered little distraction besides a steady stream of billboards advertising motels, gas prices and the enormous pecan rolls at Stuckey's. Even though this was the first time Joey and I had ever been outside the urban sprawl of southern California, we'd seen all there was to see.

When the journey first began, we were more than ready to embrace the unknown, rubbernecking across the deserts of California and Arizona, making faces at other drivers, counting license plates and playing tug-o-war with Misty Two, the springer spaniel puppy we'd picked up from a breeder in Carlsbad on the way out of town.

At every truckstop, we explored the fascinating hodgepodge of gimcrack wares and collected a variety of commemorative shot glasses and other souvenirs. But after two days confined to the car, we were dulled to the grandeur of the open road and just ready for the trip to end.

Bored, we played slapjack instead.

As I dealt the cards onto the heart of Texas with my right hand, my left hovered over the desultory pile, poised for the jack.

"Is this gonna be the one?"

I taunted Joey by flicking the edge of each card with my thumb, drawing out the process until he quivered with anticipation.

"Or maybe this is it…"

"Slapjack!" Joey shouted joyfully and hit the stack.

Not to be outdone, I slammed my hand down too.

Joey wailed from the impact. "Not so hard!"

"Don't be a wimp," I sneered. "It's called slapjack, not patjack."

"But it hurts."

"Crybaby." I laughed.

"No, I'm not!"

"Little pussy crybaby!"

"Hey!" Rick yelled over his shoulder. "Keep quiet back there! Your father's sleeping!"

In the rearview mirror, I snickered at Rick's menacing bucktoothed reflection. Half-Japanese and half-Mexican, his skin was dark, he had slanted eyes and front teeth that extended grotesquely over his bottom lip. He was always trying to boss me around, but I didn't take him seriously.

I leaned over and whispered in Joey's ear, "Pussy."

"He's calling me names again!" Joey tattled.

"I'm warning you," Rick seethed. "Knock it off!"

"Pussy, McPussy."

"Goddamn it!" the old man grumbled from the passenger seat. "Louis! Stop being an asshole!"

"I'm not doing shit!" I was quick to defend myself.

"Bullshit. Lay off your brother."

"Whatever." I picked up the cards. "How about we start a new game?" I squeezed the stack between my thumb and forefinger. The cards sprayed over the seat and onto the floorboard. "52-Card Pickup!"

While Joey scrambled to collect the deck, I put my headphones on. Anthrax blasted into my eardrums. Misty Two crawled onto my lap and we surveyed the infinite Texas prairie together. I lit a cigarette and cracked the window. The cold, moist air whipped against my face.

We were driving into a storm. That morning I'd watched the sun rise and continue its ascent across the clear winter sky, beating down against the passenger side of the car. But with so many miles behind us, the temperature had dropped and the sky had grown hazy. In the distance, monolithic clouds, fat with rain, loomed and a light drizzle pelted the windshield.

Although it was a drag to be trapped in the car for two solid days, with two more days to go until we reached our destination, I was intrigued by the change of scenery. I'd always been fascinated with geography. I had all the state capitals and major cities memorized, as well as bodies of water and other significant landmarks. When my grandparents sold their house and bought an RV to travel around the country, they sent me photos of all the state line markers and points of interest along the way. I'd paste these snapshots in my notebook with pertinent facts copied out of my mother's outdated encyclopedia set. I was a major nerd about it and had always longed to go out into the world and see it for myself. But now that it was before my eyes, I was mostly disappointed that there wasn't more to see.

As the rain began to fall steadier, I felt a warm sensation on my thigh. I looked down. There was a wet spot on my jeans.

"What the fuck!" I pushed the puppy away. "The fucking dog just fucking pissed all over me!"

Rick and the old man erupted in laughter while the puppy yapped proudly in the excitement.

"Don't laugh, you assholes," I bellowed. "This isn't fucking funny!"

"Serves you right." Rick guffawed.

"Motherfucking dog!"

"Calm down," the old man said with a raspy cackle. "It's just puppy piss. Puppy piss is as clean as tap water."

"We gotta pull over," I shouted hysterically. "Right! Fucking! Now!"

Rick was having a good laugh as he veered onto the shoulder. Before the car had even come to a complete stop, I flung the door open and waddled to the trunk. I pulled out my other pair of jeans and a fresh t-shirt. I leaned against the side of the car and changed while Joey walked Misty Two in the yellow scrub along the side of the interstate. The wind was blowing cold and the raindrops fell like missiles. When eighteen-wheelers roared past, the earth trembled under my feet.

"You better make sure that goddamn dog pisses out," I yelled, in between bouts of shivering fits.

Once we'd resumed our positions in the backseat,

Rick lit a cigarette with his Zippo, snapping it open dramatically between his fingers, and mumbled under his breath about how much time we were losing with all the distractions. He eased the car back onto the highway, accelerated to the speed limit and set the cruise control at sixty-five. Since we'd crossed into Texas, Rick had been going off about the legends of the Texas Rangers and didn't want to risk getting pulled over, especially with California plates.

Rick took all the fun out of the trip.

While driving through Arizona, I saw billboards advertising the Thing. "What is the Thing?" I wanted to know. After so many signs extolling the spectacle of the Thing, I was really curious. The Thing? The Thing? What is The Thing? "How can you not want to know what the Thing is?" I asked repeatedly. But despite my multiple requests, I never found out. "It's bullshit, that's what the Thing is," Rick said as he sped past the exit that led to the mind-boggling enigma.

During our third night on the road, I began to campaign for a motel room. It was almost impossible to sleep for more than a few hours in the moving car. And the billboards along the highway offered plenty of encouragement.

"$22.99," one sign advertised. "Or better yet, $19.99." I read them off, one after another. "That's a major deal," I pointed out when I saw a room for sixteen bucks and change.

Even though Rick was deadset on not stopping until we reached Mississippi, halfway through Texas, his endurance began to wane and the monotonous pitch-black night of the highway lulled him into a drowsy stupor. After he swerved into the passing lane and almost sideswiped a semi, the old man declared, "We're getting a room!"

We stopped at a Holiday Inn outside Dallas. Joey and I had never stayed in a hotel before. We flipped through the cable channels and ordered room service.

"I'm getting the club," I declared. So far on the trip I'd eaten grilled cheese sandwiches exclusively, but seeing as how they were only serving cold plates that late at night, I thought I'd try something different.

"I want a club too," said Joey.

"Copycat!"

"You can't have a club," Rick told him. "It's too much food. You'll never finish it."

"But I want what he's having."

"No. Pick something else."

I taunted him in song. "You can't get a club, cause you're too lame to be a member..."

"That's it," Rick said. "I'm sick of you picking on your brother. You can't get a club either."

"I can get whatever the hell I want," I said, my words steeped in indignation.

"I'm the adult and I said, No."

"Bullshit. You can't tell me what to do. You're only four years older than me. I don't hafta listen to you."

"Wanna bet?"

When the old man came out of the bathroom, I pleaded, "Dad, tell Rick to stop bossing me around. I want a club sandwich."

"Me too," Joey whined.

"Don't you start, Joey," Rick snapped. "Claude, you gotta tell Louis to start minding."

"Or what?" I challenged. "You gonna leave me on the side of the road?"

"I just might."

"For fuck's sake!" the old man shouted. "Everybody get what they want! I've had enough bitching and moaning for one day." He grabbed his field jacket and headed out the door. "I'm going for a six-pack."

"Wait for me," I said. I didn't want to be in the room with Rick while he was in one of his moods.

Later that night, as Joey watched TV on the bed next to Rick, I stood on the balcony outside smoking with the old man. In the chill of the desert night, our exhalations formed clouds above our heads like noxious think bubbles.

"Seems like we'll never get out of Texas," the old man said as he scratched his grizzled chin. In only three days, he almost had a full beard, mottled like dirty concrete.

"I can't believe we're so far away from home," I said.

"Rosemead's not your home anymore." He pitched his butt into the bushes below. "Alabama's your home now."

"If you say so," I snorted a cloud of visible contempt.

"Don't be such a sourpuss. You're gonna love Alabama."

"Yeah, right."

All I knew about the South was what I'd seen on TV, *The Dukes of Hazzard*, *Roots*, *Deliverance*... So that's what I expected: racist, good ole boys, playing banjos and speeding around the countryside in souped-up muscle cars, murdering and sodomizing strangers. Despite the old man's assurance that I shouldn't believe everything I saw on TV, my enthusiasm wavered from one moment to the next. But the truth was,

I was ready for a fresh start.

I wasn't leaving much behind in Rosemead. Just bad memories and the rest of my crazy family. I figured I could write my own ticket in a podunk Alabama town. Nobody needed to know that I was born in the crappy part of a crappy suburb on the wrong side of Hollywood. But while Rosemead was nothing like the Los Angeles depicted in movies and television, I looked totally LA. It was 1986. My style was an amalgam of punk and heavy metal. My hair was long and my pants were tight. My ears were pierced three times in my left and once in my right. I wore the same Iron Maiden shirt almost every day and never left the house without at least one bandana tied around my ankle.

How could I not ride into town and just take over?

Shit, in my mind, as soon as these bumpkins in Alabama got a look at me, the guys would idolize me, the girls would lust after me and all their parents would fear me.

I would finally become the person the audience in my head had always cheered for.

All the way across the country, as I sat in the backseat of my father's low-rent Cadillac, alternately picking fights with Joey, talking back to Rick and zoning out to the soothing sounds of heavy metal on my Walkman, I felt it in my gut, a rising excitement that everything was about to change.

For better or worse, once I fulfilled my destiny, the name Louis Baudrey would be synonymous with infamy.

TIMBER

We started the new year in Saks, a small community just north of Anniston near Fort McClellan, where the old man and Rick were supposed to report for duty in a few days. Before we left California, the old man had rented a three-bedroom brick house on the main road. I called dibs on the room with a window facing the street. The old man took the small, cell-like room in the back of the house while Rick and Joey shared the master bedroom.

When we moved in, the utilities hadn't been turned on yet and our furniture was still in transit, so we only had what we'd packed for the trip. We spent the first couple evenings huddled around the fireplace in the empty living room trying to stay warm.

The cold was shocking. Only the old man, who had grown up in Vermont, had ever experienced this kind of weather before. The rest of us had lived our entire lives in the moderate climate of southern California. Rick tried to act like it didn't faze him, but I saw him shivering too.

During the day, we explored the town and countryside. In the backseat of the car, Joey and I absorbed our new surroundings from behind glass. I knew Saks was going to be small, but I wasn't prepared for just how remote it was. We drove through abbreviated pockets of civilization scattered far and wide, separated by hills and long stretches of thick forests.

Trees, trees, trees… as far as the eye could see.

There were so many trees, they formed canopies over the roads.

When the woods gave way to farmland, we traveled through wide-open fields littered with bales of hay, tractors and dilapidated barns overwhelmed with kudzu. Along the highway were rows of mailboxes far from any visible house. Even though it seemed like we were in the middle of nowhere, we passed BBQ joints and other roadside establishments that sold everything from mufflers to hairdos to religion.

In Alabama, the churches resembled warehouses, with signs that announced sundry denominations: Assembly of God, Church of God, Church of Christ, New Home Missionary, Open Door Fellowship, First Congressional Methodist, Pentecostal Assembly Covenant Life Ministries…

I'd never seen so many crosses in my life. There were almost as many crosses as there were trees.

And white people. Everywhere we looked, in the other cars on the road, in stores and at restaurants, we saw more white people than we'd ever seen before in one place besides TV. No Mexicans. No Asians. Just Caucasians. And the occasional blacks. But what was even more bewildering was how excruciatingly friendly they all were. We were strangers in these parts, and yet, when we entered a place of business, we were greeted with the sing-song drawl of a welcome: "How y'all doing?" They sounded like extras from *Hee Haw*.

Not that our accents didn't stand out as well. All we had to do was open our mouths and we'd get, "Y'all not from around here, are you?"

No siree.

The main part of town, which was only slightly more congested than the countryside, was a four-lane highway lined with shopping centers and fast food restaurants. After noticing the lack of foot traffic, I figured out why: there were no pedestrians because there were no sidewalks to walk on. Just ditches on either side of the road. This was a huge disappointment to me. How was I supposed to get anywhere? Back in LA, my former stomping grounds were so ingrained in my memory, I could move through the streets and alleyways in my imagination without ever getting lost. I could count the number of houses on our street and name each occupant. The day my brothers and I realized we could go past the four block radius of our folks' bailiwick and we wouldn't fall off the face of the earth, we never looked back. We explored the depths of our neighborhood on foot and on bike. And if a destination was further than we could manage by tread of shoe or tire, there was always the RTD bus.

In Alabama, there were no buses on the road. Just big rigs among the pick-up trucks that outnumbered cars twofold.

Even the dirt was different. All my life I'd thought the universal color of dirt was brown.

But in Alabama, the ground was red.

Alabama... my new home. The differences were both intriguing and frightening.

The second night we were in the house, there was a major storm. The kind of storm that left castaways. Joey and I watched the weather through the windows, impressed that nature could cause such a ruckus. Lightning strikes illuminated the gesticulating landscape and the eruptions of thunder shook the house as if the gods were bowling for dollars. Rain and hail fell from the sky sideways. The pines hissed like serpents in the wind and the barren branches on the trees swayed and lurched like madmen. When the weaker branches fell onto the roof, they scratched against the shingles, creating a terrifying sound that made us think of Freddy Krueger's fingertips.

We went to sleep that night expecting to wake up to widespread carnage and destruction, but in the morning, when we looked outside, the landscape was a panorama in white.

"Snow!"

Joey and I put on our warmest clothes and ran out into the winter wonderland with the puppy yapping at our heels. Despite the chill that penetrated our bones through our light coats, we tried to make a snowman. The result was less than impressive. The white stuff that had collected on the ground was more slush than powder. Mixed with dirt and pine needles, our Frosty looked more like a fudgsicle that had been dropped in the grass.

That morning, the old man and Rick reported for duty at the fort. Joey and I were home alone. The electricity was still off and our stuff hadn't arrived yet. We sat around the cold hearth, talking about starting a fire. Since we had no money to buy a firelog at the Magic

Mart down the street, we decided to take matters into our own hands. I grabbed an ax left behind by the previous tenants and we walked around the backyard looking for an easy kill.

The cold stung our cheeks and chapped our lips, as it creeped deeper into our bones. The air was ripe with the smell of burning wood. Trails of smoke spiraled from the chimneys of our neighbors' houses.

Determined to get our own fire that would burn just as bright and warm, I surveyed the trees until I found a narrow pine. I patted the scabrous trunk and assumed the position of a homerun hitter. As I hefted the ax over my shoulder and swung furiously at the tree, the blade ricocheted off the bark with hardly a score. After several more unsuccessful whacks, I took off my coat. Cutting down a tree was a lot harder than I thought. I spat in my hands and rubbed them together, like I'd seen in the movies.

While Joey stood shivering, I tattooed the trunk with all my might until I finally managed to chisel a gash in the wood.

"I think this might do it," I told Joey. "Help me push it over."

Against our combined weight, the tree wobbled and swayed, but stood firm.

"Harder!" I shouted.

We kept pushing until the pine finally gave way. It snapped the branches off the surrounding trees as it fell to the earth with a pathetic thud.

"TIMBER!" we hollered like victorious hunters and stood over the spoils of our labor. Soon the chill returned and froze the beads of sweat on my forehead.

"C'mon, let's get this back to the house and start a

fire."

As we dragged the hewn tree back to the yard, a bearded man accosted us.

"What do y'all think you're doing?" he demanded.

Startled, we dropped the tree and stared at the man. It was clear he was pissed off about something. But what?

"We're just chopping down a tree," I said, matter-of-fact, with more than a tinge of pride.

"Those are my trees!" the man protested. "Y'all can't just cut down any tree y'all see."

"But there are so many," I said. "We only took one."

"That don't matter none. If I catch y'all cutting down my trees again, I'll tell your pa. Y'hear?"

I squinted at the funny-talking man, unsure if I could tell him to fuck off. How did he know who my "pa" was? He didn't know me and I didn't know him. I assumed he was crazy since he wasn't making much sense. How can you own a tree in a forest?

Still, I remembered that I'd promised to be on my best behavior in this new land, so I said, "Sorry, man."

Figuring my feeble apology would resolve the conflict, Joey and I resumed the task of pulling the tree across the yard.

The bearded man followed us. "What y'all doing with that tree anyway?"

"We're trying to make a fire," I said, annoyed with all his stupid questions.

"But that tree's still alive. It won't burn."

Joey and I looked at each other and shrugged. "Whatever, man." We began chopping off the branches that split easily from the trunk as the bearded man stood at a distance and watched us.

"What's his problem?" Joey asked.

"Fuck him. He's crazy."

We each carried an armful of wood inside the house and filled the fireplace. Joey shoved newspaper in between the logs and I set it ablaze with my lighter. The paper burned quickly but the branches didn't ignite. I grabbed Rick's lighter fluid and sprayed the pyre with gas. This time it burned longer, but the branches just smoldered and popped.

"Why won't it burn?" Joey asked.

"Fuck if I know," I said.

"Maybe that guy was right."

"Shut up and get some more newspaper."

When we finally gave up, there was nothing left to do but crawl into our sleeping bags and wait until the old man and Rick got home.

The next day, the power was finally on. Joey and I were eating cereal at the kitchen counter when he pointed out the window.

"Hey, isn't that the guy who told us not to cut down his trees?"

In the distance, I saw the bearded man walking towards our house. There was a woman with him.

"Holy shit!"

I ran to my room. With my ear against the door, I heard the yapping of the dog, then Joey yelled, "Somebody's here!" Rick and the old man came out of their rooms and welcomed the guests cordially. Then it got real quiet. I waited for a while until my curiosity got the better of me. Not sure if I was about to walk into a firing squad, I slowly made my way to the other side of the house. Everybody was in the living room. The crazy bearded man and the woman stood nodding their heads as the old man talked. Rick and Joey were by the fireplace. They all turned to face me when I entered the room.

"Oh, here's my other son, Louis," the old man said. "Louis, these are the Sheltons."

"Hiya," I mumbled.

"Three boys, they must keep you on your toes," Mrs. Shelton said.

I knew the old man introduced Rick as one of his sons. He always did. But the idea that Rick could be related to me in any way made me want to vomit.

"You know how boys are," the old man said in his two-packs-of-Kools-a-day rasp.

I avoided eye contact with the Sheltons and returned to my soggy frosted flakes in the kitchen. I noticed a small bundle of wood on the floor by the back door.

A few minutes later, the adults walked into the room.

"Well, if y'all need anything else, we're right next door," Mrs. Shelton said.

After the neighbors had departed, the old man sighed. "Our first encounter with the locals... I think that went well."

"They seem like nice people," said Rick.

"For hicks." I snickered.

Joey set a basket on the table. "They brought us cookies."

"Cookies?" They looked like Toll House, my favorite. I reached in to grab the largest one.

"Those aren't for you," Rick said sternly and slapped my hand away.

"Oh, c'mon! I'm hungry!"

"I said you can't have any."

"Why the hell not?"

"You should be getting your ass beat for cutting down the neighbor's trees."

"What was I supposed to do?" I wondered when they were going to bring up the tree. "We were freezing to death!" I pleaded in my defense.

"Stop your bellyaching," said the old man. "This ain't cold! You don't even know what real cold is! Why, when I was a kid…"

"Yeah, yeah, yeah… I've heard it all before. Back in the dinosaur ages you used to walk to school through ten feet of snow in your bare feet."

"Watch your mouth, buster," the old man said with a chuckle.

"Whatever you say, geezer." I snatched a cookie out of the basket.

"I said no cookies!" Rick slapped it out of my hand.

"I can have one if I want!" I reached for another but Rick pushed me against the wall. "Hey! Watch it!" I shouted.

"You better do what I say or…"

"Or what?" I looked at the old man, but when it came to my conflicts with Rick, he was Switzerland.

"You can't even behave for a second, can you?" Rick asked rhetorically. "Always starting trouble…"

"Man, fuck you!" I ran to my room and locked the door.

Rick pounded a few times until the old man told him to stop.

"Don't think you're getting away with this!" Rick yelled through the wood.

I spent the rest of the morning on the floor of my room, listening to my Walkman and writing in my notebook. I never went far without a spiral pad. I filled the pages with lyrics that I copied out of my stack of rock magazines. I even wrote some of my own. It was my dream to one day have a band. I already had a guitar, though it wasn't much: a black imitation Strat the old man bought me from Toys-R-Us that past Christmas. There was a speaker built into the body, but I removed it, covered the hole with electrical tape and plugged into a Kalamazoo amp. I made a royal racket. Unfortunately, that's all I could do, since I didn't really know how to make chords or even tune the damn thing. I just positioned my fingers on the fretboard based on pictures in magazines and went to town. I was supposed to have taken guitar lessons when I was around ten, but on the day of my first lesson, when we got to the place where the classes were to be held, they told us the building had burned down the day before. Disappointed, I fiddled around with my mom's acoustic until she got pissed off at me and broke it over my head.

But I wasn't going to let my lack of technical abilities slow me down. I saw no other future for myself beyond playing music.

Later that afternoon, Rick came to my room. He apologized for being so rough on me.

"I'm just trying to help you," he said earnestly. His

breath reeked of Budweiser. "You need a role model, and I'm trying to be that for you. Don't you understand? Now that we're in Alabama, it's important we become like a real family."

"Whatever."

"C'mon, I'm trying to be your friend." He held out three of the chocolate chip cookies. "You want some cookies?"

I reached for them but he pulled his hand back. "You know the deal."

I groaned. "What do I hafta do this time?"

"You up for a little endurance challenge?" Rick smiled and his buckteeth glistened in the overhead light.

That was the way it was with Rick. He never gave up anything for free. There was always a price to pay.

"Okay. What's it gonna be this time?"

"Let's see…" Rick contemplated the sky, finger on his chin. "What's it gonna be?" he asked himself with a menacing smirk. "The match game? That's always fun. What about an oldie but goodie, like an Indian burn? A couple titty twisters? Knuckle sandwich? Pin prick? Fanny pop?"

Rick had so many tricks up his sleeve he found it difficult sometimes to decide on just one.

"Oh, I got it. Here, stick out your hands like this."

Rick unsheathed his belt. Once I had my hands in position he brought the leather strap down.

It hurt like hell and I winced from the pain. "Oh, c'mon. Do you hafta hit so hard?"

"You want the cookies or not?" Rick laughed. "Just two more to go."

Since I'd already taken one lick, I suffered through

the second, which stung even more than the first. But it was the third lick that was always the worst, because it took the longest. As I writhed in anticipation, doubting my resolve, Rick held the belt high and psyched me out a few times, just to make things more interesting. With his face stretched in that sinister, bucktoothed grin, he said, "Pull away and no deal."

"Just get it over with already," I shouted. If I gave up before the third lick, I'd forfeit and get nothing for the previous two. I knew the deal well.

"I only dish out what I can take myself," Rick said and slapped his own palm with the belt. "Don't you want to be tough like me?"

Not really. I just wanted some fucking cookies. "Hurry up!"

"Then don't move." When he was good and ready, Rick unleashed the final blow.

Although my palms burned from the lashings, I scarfed the cookies and quickly forgot the pain. But once they were consumed, I was overcome with regret. Every time I fell for one of Rick's endurance challenges, I swore I'd never do it again. But he knew my weakness. Sugar had always been my downfall.

"Tastes better when you earn it, doesn't it?" Rick laughed as he walked out of my room.

THE NEIGHBORHOOD

Five days after we moved into the house, a cargo van was parked in front, blocking traffic on the narrow two-lane road. To expedite the process, we helped the movers carry the boxes and furniture. While I was walking back and forth, I noticed a tall kid standing along the edge of the Shelton property line monitoring our activity. He had a skateboard under his arm. With each trip from the van to my room, I glanced furtively in the guy's direction. Eventually, he walked over.

"Name's Casey Payne," he said. "I live across the street."

Casey looked to be the same age as me. He stood ramrod straight but his gangly limbs seemed to move against his will. A mess of blonde curls fell forward into his eyes. As he talked he pushed the unruly tuft to the side, but it immediately swung back into place. From his initial greeting, he talked a mile a minute.

"Y'all from California, huh? Welcome to Sucks, Alabama—the armpit of the universe. Hey, do you skate? All my favorite skaters are from California. This is a Gonzales." He held up the skateboard without pausing. "It's not mine. I'm just borrowing it from my friend

Brett. He's an awesome skater. He can do all kinds of tricks. Right now I'm saving up for a Powell-Peralta board. Say, y'all need any help?"

The old man and Rick were happy for the extra hand. Casey kept talking as he worked, bossing the movers around and making sure the boxes ended up in the proper rooms.

When our possessions had been transferred and the van departed, Casey hung out in my room, fiddling with my guitar while I rummaged through the boxes that covered the floor. It was a relief to have my things again.

"My dad's got a Martin acoustic," Casey told me as I sorted through my tape collection. "But I want a Les Paul." He hit a chord and bent the strings. "So I can really wail!"

"What kind of music are you into?" I asked, after I found my Suicidal Tendencies tape. "You like hardcore?"

"Yeah, I like all kinds of stuff."

"Here, check it out." I handed him my Walkman.

Casey put the headphones over his ears and I pressed play. The music came on with an immediate eruption of cacophonic screaming and dissonant guitar squeals. He flung the headphones off his head.

"What's wrong?" I asked. "That shit rocks."

"I just never heard that song before."

"You like Metallica? How about Anthrax?"

Casey stood up. "Yeah, maybe later. Say, you wanna see something cool?"

"Sure."

I followed Casey across the street and down a gravel driveway to a two-story pink house.

"That's where I live," he told me.

I laughed. "Dude, your house is pink!"

"My mom picked out that color," he said ruefully. "But that's not what I wanna show you. C'mon."

Casey led the way past a decayed fruit tree and a car covered with a blue tarp to a dilapidated shed.

"Follow me," he said.

We climbed up a wooden fence onto the roof. At the edge we looked out over a field.

"See that?" Casey pointed at a large figure standing in the weeds on four legs.

"Is that a horse?" I asked.

"That's Sir Bob," he said proudly. "Wanna ride him?"

"Okay."

We climbed down the side of the shed and slowly approached the large animal.

"Don't wanna spook him," Casey whispered. "He can get kinda ornery."

"He's not gonna bite, is he?"

"Nah," Casey said assuredly and patted the horse's flank, which was taller than me and almost as wide as a small car. He grasped the mane, mounted effortlessly and reached his hand down to help me up.

"Don't we need a saddle or something?" I asked, trying to sound like I had some idea of equestrian etiquette.

"He don't mind."

After we'd trotted around the field for a while, Casey yelped, "Hiyah! Giddy-up!" as if we were about to take off like the thoroughbreds at Santa Anita racetrack. But the horse just kept meandering at the same pace.

"Bet you never done nothing like this in LA!" Casey asked over his shoulder.

"Not even."

Over the next week, Casey showed up at the house almost every day, usually unannounced, to invite me on excursions across the countryside. He was always up to something, chasing after one adventure or another. I was happy to join him, since it got me out of the house. Sometimes Joey tagged along too, although Rick kept him on a short leash. He said I was a negative influence on my little brother. But I didn't mind not having him around, cramping my style.

When we weren't roaming over the hills and through the woods, Casey and I sat on the guardrail in the Magic Mart parking lot watching the customers come and go. He greeted most by name. Casey was the friendliest kid I'd ever met. He seemed to know everybody in Saks, even waving at cars that drove past on the road.

When he introduced me, Casey made sure to mention that I was from Los Angeles. I could tell he was looking to benefit from my exotic origins. I didn't mind, but the people I met seemed to regard my birthplace with disdain, and me with a level of sympathy for having come from someplace other than Alabama. I learned fast that anybody from outside the perimeter of the Mason-Dixon line was a Yankee. Which made me suspect.

Some of the locals didn't take too kindly to folks from California. A few were downright rude.

"That shithole ain't fell in the ocean yet?" this guy asked me one day as I stood in his garage contemplating the carcass of a deer hung by its feet from the rafters. Half its hide had already been pulled away from the red marbled flesh. The erstwhile noble beast looked like it was in the process of pulling a sweater over its head. Below the deer, three puppies gnawed and yapped frantically at the hide, chewing the small pieces of meat that clung to the inside of the skin.

I was horrified by the sight of the corpse, yet I couldn't look away.

"Is that a buck or a doe?" Casey asked the guy.

"Why? You looking for a girlfriend?" He snickered, as if he wouldn't bother to laugh at his own joke if it weren't so funny.

"I'm just asking," Casey said. "Jeez."

"You ask too many questions. Now beat it."

As we walked back to Casey's house, I flicked my cigarette butt into the field that was the guy's front yard.

"What an asshole," I said.

"Ah, he's always been like that."

We climbed a large oak in Casey's backyard and hung out in his partially constructed treehouse. He told me his father had built the floor and two walls several years back, but after a stroke, wasn't able to complete the rest. Roofless, the treehouse was exposed to the elements and the structure wobbled under our feet as we stepped on the creaky boards.

"I've been stockpiling lumber and one day I'm gonna finish it on my own," he said. "And then I'll be styling, boy!"

In anticipation of the glory that was to be, Casey had furnished his hangout with two wooden stools and a salvaged round table. As we sat on the makeshift furniture, we perused his small collection of *Thrasher* and *Circus* magazines which he kept hidden in a paint bucket because his mother was devout Church of Christ and did not approve of his pastimes.

"She thinks this is the devil's music," he said,

pointing at a picture of Mötley Crüe.

"Mötley Crüe isn't even that satanic. You should give her a Slayer album."

"No, she thinks all music is the devil's music. She doesn't even like me to skate. But I hide my board in my box springs. I have so many stash-spots. That way, when she snoops, she might find one thing, but not everything. I keep my best stuff up here, cause she's afraid to climb the ladder."

I'd never come across this kind of religious dogma firsthand before, though I knew about it from TV and movies. "It sucks your mom's like that."

"Your dad seems pretty cool though."

"Yeah, he's laid back. Rick tries to boss me around, but I just ignore him most of the time."

"Is Rick really gonna join the special forces?"

"Nah, that's just some bullshit he's always talking about. He's full of it."

"Is he your... Uhm, I mean…"

"Is he my real brother? No. Fuck no. He's just this guy from my old neighborhood. My dad's friend." I grabbed a magazine with Megadeth on the cover. "Man, when you get your Les Paul, we should start a band."

"Fuck yeah!" Casey said with gusto.

We high-fived.

"Man, I'm glad you guys showed up. Things were getting real boring around here."

THE NEW KID
IN TOWN

On my first day of school at Saks High, I spent all morning getting ready. I was sporting my coolest threads: a dark blue button-up over my Iron Maiden shirt. The ankles of my black jeans were pinned and tucked into my Nike high-tops. I had all my earrings dangling. I'd put mousse in my hair to give it some lift. But the *pièce de résistance* was a pewter bolo tie in the shape of a cow skull that I'd scored at a Native American gift shop in New Mexico.

I was rocking it hard.

Before we left the house, the old man tried to convince me to change my clothes.

"You shouldn't draw so much attention to yourself," he said. "In the South you need to be subtle."

But I didn't want to be subtle. I wanted to make myself known and wave my freak flag as high as possible… let these hicks know I meant business.

After the old man dropped me off in the parking lot, I went to the vice-principal's office to get my class schedule. On his desk, Mr. Griffin had spread out the transcripts from my two previous high schools. He did not look impressed. During my freshman year, my highest grade was a D, and I got expelled for cutting a kid in shop class. I thought I'd have to repeat ninth grade at the continuation school they sent me to after that, but miraculously, on the first day, they had me down as a tenth grader.

Mr. Griffin pointed out that schools in Alabama were not as liberal with promoting students, but he'd abide by the School Board of LA County and let me remain a sophomore. Then he informed me that semesters in Alabama started earlier than in California and, since I hadn't completed the first semester yet, I'd have to make up the credits in summer school.

Before I had a chance to absorb these ramifications, Mr. Griffin appointed a hall monitor to give me a tour of the campus.

A guy in a letterman jacket looked at my schedule and grudgingly showed me where my classrooms were. As we walked through the deserted hallways, he asked where I was from.

"Rose– I mean, LA."

"Where?"

"LA. You know, Los Angeles. The city. It's in California."

"You must be military," he said with palpable disdain.

After the half-hearted orientation, I went to my first period. The teacher made me stand up and introduce myself to the rest of the class. I examined the whitewashed faces that stared me down. I didn't see a lot of promise. But I kept an open mind.

In the crowded hallways between classes, all eyes were on me. I felt like a celebrity. But I played it cool.

Jeff Spicoli cool.

During algebra, a girl tapped my shoulder and handed me a note. "You the new guy from LA, right?" she'd written. "I'm Denise."

I turned and smiled. She was a rocker-looking chick in faded jeans and a t-shirt with long brown hair parted down the middle.

"Yeah. My name's Louis," I wrote back. "What's up?" Just as I had expected, word of my arrival had spread like wildfire.

"Awesome. You fry?"

I was surprised by her response. I'd been smoking pot for a couple years and had tried cocaine, but I'd never done acid before. Still, I was up for anything, so I replied, "Sure."

"Cool. Meet me in the parking lot after school."

The rest of the day, I was nervous about my first acid trip. I'd heard stories about kids tripping out and jumping off buildings, thinking they could fly, having religious experiences and joining cults. I'd just seen *Helter Skelter* a few months back. Acid was some freaky shit. But I reassured myself that I could handle anything. If acid is what they did in Alabama, then I was willing to go along. The old man said I should try to fit in...

After school I walked to the parking lot and found Denise next to a dark blue Skylark. She introduced me to the chubby guy behind the wheel, "This my brother, Dale."

"What's up, dude?" I climbed into the back.

Denise popped a Foreigner tape into the stereo and pulled out a joint. She got it going with the cigarette lighter from the dash and passed it to me.

"Say. You ever been in an earthquake?" she asked, her arm on the back of the seat.

"Once, but I slept through it." I took a small hit and passed the joint to Dale. I didn't want to get too stoned, figuring they were going to bust out the acid soon. "My sister woke me up after it was over and I was all like, 'Earthquake? What earthquake'?"

Denise laughed. "I bet you seen lots of movie stars in LA?"

I had not. I'd cruised Hollywood Boulevard, but in the madness of that scene, it didn't seem likely that Molly Ringwald or Eddie Murphy would be among the freaks and tourists who mobbed the sidewalks. But I figured the truth would only disappoint them. "Oh sure. All the time."

"Wow," Denise said. "And you musta gone to the beach a whole bunch too, right?"

"The beach is cool." That much was true. Except the ocean was thirty miles from my house and required a car, or a very long bus ride.

"I just love the beach," said Denise. "I've been to Florida twice. Do you know how to surf?"

"Yeah, I surf. But I prefer boogie boards." Only the latter was partially true.

She held the joint and licked her finger to stop a run. "Say, you want a blowback?"

"What's that?" Is this when they bust out the acid? I wondered, even more worried as the weed took effect.

"Shoot, you from California and I gotta learn you a blowback? It's easy. When I blow, you inhale." She put the joint in her mouth backwards and a stream of smoke came out the other end.

"Oh, in LA, we call that a shotgun." Just as I leaned in to take the hit, we approached a stop sign. Dale pressed the brakes and I bumped my lips against Denise's mouth.

Embarrassed, I choked on the smoke.

Denise didn't seem to notice. "LA must be so cool," she said effusively.

When they dropped me off that afternoon, I walked through the house quietly to avoid a stoned interaction with Rick. As I passed his room, I heard the blip and warbled chimes of Mario Brothers behind the closed door. I thought about how much fun it would be to play video games while high on pot. But the only way I could use his Nintendo or watch videos on his VCR was to participate in an endurance game. And I wasn't in the mood for that.

I found a snack in the kitchen and went to my room. I spent the rest of the afternoon on the bed, buzzed and ecstatic, watching the ceiling spin. Black Sabbath pulsated through my head from my headphones. I'd forgotten all about the acid, too preoccupied with the accidental lip bump, wondering if it counted as a kiss, which meant I could add another girl to my list of girls kissed for a grand total of four. I knew it was an accident—it's not like she kissed me back. But our lips had touched and we weren't related, so I figured, why not? The more the merrier.

My stoned repose was disrupted a few hours later when Rick banged on my door.

"Family meeting. Now."

I followed him into the living room. The old man was on the couch with a highball. Joey was seated next to him.

There was something in the air that shaved my buzz.

"What do you guys want?"

"Your father and I've been talking," Rick began. "There needs to be some changes around here. Now that we're in a new state…"

Before he could finish, I started laughing.

"You tell him then, Claude." Rick grabbed his Budweiser and sat on the arm of the couch. "Maybe he'll take it serious if you say it."

"You need to start minding Rick." The old man drained his glass and the ice cubes rattled. "That's an order."

"What the fuck are you talking about?"

"Just do what he says and don't make trouble."

"Fuck that! He thinks he's hot shit cause he's in the Army now. But I don't have to listen to what he says. He's only four years older than me." I incessantly pointed out this discrepancy in the household hierarchy, as if the logic of my argument would eventually sink in.

"I'm still your superior," Rick said. "And you have to obey my orders."

"Bull-fucking-shit. It's easy to boss around a little kid like Joey, but you can't make me do nothing."

"See, like that, right there," Rick snapped. "Claude, he can't be cussing all the time and acting disrespectful."

"Disrespectful?" I retorted. "To who? My dad? Who do you think taught me to talk this way?"

The old man chuckled. "He's got me on that one."

"Listen, Claude. This is serious. He needs to start showing respect. Not just to you, but to me and Joey as well."

"Then tell him your big plan already," the old man snapped.

Rick cleared his throat. "You want an allowance?"

I was dubious. "What do I hafta do for it?"

"We're going to set up a point system. Each week you get five dollars. But any time you cuss or act disrespectful you get a demerit. And with each demerit you lose part of the money. Too many demerits and you get nothing."

I laughed. "You gonna make a chart with my name on it and when I'm good I get a little gold star?"

"That's what I was thinking about."

"Fuck that! I don't want anything to do with your fucking point system. Give me money or don't. I don't care. But I ain't no monkey. I don't do tricks for handouts."

"Goddamn it, Claude! He just won't stop mouthing off. You gotta do something!"

"What can I do?" When the old man got flustered his voice got higher. "Take him over my knee? He's a little big for that now."

"Oooo, an asswhipping," I said in mock terror. "I'm so scared."

"If I whipped your ass, you'd be shitting blood," Rick sneered.

"Which would be assault and I'd hafta call the cops." I smacked my lips, self-satisfied. "I know my fucking rights. You may have Joey under your thumb, but I'm not going down easy. Guaranteed. So fuck you!"

Just as I turned to leave the room, Rick came after me with raised fists.

"Dad!" I recoiled and put up my dukes.

"Come on now!" the old man shouted.

Rick halted his attack. "Claude, I'm warning you... I'm sick of him acting like a spoiled brat all the time. How's he ever supposed to mind if he isn't punished?"

"You're not going to teach that kid shit, face it. He's as pig-headed as his damn mother."

"I'll get that boy in line if it's the last thing I do." Rick shoved me against the wall. "Come on, Joey!"

Joey leapt off the couch and followed Rick back to their room.

I looked at the old man. "Why does he hafta be such an asshole?"

"He means well. That's just the way he is."

"And this is the way that I am, and you know that!"

"Just try to get along," the old man sighed as he lit a Kool. "Can't you do that? For my sake, at least?"

"Whatever." I went to my room and strapped on my headphones. *Ride the Lightning*, full blast. I flipped through the pages of a *Hit Parader* with an intensity that threatened the integrity of the binding. I just didn't get it... I mean, why was the old man letting Rick call the shots? Did he really think I could just morph into a good little boy who took it like a man?

Fuck that.

———————

Over the next few weeks, Rick became the Disciplinator. Ordained and sanctioned by the old man, his word was law. He established the house rules and enforced them with extreme prejudice, like a drill instructor on a rampage. Any deviation from the schedule or shirking of responsibility warranted the loss of privilege. And under Rick's command, everything was a privilege.

But I was determined to undermine his authority any chance I could. And for my constant insubordination,

Rick took away the thing I loved the most: junk food.

The old man rarely bought snack foods at the grocery store, but when he did, Rick stored them in his footlocker. The only way I could satisfy my craving for the sweet and salty was to give in to an endurance challenge. But I was getting better at turning him down. I stayed resolute. And I refused to give him the pleasure of hearing me complain about it. I hung out in my room at night, listening to my Walkman and reading or writing out lyrics in my notebooks.

The rest of the time I was in school.

Each afternoon, I hitched a ride home with Denise and Dale. They helped me grasp the cultural differences of Saks High and taught me how to speak Southern. As it turned out, in Alabama, "getting fried" meant "getting stoned." They also explained that they weren't "giving me rides" home, they were "carrying me" home. When they pointed to something in the distance it wasn't "over there," is was "over yonder." And when we were about to take off, we were actually "fixing" to leave. The one that tripped me out the most, though, was that soda, regardless of the flavor or brand, was called Coke.

I caught on quickly, though I never intended to add these terms to my vocabulary. I was determined to maintain my LA attitude. Besides, if I had, I would've been putting on airs. And in a small town, they told me, there was nothing more deplorable than pretending to be something you're not.

The Revival

My primary objective that first week at Saks High was to find a quiet place to sneak a cigarette between classes. I kept an eye out for where other students were lighting up, but the kids who indulged in tobacco didn't smoke. They dipped.

According to Denise, dip was snuff. She told me how to spot the guys who dipped by the lump under their mouth. Either that or the empty Coke can they carried around to spit the brown juices into. There was also the telltale sign on the seat of their jeans: a faded circle in the exact shape of a Copenhagen can.

Since dipping was the norm, there weren't the usual groups of students milling about in haphazard smoking sections, like at my old schools. But I soon discovered that the restroom on the second floor of the main building was the perfect spot for a clandestine smoke break. The hallways were less crowded and the smoke drifted easily out a jalousie window near the end stall. Every chance I had, I wandered in there and puffed away.

One day, I was alone in the restroom, leaning against the tiled wall blowing my exhaust through the frosted window slats, when the door opened. I was about to toss the cigarette into the commode but I recognized the intruders from the hallways. There weren't many students at Saks who looked metal and these three guys were the stand-outs. I had spotted them on my second day and had been waiting for an opportunity to talk to them, thinking they might be open to a new member in their small clique. They were always chatting with girls and I wanted in on that action.

I stepped out of the stall and acknowledged them with a cigarette in my hand.

"What's up, dudes. I guess this is the place to smoke."

One of the guys was tall and lanky, with long stringy hair and a sabertooth tiger earring. He pulled a pack of Marlboro Lights from his pocket. "Long as you don't get caught." He held out his hand. "I'm Clint. You're the new guy from LA, right?" As he talked, the tooth dangling from his lobe bobbed against his cheek.

"Yeah. Louis."

Clint introduced me to the other guys.

"Nice to meet you."

"How you doing?"

Very formal, their handshakes firm.

Shannon had shoulder-length blonde hair parted down the middle and feathered. "Seen you around," he said as he took a cigarette from Clint.

The third guy, Tommy, nodded and kept his distance. He didn't look much like a rocker with his short hair, but he wore a studded bracelet around his wrist. Tommy was quiet while the other two did all the talking.

"So you're from LA, huh?" Clint brushed the hair off his shoulders and set the tooth in motion. "You ever hang out in Hollywood?"

"Sure, all the time. My band used to play the Roxy." I knew this would blow them away. Their reactions were a mixture of amazement and disbelief. "It's not really a big deal," I explained. "You just have to bring in enough friends and they let you play."

Since I was supplementing my new identity with the realities of past acquaintances, this whopper of a tale was based on an actual experience, when a guy in my social studies class gave me some two-drink-minimum tickets to his band's show at the Roxy. He was the drummer. It was all ages and, since soda qualified in the two-drink clause, there was no cover charge. I went with some friends. After the performance, the guitar player told us all the sordid details of the pay-to-play shows that were de rigueur in Hollywood at the time.

To validate my tale, I entertained my current audience with some of these trivialities. Once I'd finished, they seemed more convinced. Although I exaggerated my guitar skills, I only claimed to have been a rhythm guitarist. In case the opportunity to perform presented itself, I didn't want to look like I was completely full of shit.

The first bell rang and we ditched the smokes.

"You should come with us to the revival tonight," Clint suggested as we walked out of the restroom.

"Revival?" I asked. "What's that, like church?"

"Yeah, basically," Shannon said. "The sermon's gonna be about the evils of rock and roll. They want everybody to bring their records and tapes and throw them in a pile. And after everybody gets saved, they're gonna burn 'em in the parking lot."

"A bonfire of sin!" Clint giggled and his earring spun

around the side of his head.

"That's fucked up," I said.

"Yeah. We're going to protest."

"And maybe grab some tapes out of the pile," Clint said. "It's gonna be crazy!" Clint was obviously the hyper, overly enthusiastic member of the group. "Half the school's gonna get saved. It happens every time. You should come with and check it out."

This all sounded like great fun and I was eager to join in on their hijinks, but I thought about Rick. He wasn't likely to drive me. "I don't know if I can get a ride."

"You can come with us," Shannon offered.

"Awesome!"

That evening, Clint and Shannon picked me up. Tommy was behind the wheel of an Escort, Ozzy blasting from the stereo. While we drove the short distance to the church, I played air guitar and sang along to "Crazy Train."

At Saks First Baptist, the parking lot was full of kids. Cars were still pulling into the few empty spaces available. It seemed like the entire student body of Saks High was there. We loitered in front of the church, waiting for the doors to open, and talked to a group of chicks. Clint and Shannon were goofing off, cracking jokes and acting like they were having a jolly ole time.

"So this guy who's gonna be talking tonight," one of the girls said. "I heard he used to be a roadie for the Allman Brothers."

"I thought it was Lynyrd Skynyrd," said another girl.

"Skynyrd?" Shannon asked. "Really?"

"That's what they said in my youth group."

"Wow." Clint was impressed. "I thought he was just another preacher guy."

"No," the first girl said. "He's the real deal."

"This is gonna be great! I'm so excited!" the second girl enthused. "Y'all gonna stand up tonight? I know I am."

"I stand up at every revival," a third girl said. "I've been saved five times."

Just then, a guy with a military flattop walked out the door of the church and announced loudly, "Service in ten minutes." He looked barely past his high school years, hardly an authority figure, but he held the doors open and greeted the crowd like he owned the place.

Inside, the church was packed. Teenagers and young kids stood in the aisles talking in groups. We made our way past the throngs and found seats in a middle pew. Clint and Shannon continued to make wisecracks, pulling the tassels on the dress of a girl sitting in front of us.

"Clint Hanson!" she snapped. "You best stop messing around."

Another girl looked over her shoulder and glared at us like she was sucking on a Lemon Head.

Clint stuck his tongue out at the girls and whispered to me, "Christian girls are so stuck up. Bet they ain't like that in LA, right?"

"Oh, hell no," I said. "Everybody's laid back."

"You know why Baptists don't have sex standing up?" Shannon asked me.

I shrugged.

"Cause God might think they're dancing."

I laughed and turned around to survey the masses. Behind us were two guys I'd seen at school. Casey had pointed them out to me once. They were New Wavers.

One was Casey's friend, a skater. In a show of convivial exuberance, I leaned over my chair and introduced myself.

"What's up? I'm Louis."

Brett had an asymmetrical haircut. He had several pins on his coat: The Clash, Elvis Costello and a British flag. Vic was dressed all in black, with short, cropped hair combed forward in a widow's peak.

"You guys here to get saved?" I asked sarcastically.

"Not bloody likely." Vic smirked.

"Us either. We're here to protest." I nodded at my fellow conspirators. "Maybe score some tapes out of the deal too."

"Well, then you're in luck. Check it out." Brett pointed at the large pile of tapes, records, magazines and posters in front of the stage that grew larger as more kids came forward and offered their sacrifices. The clatter of plastic resonated over the din of voices.

"I wonder if there's anything good in there."

"Probably not," Vic said. "Nobody in this town has any taste."

After a few minutes, a man walked onto the stage with a wireless microphone and the room fell quiet. "How's everybody doing tonight?" His voice boomed through the speakers set up on either side of the stage. "Y'all happy to be here?"

The crowd roared enthusiastically.

"Great to see so many of you tonight…" He fiddled with the microphone and asked, "Is this thing on? Can y'all hear me?"

The crowd roared again, this time louder.

"Alright! We hope you enjoy Brother Donny's words as he shares his experiences with the Lord. So let's get started with a prayer." He bowed his head and started to pray.

The communal "amen" was like a cue. Immediately afterwards, a man ran onto the stage like a halfback taking the field. Dressed in blue jeans, a polo shirt, and white Nikes, he had long hair. A tattoo on his forearm was visible from our seats. I glanced at Clint and Shannon. They raised their eyebrows in surprise.

Donny smiled and lifted the microphone to his mouth. "Hello, brothers and sisters!"

The crowd erupted.

"Y'all ready to talk about the Glory of God?"

The crowd screamed again.

"No," Clint quipped.

We all cracked up, but the noise in the auditorium drowned out our laughter.

"Because I know I sure am!" Donny told the audience. "It's good to see all these young faces here tonight. It fills my heart with joy to know that so many of y'all are yearning to accept the Lord Jesus Christ into your lives."

A ripple of applause broke out, followed by a more earnest effort.

Donny waited until the crowd quieted down. "Friends, I want to tell y'all a story. It's not a pretty story, but it's true. It's a story about a very bad person. A man so afflicted with evil he had nothing but darkness in his heart and selfish thoughts on his mind."

He paused for effect.

"And, friends, that man was me."

A collective gasp filled the church.

As Donny let us absorb the full implications of his words, I leaned over and whispered to Clint, "Shocker!"

A blonde chick with barrettes holding her bangs back turned and scowled. I flashed her a smile. Clint and Shannon chuckled into their fists.

"I know a lot of you think that adults don't understand what's going on," Donny was saying on stage. "That's part of being young. I've been there. It wasn't so long ago that I was y'all's age. And believe me, when I was a young'un, I thought I knew it all. Nobody could tell me nothing 'bout nothing. No siree! I had it all figured out. When people tried to offer me guidance, I rebelled and went the other way. Sometimes just to spite 'em. You see, growing up, I had a chip on my shoulder. I thought I was different because I'd lost my mother when I was eight years old. I felt completely alone, certain that nobody could possibly understand what I was experiencing. I wasn't aware of it at the time, but deep down, I was angry and confused at the world for taking my mother away. I wanted to punish everybody in it. I wanted to punish myself. I asked God, 'Why would you do this to me?' But I didn't get an answer. So I turned my back on religion. I tried to make sense of it with my father, but he was too busy and wouldn't talk about it. So I turned my back on my father. Out in the world, I searched for ways to escape the pain I was feeling inside. I was lost and turned to the only thing I knew: rock and roll. At first, I thought I'd found something that could fill that hole inside me. I plastered my walls with posters of my idols. Every day I woke up and turned on the radio. I believed all the stories I heard in the songs: the drinking and running around. Oh yeah, I bought it all. Hook, line and sinker. Rock and roll became my new religion. I went to concerts every chance I could. I grew my hair long and started smoking marijuana. Everybody was doing it, right?"

Clint elbowed me in the ribs and said, "Try it, you'll like it." While I chuckled, he repeated the comment to Shannon, who smiled.

"For most of my friends, it was no big deal. All part of being a teenager. Except I thought I was different. I wasn't satisfied with just listening to the music. I wanted more. I wanted to prove how special I was, that I was different from everybody else. My father, he didn't approve of my activities. Once, when I stayed out past curfew, he shaved my head. He cut off the one thing that made me unique... that made me who I was. I was so mad I ran away from home. I was fifteen. I didn't know where else to go, so I joined the circus. I'd always been hanging around at concerts, trying to talk to the musicians. So I did what made sense to me. I got a job working for a band. It was a wild ride. I was traveling all over the country, convinced that I was having the time of my life. We had all the vices covered: women, alcohol, drugs, and lots and lots of rock and roll. Every night we worshiped at the altar of rock and roll. I thought I was happy and living out my dreams. But what I didn't realize was that I was living a nightmare."

Donny stopped, holding the microphone next to his mouth, his breath like a heartbeat over the silent crowd. His voice was a whisper. At this point, we were all listening to his words as if it were the greatest story ever told.

"Eventually, my life started to unravel. I was sinking into a bottomless pit of sorrow. I was at the bottom. I had nothing. I was so alone and empty, I didn't have a clue who I was or why I was put on this earth anymore. I thought the music would fill that hole inside me. I thought the drugs would dull the pain. But I was still hurting. I was still confused. There was no love in my heart anymore, just hatred and misery. The path I was on only led me to nothingness. I didn't know what to do anymore.

"But then one day I opened my eyes. And I saw the pain all around me. I saw myself and the people I called friends as we really were: lost and confused souls adrift in a sea of agony. Around this time, as if by Divine Grace, I met somebody who talked to me about the Teachings of Jesus Christ. At first, I wasn't interested. But in the haze of my despair, this man's words glistened like a light in the fog. Even though I didn't think Jesus could offer me anything anymore, I went with my new friend to a church. I walked through the doors and sat down, just like y'all doing right now. And I listened to what the preacher up there was saying. It didn't make a lot of sense to me at the time, but the next Sunday I went back. And the Sunday after that. I just kept going back until I began to feel the Love of Jesus Christ entering my body. Slowly, but surely, as I let the Word of Jesus back into my heart, the power of His Love began to heal me. And then I saw the truth! I realized that everything I had been doing, all those things that had led me down this road to evil, it was all the work of Satan! I had been a soldier in Satan's Army!"

Donny stopped and looked out over the audience. "Friends, that was the day I turned my back on it all. I turned my back on the life of sin. I went towards the Light and, for the first time in my life, I felt like the richest man in the universe. I felt higher than I'd ever felt from any drug I'd ever taken. I felt more inspired by the Word of God than I had by any song I'd ever heard.

And then I received the greatest gift I could have ever asked for. After He saved me from my own despair, Jesus came to me and said, 'Donny, I got a job for you. Go out there, do what you've been doing, but do it for ME. Do it for God. Teach My Word so that others can learn from your mistakes.'"

Donny paused as a few contagious handclaps in the audience erupted into joyous applause.

"From that day forward, friends, I became a soldier in God's Army."

"Glory to God!" somebody in the congregation shouted.

A "Praise the Lord!" came from the other side of the church.

There was a "Hallelujah!" behind us.

Now that he was really going to town, Donny paced like a caged animal as he spoke into the microphone.

"Friends, we're all imperfect creatures, us humans. We're blessed with conscious thought, but in our curiosity we are also arrogant. Especially when we're young. In the world today there are so many options and decisions to make, but with all these choices, how do we decide what will bring the most Glory to God? Because that is the point of our existence, right? We were put on this earth to serve God and live in His image and bring Him Glory. But sometimes that's not easy. It can be a challenge to seek salvation in the Lord. Every day we are faced with obstacles. The influence of Satan is strong. Our minds are fragile and easily influenced. Around every corner there is temptation.

"Temptation!"

He said the word again, slower, "Temptation."

"Did he just say 'temptation'?" I asked Clint with

mock confusion. But he shushed me. Clint, Shannon, and Tommy were all leaned forward, paying close attention to what Donny was saying. I blanched. Had I gone too far? I decided to play it cool.

"Friends, there is a war going on! A war for souls! On one side is God. And on the other, Satan. We have to decide which side of the war we are on. Sure, the answer would seem easy. One offers Truth, Beauty and the Promise of Eternal Life. The other eternal pain and suffering. Simple, right? Yet we struggle to make up our minds. Why? Why is this so difficult?

"Temptation, folks. Temptation.

"It's everywhere. No matter what you think, the facts are clear: Satan loves rock and roll.

"I know it's hard to believe. How can something that seems so innocent be the work of evil? Well, Satan likes to cloak his tricks behind a veil of innocence. Like when Satan went to Eve and said, 'Eve, just eat the apple. What'll it hurt? It's just a little ole apple.' But we know what happened after that, right? Temptation! It's been a part of our lives from the beginning of time. And even though the Word of God is all-powerful, Satan is one tricky fella. He knows what he's doing.

"Satan is alive in rock and roll! This music glorifies Hell and Satan! Behind it all, there is an evil and guiding hand. Rock and roll speaks to the flesh and the flesh is weak. You might think the lyrics in the songs you listen to are harmless, but the messages are always the same: abandon the spirit and follow the flesh. Satan knows this. And he knows the flesh is his way to your soul. And when you turn your flesh over to Satan, you play right into his hands. That is how he plays his tricks. He makes you think you can find salvation in his disguises, but in reality he is taking you down his evil path where there is nothing at the end, just eternal suffering in the fiery pits of Hell.

"Friends, rock and roll is replacing the Word of God and the Teachings of Jesus. If you don't believe me, look around, everywhere you see the hand of Satan ready to snatch up all those willing victims."

"Amen!" somebody shouted.

"Speak the Truth!" Several teenagers stood up and threw their hands in the air.

"Friends, the world is coming to an end. Whether you like it or not, Judgment Day will be upon us sooner than you think. Do you want to spend your life serving the Lord or working for Satan? That's the question you must all ask yourselves tonight. Do I want to go to Heaven? And if so, what am I doing to spread the Word of God? Because if you are not glorifying the Lord, you are empowering Satan. And that's the only way you're going to get through those pearly gates of Heaven."

"Amen!"

"As sure as you live and breathe, if you die without Jesus Christ, that instant, you will burn in Hell! There is only one way to Salvation. Come to Jesus."

More kids began to rise and murmur. Others gesticulated as they raised their hands to the ceiling and shouted.

"Amen!"

"Praise Jesus!"

"All of you who want the Love of Christ in your heart, come forward. You can be saved this minute. Join me in accepting the Lord Jesus Christ as our Savior."

The guy who had led the opening prayer reappeared on the stage next to Donny and called out to the congregation.

"Come forward, those of you who want to let Jesus into your hearts and be reborn. This is the only way to the Path of the Lord. To obtain Salvation you must be born again and accept Jesus Christ as your Savior."

Those who were standing began to move towards the stage.

"That's right, children, come to the Lord! Come to the joyous power that He wants to shine all over you!"

Several more teenagers rose and staggered towards the front of the church, their faces full of reverence. As they milled about the stage, the two men shouted over their heads.

"This is your redemption!"

"Repent and be reborn!"

Soon the kids were shouting too.

"Give up on sin!"

"Accept the power of Jesus into your hearts!"

"This is fucking nuts!" I said over the confusion. I turned to my companions, expecting them to share my disbelief, but Tommy and Shannon were shuffling down the aisle. "What's up, guys? You splitting?" I stood up to join them.

"No, man, it's time to get serious about our faith," said Shannon.

I thought they were joking and laughed. "For reals?"

"We've had our fun," Shannon said, his voice strained with emotion. "Now it's time to do the right thing."

At the end of the aisle, Clint turned towards me. The expression on his face seemed to suggest I was supposed to follow them. But I sat back down. I wasn't having any of this. I watched my recently acquired friends coalesce with the other teenagers and move towards

Donny, their faces raised to the illuminated wooden Cross.

I was completely thunderstruck. I was afraid to move, in case I was swept up in the fervor of kids rushing towards salvation. But I had to get out of there. I left my seat and moved towards the back of the church. Everywhere around me kids were rising and converging in a mass before the preacher. I wandered through the enraptured crowd like the only survivor of a plane crash.

I headed to what I thought was the way out. I reached a double door and pushed the handle. It didn't open.

I began to panic.

I pushed harder.

Just as I thought that they'd locked us in, I felt a hand on my arm. My whole body tightened. But then I heard a familiar voice.

"This way. Follow us."

It was Brett. A few feet away, Vic motioned towards another door.

"What the fuck's going on?" I asked.

"The sheep are getting led to slaughter," Vic snorted in disgust. "It's always the same shit at these revivals."

"You can't pay for this kind of entertainment," Brett said with a smile.

They both seemed to be enjoying the spectacle as we made haste towards the exit.

We were almost home free, the front door just a few feet away, when three men in suits blocked our path. I recognized the flattop from earlier. The other two were older, bearded.

"Can you boys come with us for a second?" one of

the older guys said.

"What have we done?" Vic demanded.

"Nothing." He smiled. "We just want to talk. That's it."

"Do we have a choice?" Brett asked.

"You have lots of choices, son." He put his arm on Brett's shoulder. "That's what we want to talk to you about."

"But my mom's about to pick me up," Brett said.

"This won't take but a minute of your time," the second man assured us. "I'm certain she'll wait for you."

Reluctantly, we followed the men into a small room.

The flattop was the last one in. He closed the door and stood in front of it, looking pissed off. "You must think this is a real laugh riot?"

Silently, we shook our heads.

"Then why did you come here tonight? Is this your idea of fun? Mocking our faith? You know, Jesus has a special place for people who mock His Teachings."

"We only wanted to check it out, that's all," Vic said. "Is that against the law?"

"Now, now, now," bearded man number two said. "Let's not get all worked up." He asked Vic, "Tell me, son, what do you think happens when you die?"

Vic screwed up his face. "Why you asking me that?"

"Because, I'd like to know your opinion. You seem like a smart fella."

Vic straightened his back and thought about it for a moment before he answered, straight-faced, "When we die we rot in a box in the ground and turn into worm food."

"You don't believe in a higher power?" asked the first bearded man. "A life beyond the flesh?"

"No. I don't believe in Santa Claus either. Or the Easter Bunny. Or the Tooth Fairy."

"That's kind of sad if you ask me," the flattop remarked snidely.

Vic glared at him. "Well, it's my life."

"How about you?" The second bearded man pointed at Brett. "What do you think happens when you die?"

"I dunno…" Brett pondered his human condition. "I guess our essence… it just like floats out into the cosmos."

"Our essence?" he asked. "You mean our soul?"

"Nah… More like an energy form. Or radiation… something like that. When we die it leaves our body and connects with other energy forms and floats away into space."

"That's an interesting concept. And you?" he asked me. "What do you believe?"

I couldn't help but smile under their scrutiny. "It's cool. I've already been baptized. Lutheran."

The flattop waved his hand through the air, as if to wipe away my claim. "And you feel that just being baptized is enough?"

"Isn't it?"

"You may not be aware of it," the flattop said. "But you are drifting away from the Lord. All three of you are flirting with evil. If you want to stay on the righteous path you need to be saved in order to be absolved of your sins. The Bible says there is only one true way to Heaven…"

He paused and looked at us as if we were eager to know the answer. But we just stared dumbfounded until he continued.

"And that is by accepting Jesus as your Savior.

Everybody else will burn in Hell."

I laughed. "So what you're saying is that Buddhists and Hindus and Muslims and anybody else who doesn't believe that Jesus is the son of God are gonna burn in Hell?"

"Only those who believe in Jesus will enter the Kingdom of God."

"But what if you don't believe in Heaven?" Vic pointed out. "Then it doesn't matter."

"If you haven't accepted Jesus into your life and you leave here tonight and die in a car crash, then you will burn in Hell," the flattop said ominously. "That's a fact."

There was something in his face that made me shiver. It seemed like we would never get out of this room unless we played along.

"Well, if we're gonna burn in Hell we might as well get going," Brett said. "My mom… you know, she's waiting and all…"

"Yeah," Vic added. "Can we go now? My mom's expecting me too."

"Look, y'all seem like bright boys," said the first bearded man. "Let's make a deal. Why don't you boys come back tomorrow night and hear the message again. If you still feel the same way, then you have nothing to worry about." He smiled. Mr. Reasonable. "But you need to give it a chance. That's all we're asking."

"Sure thing," Vic said.

"Yeah, no problem," said Brett.

We moved towards the door and the flattop stepped away to let us pass.

"We'll come back tomorrow. For sure."

"Think really hard tonight, boys," the man continued as we exited the room. "Think about where you want your essence, as you call it, to go when you die. Do you really want to rot in a box? That doesn't seem very pleasant to me. Jesus promises eternal life. That's a much better deal, isn't it?"

"Yep."

"You're right. I never thought about it like that before."

We left the church quickly. Outside, the parking lot was full of ecstatic teenagers. I looked around for Clint and Shannon but they were nowhere to be seen. "I guess I lost my ride."

"My mom should be here eventually," Brett said. "I'll ask her to drop you off."

We stood at the far end of the parking lot, away from the reborn congregation, silently watching them pile into cars and drive away, blowing their horns and shouting "Amen" and "Praise the Lord" out their windows.

"Robots following the leader..." Vic muttered.

"Are you guys really going back tomorrow night?" I asked as I lit a cigarette.

"No way!" Vic said. "Fuck these Bible thumpers."

I felt stupid for even suggesting it.

Brett sighed. "I woulda said anything to get outa that room."

"For sure. Those dudes were freaky." I smoked and shivered against the moist chill.

After Brett's mom dropped me off at the house, Rick called me into the kitchen. The old man was washing dishes as Joey did his homework at the table.

"Where the fuck were you?" Rick demanded.

"What? I went to church. I left a note."

Rick held up the paper I'd taped to the fridge. "You wrote, 'Gone to protest a church.' How is that going to church?"

"I was still at a church. What's the big deal?"

"You didn't ask permission. Why do you think you can just leave whenever you want? And why is your father doing the dishes?" He pointed at the old man, elbow-deep in suds. "You were supposed to wash the dishes when you got home from school."

Rick had set up a daily schedule of household responsibilities and according to the chore list I was on KP Duty.

"But I didn't even eat dinner last night," I pointed out.

"That doesn't matter!" Rick turned to the old man. "Claude, stop washing the dishes. That's his chore! He's getting away with murder around here and I'm sick of it. You slaved to make a meal last night and he was supposed to wash the dishes. You already let him slide and said he could do them before school. And look! They're still dirty!"

"You call that a meal?" I snorted. The night before, the old man had made a big deal about cooking an authentic Southern meal of black-eyed peas and collard greens, but I'd turned my nose up at the food. "I'd just as soon pull up grass from the yard."

"We live in the South now. That's what we eat."

"I may be forced to live in the South, but I don't eat that shit."

"I've had enough of you whining about what you can and can't eat. You eat what's cooked or you don't eat at all."

"Well, I didn't eat it and that's why I'm not washing

the fucking dishes."

"Claude! I'm warning you. You can't let him talk back to me! He's working my last nerve."

I laughed. "You've been working on that same last nerve as long as I can remember."

"C'mon, you two," said the old man. "Can you just try to get along? I'm tired of all this bullshit. Why can't I get some peace and quiet?" He wiped his hands on a towel and went back to his room.

I looked at the dishes lined up in the drainer and smiled smugly at Rick. "Dishes are done."

"Just wait," he seethed dramatically. "I will break you."

"Whatever, Rambo." I laughed. "You think you're badass, but you ain't shit. Just a lot of big talk and nothing to back it up with."

"Wanna try me, motherfucker?"

"Go ahead. I'll have you arrested for assault."

"What makes you think the cops won't take my side?"

"Uhm, let's see… maybe cause you're just some dude living here and I'm with my father and my brother."

"I have more right to be here than you. And the cops'll back me up on that."

"Care to make a wager?" I started to walk away.

"This isn't over. I'm still thinking about what your punishment will be."

I scoffed at his threat. "I've been over this shit since before it started. So fuck you." I ran to my room and slammed the door.

———

The next day at school, I passed Shannon and Clint in the hallway. They were talking with an even larger group of girls. It seemed that getting saved had increased their popularity with the chicks.

"What happened to you last night?" Clint asked. "You just took off?"

"No, man. It was fucked up. I got locked in this room with Brett and Vic. They wouldn't let us out until we promised to go back tonight."

"Well, you're going back then, right?"

"Nah. I was just trying to get outa there. The whole thing was too wacky for me."

"If you told them you'd go back, you hafta do it," Clint said. "You can't just lie to the pastor."

"That's like lying to God," added Shannon.

I hesitated, "I dunno... I'm cool with the religious scene and all, but, you know..."

"C'mon, we're going back tonight," said Clint. "You should tag along. I mean, what'll it hurt?"

"Are you guys really gonna stop listening to metal?" I asked.

"You heard Brother Donny last night," said Shannon. "That music glorifies Satan."

"It's not like we are turning our backs on who we are," Clint assured me, as if he were my confidant. "Look, we're just giving up certain things that get in the way of worshipping God." Clint moved in closer and I took a step back. All this touchy-feely stuff was weirding me out. "You probably don't realize how important this is... Come with us tonight so you can learn about living with Jesus."

Shannon nodded. "And really, you need to stop hanging around those guys Brett and Vic. They're bad news."

"Yeah, stick with us," Clint added. "We'll keep you straight."

I didn't know what to say. I wanted to be friends with Clint and Shannon. And I wanted to hang out with chicks. But…

"So you're coming tonight?"

"I'm not sure."

"We'll stop by your house around six-thirty," Shannon said. "Think about it."

I promised to mull it over and spent the rest of the day with all this God stuff on my mind…

It wasn't like I was without religion. From the day I was born until I was thirteen, church had been a Sunday ritual. First, we were Mormons. But I didn't remember much about it, just things like Postum, the coffee substitute the old man drank each morning, the undergarments they wore, the bins of flour and oatmeal in the store room that we kept in case of an apocalypse, and that one day I would have to ride a bike around as a missionary. I remember being somewhat excited about getting baptized. They said the Holy Spirit would come to me with a gift. I always wondered what I'd get, secretly hoping for a remote control airplane. I was pretty disappointed to find out later the gift was a metaphor. Too young to appreciate symbolism, I felt ripped off.

When I was seven, a year before I was supposed to be baptized, my mother had a dream that Beelzebub came to her and told her she was on the right path. And since the Mormon path was the path she was on, she decided to find another one.

After that, she dragged all five of us to a different house of worship each Sunday. As a spiritual vagabond, she was open to all faiths. In her search for a new religion, we explored the Methodists, the Presbyterians, the Episcopalians, even the Jehovah's Witnesses. She finally settled on a Lutheran church in Alhambra that had a private school where the members could send their kids free of charge. From then on, the Bible was a daily reality. Part of our schoolwork included memorizing entire passages, various creeds and assorted prayers. Every morning we went to chapel. In the afternoons, there were youth group activities and Boy Scouts. And of course, Sunday was the big day, with Sunday school followed by regular church service. If that wasn't enough church to last a lifetime, there were the special holidays: Easter Sunday, Palm Friday, Good Friday, Ash Wednesday... Church was exhausting and I hated spending what felt like six days at school.

But just as I was approaching communion age, the old man moved out of the house and Mom was too embarrassed to be seen at the church without her husband. So that was the end of my religious career.

Since then, I hadn't thought about it much. And when I did, it just seemed like a lot of work.

When I got home that afternoon, Rick announced my punishment. "You're grounded for two weeks."

"What the fuck are you talking about?" I snapped. "You can't fucking ground me."

"I can and I just did. Watch your mouth or you're gonna make it three."

"Fuck you!" I took off for my room.

"That's it!" he yelled after me. "You just got three weeks!"

A few hours later, I heard the sound of tire tread

on gravel. I looked out the window and saw Tommy's Escort. I peeked into the hallway. Rick's door was open and Joey was alone on the bed.

I put my finger to my lips and crept slowly past their room. At the front door, I heard Rick's voice.

"Hey!" he yelled. "Stop!"

But I was already in the car by the time he made it to the porch. I saw him shake his fist as we pulled out of the driveway.

"I knew you'd come around," Clint told me.

At the church, we waited for the service to begin and talked to the girls from the night before.

"So you're gonna stand up tonight?" one asked me.

"I dunno." I was determined to just get through the night, hoping I wouldn't have to make a decision.

"Well, at least you're here," another girl said cheerfully. "It's a step in the right direction."

The sermon that night was the same as the previous night: "My mother died... Rock and roll is the devil's music... Temptation! Be saved or burn in Hell! Blah, blah, blah..."

When Donny asked the congregation to come forward and get saved, I remained seated. I tried to resist the pressure to go to the front of the church, but I was surrounded. Clint, Shannon, Tommy, the girls—even random strangers were coaxing me out of the pew.

"This is what you hafta do," Clint said.

"To be right with God," added Shannon.

I thought about just making a mad dash through the crowd, but there were too many bodies in the way. I knew I'd never make it.

A girl leaned forward. Her hair fell across my shoulder. "You just don't know how much this is gonna change your life." She smiled and her eyes twinkled.

Slowly, I stood up. Shannon and the girl put their hands on my shoulders. Clint walked me down the aisle. I stood in a group of teenagers who wept and spoke in undertones. I thought, If I cross my fingers will it still count?

"Join me in prayer." Donny raised his hands over our heads. "Lord Jesus, I know that I am a sinner, and unless You save me, I am lost forever. I believe You died on the Cross for me. I come to You now, the best way I know how, and ask You to save me. I now receive you as my Savior. In Jesus Christ's name. Amen."

Amen.

After the service, in the parking lot, the collection of tapes, records and other memorabilia had grown into an impressive pile. A large crowd gathered around it, waiting for the bonfire to begin. Clint and Shannon were all excited about their new faith, talking about forming a Christian rock band, throwing out ideas for names based on scriptures from the Bible. They even talked about giving up cigarettes. After the ordeal with getting saved, I was desperate for a smoke. But I was hesitant to light one up and risk immediate condemnation, already fearful that I'd be thrown onto the pyre if these kids knew I'd only gotten saved to go along with the demands of my new friends. I regretted my decision almost immediately. I just kept smiling and nodding my head as everybody celebrated their surges of faith.

Then the articles of sin were doused with gasoline and ignited. The flames shot up twenty feet into the dark sky. The air smelled like burning tire rubber, but with none of the excitement.

When I got home, Rick was not impressed with my supposed newfound faith. He increased my punishment to a month.

"I hope it was worth it," he said, standing over me with that evil grin of mischief.

As I lay in the dark, I thought, Had I scored a couple tapes out of the deal, it just might have been...

Southern Girl

The day after the revival I could barely walk down the hallway at school without well-wishers congratulating me on getting saved. I was hoping to keep the experience a secret, but since half the school had been there, my rebirth was public knowledge. Everybody wanted to know which church I would be attending now that I had found the Lord. Of course, I hadn't thought that far ahead. I was more than a little chagrined I had to do anything besides stand up and go along with the masses.

Just as I was beginning to think I'd made the hugest mistake of my life, a girl walked up to me and said, "Hey, you're going to church with me this Sunday!"

Before I could think of a reply, she handed me a folded piece of paper and turned heel. As she walked away, switching her hips in acid-washed blue jeans, she smiled over her shoulder. I held the torn sheet of loose leaf and lingered with her perfume until the final bell peeled, wondering if each time a Southern girl talked it sounded like a bird was singing.

All through class I studied her handwriting. Maybe this getting saved business wasn't such a bad idea after all, I thought. For the rest of the day, I kept an eye out for her in the hallways. I wanted to find out more about this Missy Walker chick…

"Missy Walker? Oh, she's a slut," Casey told me after school while we hung out in my backyard listening to Dead Milkmen on his boombox. Since he was tapped into the scuttlebutt of Saks High, I figured he could give me the lowdown on Missy before I called her that evening.

"But she's only, like, what, fourteen?" I asked. "How could she be a slut already?"

"Hey, that's just what they say. She's easy. Been around the block. Known to go where most girls never dare."

I looked at him dubiously.

"I don't know from personal experience or anything. But this guy Mark Shelby said he did it with her."

"One guy and she's a slut?"

"Yeah, but then, the next week she made out with Gary Durham in the parking lot of the skating rink."

"So she's been around the block." I tried to play it off. "Who hasn't? In LA, this stuff is no big deal."

"I don't know how they do things in LA, but, in Alabama, if a girl gives it up wham-bam-thank-you-ma'am, she's a slut." Casey flipped the tape over and hit play. "Still, that doesn't mean you shouldn't go for it. Missy's got great tits." He flashed a lascivious smile and sang along to the tape: "My girl has a pet duck, and my girl is a heck of a *fuuuuuu-riend*."

I didn't put much credence behind what Casey told me. After years of bragging about faux lays, I knew most guys were full of shit. Nobody over ten wanted to be a virgin. I certainly didn't. That's why I'd been lying about it for years, claiming three imaginary notches in the proverbial belt. Now that I was in an entirely new state, I upped the number to five. And if Casey or anybody else had asked for specifics, I could have happily obliged. I'd defended my allegations so many times over the years that I'd become quite deft at subterfuge. Back in my old neighborhood, it wasn't enough to just claim to be experienced. Anything less than actual proof was suspect.

The key to a convincing tale of conquest was to offer some context for the encounter.

Explicit descriptions were vital: "One time I met a girl at Legg Lake," went one of my stories. "This girl was so hot to trot, man, we snuck behind some bushes and did it doggy-style. She was older. Like fifteen. Way more experienced. Moaned so loud I thought we were gonna get busted."

Sensory details made the anecdotes more realistic. "Once, in Pasadena, I met this chick whose mother bought Avon from my mother. While they went over the makeup samples, we boned in her bedroom closet. She already had a hairy pussy that smelled like the seafood section at Alpha Beta."

Since I didn't go to school with the other kids in my neighborhood, I was able to claim one of my classmates as an early feather in my cap, a little game of doctor that went too far. "I wouldn't say my first time was a mistake, but it sure was for her. She had a bald pussy that was so tight, I wasn't sure if I was even gonna be able to stick it all the way in."

But the truth was, I'd only kissed three girls. For a little while I had a girlfriend, this Chinese girl whose sister was friends with my sister. I was thirteen and Kim was twelve. Her parents owned a liquor store. She came over my house every day with a bag of candy and a pack of Marlboros. Even though she was a year younger than me, Kim seemed ready to go further than just kissing, making not-so-subtle suggestions and constant innuendo. At the time, I'd only kissed one girl. I was too confused by what was happening with Kim to try anything besides a little second base action. When we made out, I kept my entire pelvis region as far from her as possible so she couldn't tell I had a hard-on. I liked Kim, but all my friends made fun of me for going out with an Asian girl, so I broke up with her. After that, I kissed a sixteen-year-old girl who partied with my friends. But she was real drunk.

Still, if I was going to be the stud I always knew I was destined to be, I needed more practice. And this Missy girl seemed like a perfect candidate. The first of many, I hoped, thinking I'd be collecting phone numbers every day from all the girls who wanted a piece of the action.

That evening, I studied the keypad of the phone for several hours. A few times, I dialed the first six digits, but I chickened out before I pressed the final number.

The next day at school, Missy stopped me in the hallway. She was with a friend.

"Hey, mister, why haven't you called me yet?" she asked sternly.

"Oh, sorry," I stammered as I tried to come up with a viable excuse.

Missy laughed a throaty chuckle through a wide lipstick smile, like she knew I would come up blank. The day before her lips were pink. This day, they were a deep red.

"I get it. You're busy. Sure." Her expression suddenly turned severe. She looked me straight in the eye. "But you better not leave me hanging tonight, otherwise I'll find out where you live and kick your butt."

Her friend giggled. "I don't think you'd stand a chance," she said. "He's pretty tall."

"But I'm a good fighter," Missy said. "Watch this."

She lifted up her leg as if to kick me in the groin but stopped short, leaving a dust mark on the front of my jeans.

The other girl guffawed. "You soiled him!"

"Here, let me wipe it off for you," Missy said coyly.

My face burned crimson as she brushed the front of my pants.

"There. All better."

The bell went off and I walked away like a misguided automaton.

During my next class, as the teacher went on and on about whatever it was she assumed we were supposed to learn, I kept thinking about Missy... There was something about this girl, the way she looked up at me through that bouffant do, her eyelids dusted with blue shadow, those lipstick lips, the petite but shapely figure...

Casey was right about her tits. I could tell they were the size of pomegranates. And, I didn't know it at the time, but I had a thing for pushy girls who wore too much makeup and smelled like exotic flowers.

As soon as I got home that afternoon, I called her and we talked for hours.

The next Sunday morning, even though I was grounded, I snuck out my window when Missy's stepfather pulled up in a beat-up Lincoln.

Missy and I sat in the backseat. She had on her Sunday finest, a long-sleeved purple dress with puffy shoulders and a high neckline.

During service at Blue Mountain Baptist Church, my mind was a million miles away. I went through the motions, standing when the rest of the congregation stood and bowing my head when it was time to bow heads.

Between the morning and evening services, I joined Missy and her family for lunch at their house. After we'd eaten, Missy and I sat on the living room couch and talked. At one point she whispered, "The coast is clear."

It was time to make my move. Slowly, I eased my arm over her shoulder. I didn't want to appear over eager, but she anticipated my gesture and scooted closer, turning her head so we were face to face. Our lips met and I tasted her lipstick, a mixture of bubblegum and wax. She explored my upper palate with her tongue. I put my hand on her thigh and felt the polyester against pantyhose. As she molded her body closer, I moved my fingers across her hips, up her arm, over her shoulder and onto her chest, like a trip through Candy Land. I stroked her breasts gingerly at first, almost accidentally, but she moaned at my touch so I kneaded the mounds like handfuls of dough, alternating diplomatically between the two.

When she placed her palm on my stomach, her touch was electric.

My pants bulged.

As we were making out, I began to feel liquid trickle against my inner thigh.

At first I thought I was leaking, unsure if I was

pissing myself or the head of my schlong had ruptured like a blister from all the swelling. I tried not to think about it and concentrated on Missy's mouth. But then I felt a stream slowly moving down my leg.

"Can I use your restroom?" I disentangled myself from her arms, figuring a good piss would mitigate the throb.

In the bathroom, I checked my underwear. I was relieved the moisture was only pre-cum. Still, I tried to take a leak. But my hard-on wouldn't subside long enough to point it towards the toilet. So I tried to reason with my prick: C'mon, there'll be plenty of time for this later. I filled my mind with the least enticing images I could conjure on such short notice: naked old ladies, scenes from *Faces of Death*... anything to trick my penis into obedience. But the muscle flexed defiantly, demanding satisfaction. I was more than willing to fulfill its needs, but how? For a second I considered lying facedown on the floor of the bathroom and just getting it over with, but there wasn't enough space.

Not knowing what else to do, I shoved some toilet paper into my underwear and spent the rest of the day in boner limbo.

After lunch, we went back to the church. I was grateful I'd worn a long shirt. Throughout the evening service my cock throbbed painfully, bound like a wound in my tight jeans. Every movement was a knife in the gut.

When Missy's stepfather dropped me off at home that evening, I stood on the porch and waved as the car pulled out of the driveway. Once the taillights faded down the road, I ran to my room. I locked the door and rubbed my burning hard-on against the mattress. In thirty seconds flat, the sperm that had accumulated in my testicles all day traveled through my aching dick like a burst water main. My pants were soaked.

I was changing my clothes when Rick banged on my door.

"What the fuck do you want?" I asked testily as I let him in.

"You think you can get away with murder, don't you?" Rick seethed.

"I went to church!" I yelled in his face. "You can't stop me from going to church."

"You're grounded. That means you can't leave the house."

"Yeah, and what happens when I tell them why I can't go to church, huh? You want a lynch mob down here? They'd just love your heathen ass."

Rick glared at me, though he expressed no sense of fear. "New rule. Lights out at nine."

"What the fuck are you talking about? I'll turn my lights off when I'm ready."

"Lights out! Now!" Rick hit the light switch and slammed the door.

I turned on the lamp by my bed.

In seconds, he was back. "What did I just say?"

"Ah, fuck off." I lit a cigarette and exhaled a cloud in Rick's direction.

"That's it." Rick snatched the pack of cigarettes off my dresser. "No more smoking for you."

"Whatever." I puffed the one in my hand grandiosely.

"You little bastard." Rick slapped at my burning cigarette. The cherry burst into fragments and flew across the floor.

I laughed as he stepped on the smoldering embers. "You burned your little piggies."

"Didn't feel a thing." Rick turned off my lamp and stormed out of the room.

"Don't forget to slam the door!"

I heard him in the old man's room, yelling, "He's too young to be smoking anyway! You better not buy him anymore! I've had enough! If things don't change around here, I'm warning you..."

Blah, blah, blah. Rick was a broken record with all his bullshit threats.

The next morning, I swiped a couple Kools out of the old man's pack and sat down at the kitchen table, smoking leisurely until Rick walked in.

"Where'd you get that cigarette?" he demanded. "Did you steal it from your father?"

"No. I have my sources," I said with a coy smirk. "You can't lock up every cigarette in the world."

"I'll lock up every cigarette in this house."

I laughed and raised my fist with the butt between my fingers. "Hey, Rick, you know what? You're number one."

"Claude!" Rick yelled down the hallway. "I thought we agreed he wasn't smoking anymore!"

"Goddamn it!" the old man shouted. "I didn't give him shit."

"I'm warning you, one of these days... I'm gonna do it. I swear. He just keeps pushing me and pushing me..."

I played it cool, but the ban on smoking was a major blow.

Over the next few weeks, I maintained a rudimentary habit by smoking butts out of the ashtrays, even Rick's, with the tips wrinkled and creased from his buckteeth. I pocketed change whenever I found it lying around, and the few times I was home alone, I snooped through drawers for money.

Every night, Rick came to my room to see if I was ready to capitulate. He offered me all the things he was denying me: candy, chips, soda, cigarettes, a later curfew... But I turned them all down. Although my mouth watered at the thought of junk food and my entire being craved the cigarette smoke he blew in my face to tempt me, I told him that I wasn't hungry, or that I was thinking about quitting. Just to get him off my back.

The resistance took everything I had.

THE CULT OF
TEDDY RUXPIN

Even though I went to Blue Mountain Baptist Church with Missy twice a week, over the next few months I realized that I wasn't cut out for the Born Again lifestyle. I had tried to get along with the Christians, but there was a major disconnect. It was obvious I didn't fit in. I talked too much. I cussed too much. I made crude and blasphemous comments without thinking. And I absolutely refused to give up my music. So far, my only sacrifice had been not wearing rock t-shirts to school.

With every act of piety I had an ulterior motivation. When I got a ride home in Tommy's Escort with Shannon and Clint after school, it wasn't to discuss our future Christian metal band—I just didn't want to take the bus. I only quit sneaking smokes around campus because a teacher busted me before I could flush the evidence. And I went to church with Missy for one simple reason: to go back to her house after morning service and satisfy my insatiable desire to get past the satin threshold of her panties.

Shortly after the revival, I looked up the words "atheist" and "agnostic" in the dictionary. I went with agnostic because I liked the way the word rolled off my tongue.

Ag-nos-tic!

I saw the possibility of a higher power, though I wasn't sure what that was. Maybe I was supposed to have been a Buddhist or a Hindu, or a pagan that worshipped stones. While I couldn't honestly say what I believed in, I was certain, or at least as certain as a fifteen-year-old can be, that I did not believe in the Christian God anymore.

I'd moved past organized religion.

So one day I just said fuck it. I gave up all pretense and showed up to school in my Iron Maiden shirt. And instead of meeting up with Clint and Shannon at Tommy's car in the parking lot, I waited for the bus with Casey.

My final act of becoming un-Born Again was joining the Cult of Teddy Ruxpin.

The Cult of Teddy Ruxpin was the brainchild of Brett and Vic. For several weeks after the revival, I said hello to them in the hallways. Then I discovered we had the same lunch period and started eating lunch at their table. I was embarrassed to admit I'd succumbed to peer pressure and gone back to the church, but they never asked me about it and I never brought it up, although I was certain they knew I'd gotten saved.

As the outcasts of Saks High, Brett and Vic found great pleasure in being contrary. Since the Christians were always talking about devil worshippers and cults, they decided to start a cult of their own. The stuffed talking bear was the most absurd icon they could think of to worship. They scrawled, "Teddy Ruxpin Rules" all over school. On desks, cafeteria tables, their lockers and the bathroom walls. Although there were slight variations, such as, "Teddy Ruxpin Is God," "All Hail Teddy Ruxpin" and "Teddy Ruxpin Is My Savior," the message was always the same.

They knew it was stupid, but it alleviated the boredom. And it pissed off the Christians. So that made it worthwhile.

Like me, Brett and Vic were trapped in small town Alabama because they were military brats. But while my father was only a reservist and didn't have to transfer every three years, their fathers had travelled all over the world with them in tow. I envied their globetrotting pasts.

Before coming to Saks, Brett's father was stationed in Germany. That's where he told me he was from when I first asked. Though later he clarified it with, "I'm from everywhere and nowhere all at once." He was a suicidal skater. His arms and legs were covered with scrapes and scabs and bumps and red marks. Almost every day there was a new injury from some aerial mishap. Brett didn't care about much, besides skating. Before I showed up, Vic was his only friend.

Vic's father retired from the military in Saks. "After living in Japan, Europe, Alaska and Hawaii, this is where my dad decided to settle down," he said ruefully, shaking his head at the bad luck. Vic dressed in black every day: black jeans, black t-shirts, and scuffed black combat boots. He was a punk rocker and had a massive collection of punk and new wave records, courtesy of an older brother who lived in New York and hung out at CBGBs.

Vic made me tapes of all the essential punk albums by the Sex Pistols, Black Flag, the Ramones, Gang Green and the Stooges.

I was blown away by the new bands I was discovering. Punk was all about extremes. And I liked extremes. The anti-authority lyrics were the perfect soundtrack for what was going on in my head. The best part, though, was that I could almost play a punk song on the guitar. I knew I'd never be able to jam like Randy Rhoads or Eddie Van Halen, but most punk songs didn't even have guitar solos. It didn't matter if I could play the guitar or knew how to sing. It was just about attitude, and I had plenty of that.

————————

During lunch, the Cult of Teddy Ruxpin sat at our table in the cafeteria and discussed the important matters of the day, like which Sex Pistol was more of an anarchist.

"Sid was a true anarchist," Vic argued.

"But Johnny Rotten wrote all the lyrics," Brett pointed out.

"Johnny was only a fashionista with a reggae bent. Fuck PiL! Sid was the real rebel in the group."

"But Sid couldn't even play his instrument."

"Exactly! That's a true anarchist. Sid was the spirit of the band. Johnny Rotten was just the voice. The message was all Sid's, even before he joined the band. Without him there would never have been—" Vic stopped short.

Four burly jocks in letterman jackets walked up to our table.

"Well, well, well… what do we have here?" one of the guys said. "You the ones been writing all that Teddy

Ruxpin crap around school?"

We snickered at the way he said "Teddy Ruxpin" with such disdain in his country drawl.

"What y'all doing is blasphemy," he added. "The only one that rules is God."

Vic and I smirked while Brett laughed out loud.

"You think that's funny, freak?" He got in Brett's face. "Is God funny to you?"

"It's kind of funny, yeah," Brett said.

"I think we need to have a little chat." The guy grabbed Brett by the collar and pulled him through a side door.

The other jocks stood over Vic and me in case we tried to make a move.

"What's your problem?" Vic demanded.

"You're my problem, loser."

"You shouldn't be mixed up with these two space-cases," one of the jocks told me. "We thought you were smarter than that."

I was surprised they had noticed me. A little flattered even. But I said, "I guess I'm not that smart after all."

In the corner of my eye, obscured in the small frosted glass of the door, I saw a flurry of movement outside.

A few seconds later, Brett came back in, his face drawn up. He walked past us without saying a word.

"Hey!" Vic and I ran after him. "Slow down, man. What happened?"

"The fucker punched me!" Brett said over his shoulder and kept moving.

"That's fucked up!" I told Vic. "We should do something."

"What's the point? It's not going to change the fact

that they're always going to be assholes."

I looked back at the jocks, high-fiving each other.

"Motherfuckers," I said under my breath.

From that day on, I became the self-appointed Minister of Propaganda for the Cult of Teddy Ruxpin. I spent most of my class time coming up with new slogans like, "Teddy Ruxpin Died for Your Sins," "Praise Be To Teddy Ruxpin" and "If I Were A Stuffed Bear I Would Be Teddy Ruxpin."

Within a week, Teddy Ruxpin-related graffiti around campus had quadrupled.

The Magic Mart
Showdown

In American history class, sitting next to a rarely used chalkboard, I picked up a piece of chalk off the ledge and wrote, "Teddy Ruxpin Is The Way" in small letters. As I contemplated my latest catchphrase, somebody handed me a note.

"Erase it or you're dead meat."

I looked over my shoulder. One aisle over, a guy was glaring at me from under the brim of his baseball cap. I ignored his demand and spent the rest of class staring at the teacher, though I could feel his presence behind me. When the bell rang, I rushed out the door.

Later that day, Missy and I were making out during break. She was sitting on a banister while I stood between her legs, my hard-on pressed against her thigh. When I came up for air, I looked over her shoulder and noticed the guy from class. He was at the other end of the concession area, next to the garbage can, into which he spat a trail of brown fluid and wiped his lips with the back of his hand.

"Who's the redneck?" I asked Missy, nodding at the spectator.

She turned and sighed. "Oh, *god*, that's Waylon."

"Waylon? Who's Waylon?"

"He's just this *boy*." She said it as though she couldn't be bothered to explain such an inconsequential detail, but I sensed there was more to the story.

"Why's he eyeballing us?" I asked.

"Well, we kinda dated before you showed up. I don't like him none, but he still thinks I'm his property."

"Does he know you don't like him anymore?"

"I told him it's over. What else am I supposed to say? He knows I'm with you now, but he won't listen. Keeps calling me on the phone, being a real bug." Missy smiled. "Hey... Are you jealous?"

"No, I uh..."

"I wouldn't worry none about Waylon. He's no match for you. I even told him you have a bigger dick." She giggled mischievously.

"What!" I pulled away. "Why'd you say that?"

Missy chortled louder.

I looked her dead in the eye. "You're just fucking around, right?"

"Who cares? Waylon's an idjit."

The next day, on my way to algebra, Waylon turned the corner and blocked my path, flanked by two guys.

"I don't care how they do things in LA," he said, his voice full of contempt. "But I'm calling you out." He looked over each shoulder as if he needed reliable witnesses for the challenge. "Meet me behind the video store after school."

I remained calm, even though I was shitting bricks.

"Sure, I'd like to do that, but, uh... here's the thing... I gotta catch the bus home and it leaves the school parking lot at precisely three-fifteen. That bus driver lady... man, she's a real bitch. Won't wait for nothing. So unless you can kick my ass in less than five minutes, that's not really gonna work for me."

Waylon wrinkled his brow and looked at his buddies. "You live by the Magic Mart, right? Meet me behind the store at four. You're getting your ass whupped this afternoon come hell or high water."

"Sure thing," I said and shook Waylon's outstretched hand.

As I walked into the classroom, he said, "You better be there, if you know what's good for you."

I spent the rest of the day in a mild panic, thinking of a way out of the contretemps.

On the bus ride home, Casey arranged all the details of the fight, telling anybody who would listen to show up behind the Magic Mart.

"What are you, fucking Don King or something?" I hissed. "The whole school doesn't need to know about this."

"Why not?" Casey asked, nonchalantly. "That way you know it'll be a fair fight."

"And what if all Waylon's friends jump in? Who's gonna be on my side? You?"

Casey scoffed at my concern. "Waylon's just pissed off about the whole Missy thing. I told you not to get mixed up with that girl."

"It's a little too late for that now, don't you think?"

Even though Casey seemed to think I had half a chance, I didn't see the point of walking around with a black eye or a busted lip just to prove I wasn't chicken.

I had no problem being a coward.

After we got off the bus Casey asked, "Wanna hang

at my house before we go over to the Magic Mart?"

"Nah, I'm gonna go practice my bob and weave." I assumed a boxer's stance and shadowboxed a jab and an uppercut combination. "Float like a butterfly, sting like a bee."

I laughed uncomfortably and walked across the lawn to my house.

"I'll see you at Magic Mart!" Casey hollered after me.

In the kitchen, I was surprised to see Joey. Rick rarely let him out of the room when he came home from school. I only saw him in the mornings and at dinner. The rest of the time he was on the bed with Rick, watching him play video games.

"Where's Rick?" I asked.

"Sleeping." He was wearing a new striped button-up.

"Where'd you get the shirt?" I asked.

"Rick bought it for me from Martin's."

"You look like a dork."

I plopped down in the old man's easy chair and turned on the TV. Joey sat on the couch. I found an afternoon special about the perils of teenage pregnancy, though I could barely follow the storyline. I was too busy watching the hands of the clock as they moved towards and then past four.

Five minutes after the hour, the phone rang.

Slowly, I got out of the chair.

On the sixth ring, I picked up.

"Hello."

"Hey, man. It's Casey." His voice was frantic, as if he was getting pummeled in my stead.

"What's up?" I feigned a casual tone.

"Where are you?"

"Oh, man, you know, kicking back at the pad, vegging out in front of the tube. This show I'm watching is pretty interesting. They're about to throw this girl out of school for getting knocked up. She's thinking about having an abortion. Some messed up shit…"

"What you talking about?" There was a crackle on the line as Casey seemed to fumble the receiver. "We're all down here waiting at the Magic Mart. You gotta get down here!"

"Yeah, I don't think that's gonna happen."

"What?" Casey sounded offended, as if I was letting him down. "But you gotta," he said. "Waylon's waiting for you. You said you'd be here."

"Why? So I can get my ass kicked? Fuck that."

"They said it was gonna be a fair fight!"

"I don't care. Tell them I said to fuck off."

Click.

Thirty seconds later the phone rang again. I let it ring for a while before picking up. "Still not coming."

Click.

Ring. Ring. Ring.

"Do you just feel like wasting all your dimes?" Before I dropped the receiver into the cradle, I heard Waylon's voice.

"Boy, you bet–."

Click.

Ring. Ring. Ring. Ring. Ring. Ring. Ring. Ring. Ring.

When the phone stopped ringing, I hoped they'd given up. But I knew there was little chance of that. Not with a bloodthirsty crowd waiting to see me get a proper beatdown. I switched the ringer off and went back to the TV.

The girl was at the abortion clinic having second

thoughts. A montage of what had led to that moment flashed across the screen, the inspirational moment in the story. Would she or wouldn't she go through with it? That was the question.

Misty Two started barking. Five seconds later the doorbell rang.

"Fuuuuuck," I groaned.

I went to the window and pulled back the curtain slightly. On the porch, Casey stood in front of the door with Waylon behind him. Four other guys were milling around in the driveway.

Casey rang the bell again and banged on the door.

"Louis!"

Joey walked out of the living room. "Someone's at the door."

"No shit," I said. "Tell them I'm not home. But don't open the door." I grabbed his shirt. "No matter what, don't open that fucking door. Got me?"

Joey nodded and looked out the peephole.

"Nobody home," he yelled through the wood. "Go away."

Casey banged louder. "Hey, Joey. Tell Louis to come out! We know he's in there."

Joey looked at me. "They know you're here."

I looked out the window. Waylon saw me peeking.

"Boy, you best be getting out here or I'll come in there and whup your ass." His face was clenched in anger.

The guys who had been loitering in the driveway ran to the porch to see more of the action.

"Go ahead, huff and puff and blow my house down!" I shouted. "I ain't coming out. So fuck all you mother-fuckers!"

"Louis, just let me in so I can talk to you for a minute," Casey suggested.

"Tell them to fuck off," I told Joey.

Joey stood next to the window and recited every cuss word he knew: "Fucking assholes! Jerks! Mother-fuckers! Stupid cocksuckers! Bitches!" When he ran out of curses he repeated the list.

I laughed and slapped him on the back. "I don't think they can hear you. Louder!"

Joey stuck his head against the glass and unleashed another salvo of invectives. "Fuck you guys! Bunch of assholes! Dipshit motherfuckers!"

I giggled maniacally.

"What the hell's going on in here?" Rick emerged from his room, bleary-eyed.

"Nothing," I said. "Under control."

"Who's there?" Rick looked out the window.

"Hey, Rick!" Casey shouted.

As Rick opened the door and stepped outside, I assumed my goose was cooked. I watched him confer with Casey and the other guys, nodding his head as if he were seriously considering Waylon's cause. He lit a cigarette, flicking the Zippo open between his fingers.

"We came for an honest fight," Waylon said. "But he won't face me."

I closed the curtain and slid down the wall onto the floor. It was only a matter of time before Rick dragged me outside to face the pack of rednecks. I was sure of it.

"Uh, oh," Joey said.

"What?" I sat up and peered through the window. "Oh shit."

"Dad's home."

When the old man pulled into the driveway,

Waylon and his posse immediately gathered around the car. Rick stayed on the porch.

The old man looked baffled as he regarded the mob of teenagers. "What's going on?"

Waylon stepped forward and extended his hand.

"Sir, my name's Waylon. And I'm here to defend my honor."

"What the hell are you talking about?" The old man glanced at the outstretched hand but made no move to acknowledge the formality.

"I'm here to fight your son." Waylon folded his arms across his chest and straightened his back. "He accepted my challenge but he won't come out and face me like a man. So I'm asking you, sir, to send him out."

"If he doesn't want to fight, how can I make him?" the old man asked.

"But, sir..."

"What am I supposed to do? Drag him out?"

The old man looked at Rick.

Rick shrugged.

"You all need to get off my lawn." The old man grabbed a bag from the back seat and headed towards the house. "Go on, get!"

When he walked through the door with Rick, I tried to laugh the incident off.

"I told you not to mess around with these rednecks," said the old man.

"I didn't do shit!" I pleaded.

"Everywhere you go, you piss people off," Rick said. "You're lucky I didn't turn you over to them."

"Yeah, thanks for that," I said.

Just when I thought he couldn't get any more low down, Rick pulled a cheap shot like making nice.

"Oh, they would have eaten you alive for sure! But I couldn't let that happen to you." Rick laughed. "After all, your ass belongs to me."

ANOTHER STATE OF MIND

Saks was an electromagnetic wasteland, too remote to pick up a signal on the TV without cable. Since Rick spent his days lounging around the house watching the tube when he wasn't playing Nintendo, for the first time I had access to MTV as well as shows like *Night Flight* and *USA Up All Night*. I shared a small set in the living room with the old man. As soon as he finished watching the news, it was all mine. On weekend nights, I scoured the dial for videos, weird movies or anything with a little T&A.

I was flipping through the channels one Friday night when I stumbled on a show with punks sporting mohawks and studded leather jackets. I watched transfixed as the story unfolded. It was some kind of documentary about two punk bands from LA touring across the US and Canada in a school bus covered with anarchic graffiti. At each stop, they played shows in dingy clubs and warehouses, featured in long concert footage with a detailed demonstration on the techniques of slam dancing. There were interviews with kids from all over the country. People with spiked hair, buzz cuts, mohawks, pierced noses and tons of make-up discussed their local scenes and what it was like to be a punk when the world around them refused to accept their music, their style and their way of life.

The movie covered all kinds of punks, from the drunk, rowdy types to the straight edge movement in DC. There were even Christian punks.

While they were in Canada, the bands stayed at a house called the Calgary Manor, where a bunch of punks lived together. They talked about running away from abusive parents and broken homes to form their own community around punk rock. In the backyard was a half-pipe. Bands played in the living room. They made meals and ate together, like one giant family.

A family of outcasts.

This was the life for me, I thought, immediately overcome with the realization that something else existed out there. A punk rock life was everything I ever wanted: freedom, chaos, style and an aggressive soundtrack.

Inspired by the movie, I amped up my freak style. With a marker, I drew an anarchy symbol on a ripped piece of a white t-shirt, wrote "F.T.W." underneath and safety-pinned it to the back of my jean jacket. I drew crazy designs on my arms with a black Paper Mate. I painted my fingernails with Missy's red nail polish. I died my hair green with food coloring. I pierced my right ear a second time and inserted a long teardrop pearl earring.

As my transformation continued, I started getting dirty looks in the hallways. People averted their eyes. I heard snide comments behind my back.

But I didn't care. I reveled in their contempt.

———————

A few weeks after my confrontation with Waylon, two of his redneck friends stopped me in the hallway.

"Look at this freak," the first one said to the other.

His sidekick chuckled like a buffoon.

"Thanks," I said. "Happy to be of service."

Redneck number one gestured at my ears. "Look at all that purty jewelry."

The second guy stepped forward. It was his turn to get a lick in. "Boy, you a fag?" he asked.

I smiled. "Why yeah, I am a fag. And I have AIDS too. Why don't you kick my ass so I can bleed all over you."

I might as well have socked them both in the kissers.

"Boy, you best stay the hell away from me!" the first one sneered.

I laughed as they did the cowboy shuffle down the hallway.

It amused me to no end that I could do almost anything and the small-minded hicks would react as if according to a playbook.

Hook, line and sucker.

The Ladies from the State

I was in chemistry class when a hall monitor came for me. I followed her back to the principal's office, where I was led into a small conference room. Two women stood up when I entered.

"My name's Clorise," the first one said. "This is Sandra. We're from the Department of Human Resources. We'd like to ask you some questions. Is that okay?"

"Sure." I racked my brain for a reason that I would be on the hot seat, but I drew a blank. "What's up?"

"How are things at home?"

"Fine," I said slowly. "Why do you ask?"

As if she sensed my alarm, Sandra said, "There's nothing to worry about. We just need to find out some things about your home life." She came across as the friendly one.

Clorise was all business though. "Does your father keep his dog in a cage?"

This struck me as an odd question. What did Misty Two have to do with anything? "He has a carrier that he puts her in sometimes," I clarified. "But the dog goes where she wants most of the time. Why?"

"No reason." She nodded and wrote something down.

"Why is your brother's head shaved?"

"My dad thought that's how people look in the South. I had to cut my hair too. It used to be a lot longer."

The whole time we were talking, they were taking notes.

"Who is Rick?" Clorise asked. "And what is his connection to you, your brother and your father?"

"Uhhmm." I didn't know what to say besides what the old man told everybody.

"Is he really your adopted brother?"

I cringed at the thought of perpetuating the ruse. "No. But the only reason my dad says that is cause he knows how racist people are in Alabama and if everybody thinks he's adopted, they won't hate him for being half-Japanese."

The ladies exchanged a glance.

Sandra gestured at my clothes. "Can I ask why you're dressed this way?"

I looked down at what I was wearing that day: a sleeveless white t-shirt with an anarchy symbol scrawled on the front with a red magic marker.

"What? This is just my style."

She pointed at my high-tops. I'd written the word "FUCK" on the front tip of my right shoe, and on the left, "OFF."

"You have 'death is the ultimate high' written on the side of your shoes… Are you suicidal?"

"No, that's from *Miami Vice*. When Crockett and Tubbs went after these punk rock thugs, that's what they had spray-painted on the side of their car. I just thought it was a funny expression. It's not supposed to mean anything."

"Are you sure you're not having any problems at home?"

I shook my head. Since I couldn't think of what they might have on me, I decided to force their hand.

"Am I in trouble or something?"

But that was the end of the interview. They stood up and thanked me for my time. I went back to class.

That afternoon at home, Rick was in a rage. The ladies had visited Joey's school as well. Their final stop was the house.

"Somebody called them," Rick fumed. "When I find out who, I'm gonna burn down their house!"

The old man was concerned but calm. "Did you say anything to them?" he asked Joey.

"No."

"Did you say anything?" he asked me.

"They were on me about my clothes and shit," I said. "But I played it cool."

"Well, then don't worry about it," the old man told Rick. "It's just small town curiosity. We're an unconventional family."

"But this is a free country!" Rick hollered. "You can't just go to people's homes and harass them like the fucking Gestapo!"

All evening Rick ranted about the social workers. As he pounded Budweisers, his violent tendencies were directed toward Joey. I heard him whimpering and occasionally crying out in pain. The old man banged on the door a few times, but it did little good. When Rick got that way, he was uncontrollable.

Later that night, I heard him yelling at the old man,

"This is Louis' fault. You know that, right? It's the way he dresses! He looks like a freak with all those earrings and his nails painted. You need to put your foot down. Or I will. He needs to shape up or ship the fuck out. You can't let him do anything he wants. Somebody needs to be in charge around here."

I put on my headphones and waited out the storm.

RTD

When I told Casey about the visit from the ladies the next day, he wasn't surprised.

"Just look at yourselves!" he said. "You guys ain't exactly the norm around here. Your dad looks like your grandpa. You dress like you wanna piss everybody off. Joey's a skinhead. And Rick... I mean, where do I start?"

"Sure, Rick is kinda weird, but..."

"Look, that's what I've heard other people say. C'mon... This is Alabama. You guys are a total freakshow. And Rick is the king of the freaks."

It was true, there was nothing subtle about Rick. He talked weird and looked strange. Short and skinny with a buzzcut, he wore coke-bottle glasses that made his slanted eyes look even more beady. And those front teeth... He stood out like a sore thumb in Saks. Every day he wore his government issue camouflage uniforms and told anybody who'd listen that he was going to join the special forces. Rick's bravado was embarrassing to listen to all the time, but after being around him so long, I was used to his flamboyant demeanor.

Growing up, Rick was a constant fixture at our house. His family lived two doors down. Because he was older, Rick presented himself as a guardian for my brothers and me. When we ran the streets after school, he promised to keep us out of trouble. "Don't worry, Mrs. Joan," he used to tell Mom earnestly each time we left the front yard. "I'll look after the rugrats."

As far as she could tell, Rick was a good influence. In front of adults he was careful to mind his manners, but once we were out of view, Rick became a ceaseless provocateur. A twisted Peter Pan to our Lost Boys. When we weren't embroiled in an epic game of Ditch 'Em, we'd ride our BMX bikes to San Gabriel High and climb the roofs. In the empty dirt lots around town, we'd carve out off-road courses with abandoned shopping carts and practice jumps. We'd scale the fence that barricaded the Alhambra Wash and ride through the concrete channels that drained into Whittier Narrows, where we'd play Rambo in the scum-laden, swampy water. And since there usually weren't enough BB guns to go around, one of us would be the human prey while the others took pot shots from the trees along the gravel bank.

Rick organized some of our best adventures.

He was our friend.

We looked up to him.

But everything changed the summer before his senior year. Rick was riding his Mongoose across New Avenue when he was broadsided by an RTD bus. Never even saw it coming. Projected almost thirty feet, he survived, miraculously, with multiple broken limbs and lacerations over his torso and face that required hundreds of stitches. He was in the hospital for a month. The doctors said he was lucky to be alive. The bus hit him so hard, the frame of his bike was bent in half.

Rick was never the same after the accident. When he got out of the hospital, there were no more games of hide and seek. No more Ditch 'Em. No more bike rides. He began to act like a military man and talked about joining the Army as soon as he graduated. The old man brought him several pairs of uniforms home from the reserve center and Rick wore them every day with cut-off t-shirts. His nickname at school that year was Major Tom. He started reading *Soldier of Fortune* and talked about joining the Green Berets.

After his folks replaced his mangled bike with a moped, he drove out to the reserve center in El Monte to visit the old man. He had gone there with us in the past, during summer vacation, when the reservists brought their kids to work. But this time, my older brother Nate and I weren't invited. Rick wasn't interested in us anymore. Now that he planned to sign up, he perceived his time at the center as a prerequisite for his future career.

True to his word, upon graduation, Rick shipped off for Fort Jackson in South Carolina.

It was while Rick was gone that the old man split the scene with Mom. Joey and I were already living at his apartment in Baldwin Park when Rick got back from basic training and moved in with us. A short while later, the old man announced the move to Alabama and that Rick was coming with us. When I asked why it wouldn't be just the three of us, he said Rick helped with the bills. "Your mother is draining me with alimony and child support for your brother and sisters. I need all the help I can get."

I knew the old man was broke. We never had money. The summer Joey and I moved into his bachelor pad, we rarely had anything to eat but the bare essentials. When his payday was just a few days away, the old man risked an overdraft charge and wrote a rubber check at the grocery store. But nothing changed after Rick moved in. His financial contributions didn't make much of a difference, as far as I could tell. My pockets were always empty. The only time I had spending money was when I swiped it from the old man's dresser.

In California, I was broke. In Alabama, I was a pauper.

At school, I rarely had lunch money. I had to eat the disgusting free meal in the cafeteria. I couldn't even get fifty cents for a drink. Most days, I just skipped lunch. So by the time I got home, I was famished.

Shortly after the social workers showed up, I was loitering by the stove, waiting for dinner. The old man was making his specialty, bar-b-que chicken and corn bread. He had been making this culinary delight since we were kids. There wasn't much to the recipe. He just filled a pan with chicken and covered it with bar-b-que sauce. But the meal was a flavor explosion.

As I stood there, the taste already on my tongue, Rick walked into the room.

"What are you doing?" he asked.

"Nothing."

"You don't think you're eating with us, do you?"

"What the fuck are you talking about?"

Rick chuckled as he opened the oven door and took a good whiff. "Mmmmm... Smells good. But that's not what you're having for dinner tonight." He reached into the cabinet and held up a can of beans. "Beans, beans, good for the heart. The more you eat, the more you fart."

"Fuck that! I'm not eating that shit."

"Oh yes you are. And don't even try crying to your dad. I make the rules now."

"Up yours, asshole."

"Don't talk to me like that or you won't get anything."

"Fuck you."

"I'm warning you..."

"You can't stop me from eating."

"Wanna bet?"

"Blow it out your ass, bitch."

"That's it, you're going to bed without dinner tonight."

"See if I care."

I walked into the old man's room. "Gimme a dollar."

"What for?"

"Just fork it over."

"I only have three dollars to my name!"

"And I just want one of 'em. C'mon, give it up."

"Goddamn it. You'd take my last drop of water in the desert too, wouldn't you?"

"Probably."

I snuck out the front door, walked down to the Magic Mart and bought a package of cookies. Back home, Rick was still in the kitchen. I walked in with my mouth full.

"Where did you get those?" Rick demanded.

"Stole them off a dead Jap," I mumbled. I knew how to push his buttons.

"Give them to me! Now!"

I shoved the three remaining cookies into my mouth. "All gone."

"Spit them out now!"

My cheeks bulged but I managed a smile.

"Okay," I mumbled and smacked my swollen cheeks with both palms, à la John Belushi in *Animal House*. The half-chewed cookie fragments spewed out of my mouth like a sprinkler all over Rick.

Momentarily stunned, he looked at the mess on his shirt and pants. He lifted up his shoes and stepped out of the crumbles at his feet.

"That's it," he seethed. "You're fucking dead."

I took off running but Rick grabbed my wrist. "Let go of me, asshole!"

"You're mine now!"

"No!" I tried to break free.

"What are you gonna do? Huh?"

"I'm gonna kick your ass!" I snarled.

"Go ahead." Rick smiled wide. "Take your best shot."

"Fuck you!" I flung my free arm through the air like a windmill. My momentum pushed him against the side of the kitchen counter. I swung furiously and connected with his chin.

"Oh, you're going to regret that." Rick pushed me against the table.

The wood cut into my back and I winced from the pain. "Motherfucker!" I charged again, but he held me at arm's length.

I knew I didn't stand a chance, so I ran away. I was halfway down the hallway when Rick kicked me in the shin. I landed on my back. The fall knocked the wind out of me. Rick was on me in seconds. Before I could catch my breath and resist, he pinned my arms down with his knees, his crotch inches from my face. In this position, I was helpless. Rick still had his hands free.

"What's wrong now, shithead?" he chuckled. "Don't you know better than to fuck with somebody who's training for the special forces?"

"Fucking asshole!" I yelled. "Get off me, mother-fucker." I writhed under his weight.

"Ride 'em, cowboy!" Rick said gleefully as he moved to the gyrations until I was out of strength. "You ain't going nowhere." Rick leaned over and slapped my cheeks. "Now I'm gonna teach you some manners."

I tried to scream but couldn't get enough air into my lungs. "I can't breath," I coughed in desperation. "Get your dick out of my face!"

"You know you like it."

"Fuck you! Lemme go!"

"Say uncle and I'll let you up."

"Fuck you!" I shouted.

Rick smacked my face again.

I winced and sputtered. "Fuck you!"

"Oh, did that hurt? It was just a little lovepat."

"Fuck you!"

"Oh, are you gonna cry? Look at your face! You're all red. Let's see you bawl like a little baby. C'mon, cry like a baby for me like you used to."

"Fuck you! Get off me."

I tried to spit at him but Rick covered my mouth with the palm of his hand. Drool spilled down my chin and cheeks. My face was burning.

"Say uncle," Rick said. "You're never gonna win. Sooner you realize that, the better."

"Fuck you," I gasped.

"You just don't get it, do you?" He squeezed his thumb and forefinger into my cheeks.

I moaned against my will.

Just then Joey walked into the hallway. "What are you guys doing?"

"Hey!" I tried to shout.

"Go back in the room, now!" Rick commanded.

"Help me!" I struggled more frantically. "Call the cops!"

"Go! Now!" Rick shouted.

Joey walked away.

"Fucking pussy!" I managed to scream as I twisted my body to jerk free.

"Do you really think he'll do what you say? I own that boy. You're just an accident. You're not even supposed to be here."

"You're the one that's not supposed to be here, asshole!"

Rick rapped his knuckles against the top of my head. "Hello? Anybody there?"

"This is assault!"

"I can beat you to a pulp and not even leave a single mark. You won't be able to prove anything. This is my house! I'm the adult. You're the child. You got that?"

"Fuck you! I ain't a little kid you can push around anymore! You Jap, Chink, fucking zipper-eyed motherfucker!" I bellowed as tears streamed out my eyes. "Fucking Jap! Jap cocksucker!"

Rick put his palm over my mouth again and pinched my nostrils with the other hand.

I panicked as I lost air supply.

"You need to realize that I am the one in control," Rick whispered inches from my face. "You're a little troublemaker. But I will break you. You will do what I say. You got me?" Rick pulled his hands away.

I gasped for air. "Okay, I give up. I'll say it."

"I have all day. I'm comfortable." He bounced on my chest and chuckled as I grunted under his weight.

"There's only one word I want to hear come out of your mouth."

I mumbled under my breath.

"What's that?" Rick leaned in closer.

With all the energy I had left, I shouted, "FUCK YOU!!!!"

"That's it!" Rick put his hands around my neck.

I tried to scream but with the pressure on my windpipe, I could only croak. I kicked and exerted every muscle to squirm out from under Rick.

In the melee, neither of us noticed that the old man had walked into the room. "Enough already!" He smacked Rick on the back with a pair of leather gloves. "Get off him. Goddamn it! Get off him! NOW!"

"Alright!" Rick stood up.

I groaned and rolled to my side, gasping for breath and coughing.

"I told you this would happen, Claude!" Rick shouted. "I warned you!"

"We can't have this!" the old man said. "It's too much."

I pushed myself off the ground and onto my hands and knees. "Motherfucker," I whimpered. I ran towards the phone and dialed 911.

"Yeah, hello?" I said urgently into the receiver. "I'd like to report an assault."

"What the fuck are you doing?" The old man snatched the phone out of my hand and immediately apologized to the operator. "Yes, sorry, no, that was just my son goofing around," he said in a calm, reassuring tone. "We're okay. Everything is fine. Yes, sorry. That was my son."

I stood trembling against the kitchen wall. "Dad,

why do you let him treat me like this?"

"Shut up!" The old man brought the leather gloves across the side of my face. "I'm telling you to knock this shit off. NOW!"

I looked at my father in disbelief. My cheek stung from the blow. The pain pulsated like a bee sting. I felt the tears coming and held them back as hard as I could. But it was too much. I ran to my room. I passed Joey in the hallway. He looked scared.

"Get outa my way!" I pushed him against the bathroom door.

As Rick bellowed to the old man, I buried my face in my pillow with my knuckles in my eyes until red turned to white.

French Camp

On a winding two-lane highway with the old man behind the wheel, I stared out the window at the landscape streaming past. There wasn't much to see. Just trees and the occasional farmhouse. The backwoods of Mississippi looked no different from the backwoods of Alabama. When we passed a sign that read, "French Camp Academy – 4m," my guts tightened. A few weeks after the fight with Rick, the old man started talking about sending me to a Christian boarding school. I thought he was only making empty threats, but during spring break we went for a tour of the facilities.

As we approached the main part of town, there was another sign designating the road that led to the academy. I closed my eyes and hoped the old man would change his mind at the last moment. When I felt the car turn, my spirits sank.

In the gravel parking lot, we got out of the car and looked around. The leaves on the trees were mint green and the dogwoods were in bloom. I cursed their existence.

"Nice, huh?" the old man said.

I hadn't said much in the car and I didn't see why I

should start talking now.

The old man ignored my reticence. "Come on, let's find the office."

I grudgingly followed him into the administration building, dragging my soles on the pebbles.

Inside, a man in a beige suit greeted us cordially.

"I'm Travis Brown," he said. "The director here at French Camp Academy. We were expecting you. Is this our new candidate?"

"My son, Louis," the old man said.

"It's nice to meet you, Louis." Mr. Brown shook my hand longer than what seemed customary, all the while smiling like we had some deep secret together.

I diverted my eyes and focused on the silver Cross pinned to his lapel. Mr. Director. He seemed more like a preacher.

"What say we have a look around the campus." He motioned us outside. "The academy is quiet during the break, so you have to imagine all the happy children running around." He chuckled.

As we strolled across the well-manicured grounds, Mr. Brown extolled the virtues of French Camp: The chapel with its steeple piercing the sky like a dagger through my dreams. The red brick houses where the students lived, decorated with mauve shutters and surrounded by hedged yards and billowy trees like the torture chambers they were. The stone façade of the classrooms and gymnasium resembled industrial factories, an assembly line of robots. And the arts and crafts area was a blight against nature. Scattered throughout the grounds were small recreation areas, an occasional swingset, a volleyball net, a basketball half-court and a concrete playground with tetherball poles. Mr. Brown was especially proud of the equestrian center, where a few horses grazed tethered to a white slatted fence.

Everything about the place was soul-crushingly dismal. I imagined it all in flames, burning to the ground.

Back in the office, the old man and I sat across from the director. As Mr. Brown talked, he shifted his focus between the two of us.

"You can read more about the academy in the brochure that's included with your application, but let me go over some of the basics, so you can get it from the horse's mouth, so to speak." He cleared his throat and folded his hands on the desktop like a ramshackle church. "Louis, I assume you're here because you've been having some problems in your old school... maybe at home..."

Unsure if he was asking a question or not, I shifted uncomfortably in the chair and studied my shoelaces.

"But we're not here to judge. We don't hold trials. That's not what we do at French Camp. Whatever it is that led you here, it doesn't matter anymore. We deal with the present."

"He's a good kid," the old man said. "He's just a bit... misdirected."

"It's normal to go through these kinds of episodes at your age. That's why we're here. To get the wheels back on the right path. If you decide to attend French Camp, you'll be treated like everybody else. If you want to be here, if you want to study, if you want to work hard and improve your lot in life, then every opportunity is available for you to do just that. We're here to meet the needs of our students. We teach respect and discipline. We push our students because we want them to excel. And sometimes that's just what they need, a push in the right direction. This is, by no means, an environment where you will be allowed to flounder." When Mr. Brown finished his sales pitch, he smiled and asked, "Do you have any questions?"

"What religion is it here?" I gestured at the Cross on his lapel.

"We respect all faiths, even the lack of faith. But all our residents go to church on Sundays and we have daily chapel services."

"Do I have to cut my hair?"

He ran his fingers in a line above the collar of his shirt. "We expect all our students to maintain a healthy appearance and adhere to the uniform requirements."

That's all I needed to hear. I tuned out the rest.

When it was time to go, Mr. Brown walked us to the car. He shook our hands. "Be sure to look through the brochure so you can make the right decision."

Back on the road, I read aloud from the tri-fold sheet: "It says no Walkmans, no stereos, no tapes. So I can't listen to music. Great. Just fucking great. No smoking. No long hair. No earrings. I'll have to wear a uniform... Oh, god." I threw the brochure onto the floorboard. "This is so fucked up!"

The old man sighed as he lit a Kool and passed me the pack.

"Do I really have to go here?" I asked, desperately. "I don't wanna be with a bunch of Jesus freaks. You know I don't believe in that shit."

"What the hell are you talking about? You were bragging about how you got saved the first week you were in Saks."

"That was only out of peer pressure. I've since renounced my faith."

"And you go to church all the time with that girl... what's her name..."

"That's different. Just cause I'm trying to bang a Christian chick, that don't mean I actually buy into it. I'm just faking for the bacon."

"Then I don't think you'll have a problem faking it at French Camp."

"Dad, why are you doing this?" I whined like a little boy, trying to whittle down his resolve. "You don't really want me to go here, do you?"

"It's just a short while. Look to the future. When you're out of school you can do whatever you want. Three years is nothing. Trust me. I've gone a decade without even noticing. Besides, you hate Alabama. This is your chance to try something new."

"I'm getting royally fucked!"

"We're not trying to reward you. You screwed the pooch, so face the consequences."

"So fucked up..."

"Don't give me that pathetic bullshit. We tried to make it work in Saks, but all you did was raise hell."

"But, Dad..."

"Don't 'Dad' me! Since you've lived with me you haven't made a grade higher than a D. I keep getting notes from your school about violating the dress code. You don't respect Rick. No matter how many times I ask you to cool it. I can't have you guys fighting all the time."

"All you have to do is get rid of Rick. That's the problem. Why can't it just be the three of us again?"

"Enough already! You're going to French Camp. Get used to it."

We drove in silence for several miles before I thought of another loophole in the plan. "How are you supposed to afford this anyway?"

"We'll manage. Don't you worry about that."

"I guess you got it all figured out then."

The old man laughed. "You're not the only smart guy around here."

Killing Time

During the day the trees bustled with the incessant whine of an orchestra of tinplate noisemakers. As I killed time on the backsteps of the vacant house next door, I wondered what could make such a racket. I'd heard something about locusts, so I half-expected a swarm of Biblical proportions to emerge from the woods at any moment.

Not that I would have cared.

Let the rapture begin!

As an infidel, I'll be the first to go. And good riddance to this world!

Once school let out, there was nothing to do but wait. Each passing day was just another day closer to French Camp. Grounded indefinitely, this stoop was my only solace. The furthest extent of my tether. But it was better than sitting in the sweltering house, cooped up without a single luxury. Rick had taken everything away and stashed it all in his footlocker. The cable box, my Walkman, the phone... I had no access to the outside world. Even Casey was banned from the house.

All day long I fought against the palpable boredom, the dull dragging of time until the old man and Rick split for their annual Army training camp at Fort Benning in Georgia.

And then, two weeks of complete freedom. My final hurrah.

It seemed hard to believe that Joey and I would have the house to ourselves. Even though the old man had asked Mr. and Mrs. Shelton to keep an eye on us, we would still be on our own. For two whole weeks!

Of course, when they got back, I was a goner. But not on my way to French Camp. No. I had something else in mind.

Calgary Manor.

I never stopped thinking about the punk utopia. A place where I could be free. The idea of it consumed me. One day, out of curiosity, I called the bus station, to see what a ticket to Canada cost. I was dismayed to learn that the fare alone was more than what I could possibly get my hands on in the near future, which was a measly twenty dollars the old man was leaving us for spending cash while they were gone.

That left hitchhiking. Which presented another clusterfuck of problems. According to the road atlas, it was approximately fifteen hundred miles from Saks to Calgary. Fifteen hundred miles was a terrifying prospect when I thought about being stuck on the side of the interstate, hoping for a ride.

And what would I need to take with me? Some clothes and a blanket? Should I bring a pillow? What about the things I used everyday, like toothpaste, soap and shampoo? I'd also need conditioner otherwise my hair would tangle. There was my jar of Stridex or I'd get pimples. What about my Walkman and tapes? And how was I supposed to carry all this crap? Wrap it in a bandana and tie it to the end of a stick?

As I tried to formulate a plan, I kept thinking of new complications. What would I eat? How would I afford cigarettes?

What the fuck?

Why did it seem so difficult to do what so many other kids had done before me?

Running away was supposed to be a tried and true method to escape a shitty life. So what was wrong with me? I thought of all those kids in the punk movie, hanging out in squats and outside clubs, with their pimply faces coated with dirt like coalminers... did they really just walk out into the night penniless with the clothes on their back?

I wanted excitement. I wanted adventure. I wanted a punk rock life. But if I was ever going to make it out the door, I needed money.

———————

I was rarely home alone, but one day, when the old man's Cimarron pulled out of the driveway with Rick behind the wheel and Joey in the backseat, I scoured the place for loose change or cigarettes. I moved quickly. There was no telling what Rick would do if he caught me snooping through his stuff. At first, I scanned what was out in the open. I moved some things around, careful to set them back right where I found them. When Rick's room proved futile, I moved on to the old man's tiny bedroom.

While I was going through his dresser, I discovered a thick stack of Polaroids. I flipped through the photos and saw hairy skin, male bodies in positions I'd only ever imagined a guy would do with a chick. And lots of dick shots. Most featured Rick. The old man was in some. There were several with Michael the Fly, Rick's friend from San Gabriel. It was a real homo-fest. I only glanced at them for a few seconds, but it was obvious Joey was the star of the show. I put them back in the drawer just as I'd found them.

I was still desperate for a cigarette, so I continued searching and went through his nightstand. I picked up a stack of letters. They were addressed to the old man. Inside the envelopes were naked photos of dudes. In one, a guy wrote about his dick size and other personal stuff. He mentioned our house and how he'd like to move in. At first, I couldn't quite make out the references, since it was obviously a reply to something the old man had written to him about. But I got the impression that Rick and the old man were looking for a roommate. The guy wrote that he liked their situation, the older man, the younger man, and the eleven-year-old boy. There was no mention of me. But then I was soon to be on my way to French Camp, so there would be a vacancy at the house.

After folding the letters back up, I left the room and resumed my stoop. Back to square one.

––––––––––

A few days before they left for summer training, Rick stood in the doorway of my room smoking a Marlboro, his eyes glazed over. He'd just come back from McGillicutty's, a restaurant bar frequented by the GIs in the strip mall outside the Fort, next to the buzzcut barber shops, the pawnbrokers and the fast food joints.

Rick was a sloppy drunk. I knew to stay out of his way when he'd been drinking. The alcohol exasperated his usual pervy disposition. Most of the time he just tormented Joey, but this night, he barged into my room instead. He held out his pack. "Want a smoky treat?"

"No thanks." Even though the second-hand smoke wafting in the air intensified my cravings, I concentrated on the article I was reading before the disruption.

"How about a candy bar?"

"That's alright," I said, absent-mindedly.

"Soda?"

"Nope."

"You sure? I'm offering..." He smiled, his buckteeth like exclamation points.

"I'm cool. Thanks."

"You're a little shit, you know that?" Rick sucked on the cigarette and blew the smoke at me. "You're going to look so cute in your little uniform and your little boy haircut... it'll be adorable. I can't wait to see."

"I'll be sure and send you a snapshot."

"I'll use it for target practice." He chuckled. "I should just hold you down right now and shave your damn head."

A wave of panic swept over me and I assumed a defensive position on the bed.

"You know you can make things so much easier on yourself. All you have to do is give me what I want and you can have what you want. It's that simple." Rick sat down on the chair next to the dresser and stretched his legs. "I'm beat." He set his beer on the dresser and unbuttoned his pants. "Life could be so easy, but you just gotta make it sooooo hard." Rick pulled out his flaccid cock and began to stroke it. Within seconds it was stiff. "Oh, yeah," Rick groaned as he moved his fingers up and down the shaft.

I shoved the magazine into my face, the print so close it was a blur.

A few minutes later, Rick stood up and buttoned his pants. "You're such a drag. I can't wait for you to get lost. Then we can start having some fun around here." Before he closed the door, he turned and smiled. "Have fun while we're gone, shithead. Cause when we get back, it's sayonara, sucka."

Vacation Nation

On the first day we were home alone, Joey and I sat around the living room. After waiting for this moment so long, once we were free, we were at a loss. Rick had made sure we'd be bored. Before they left, he'd locked up every item of consequence in his footlocker. So we just sat there, watching Misty Two chew on a tennis ball.

When the doorbell rang, Joey and I raced the puppy to the door.

"Hey!" Casey walked through the house like he owned the joint. "So I guess you're not grounded any-more."

"Free like the motherfucking breeze," I said.

"So what's it gonna be then?" he asked.

I shrugged.

"The Magic Mart?"

"Why not."

"Can I come?" asked Joey.

"Sure. Let's go."

Outside the store, we leaned against the payphones watching the customers come and go.

"Man, if we're ever gonna do anything cool, we need

a car!" Casey lamented. "I swear, as soon as I turn six-teen, I'm getting my license. Not having a car is really cramping my style."

In the distance we heard the roar of an engine. A few seconds later, an old yellow VW Bug pulled up to the gas pump, choking and sputtering, a miasma of exhaust billowing from the muffler.

"Hey look, it's Clint Hanson," Casey said.

We walked up and said hello.

"Check it out," Clint said, gesturing at the car. "I got wheels."

"Let's go for a ride and see if we can find some chicks," Casey suggested.

"Get in!"

"What about me?" asked Joey.

"Time to go home now, little man," I told him. "This don't concern you."

"You're always ditching me!" he shouted as Clint fired up the spewing turbine.

We drove around for a while and cruised the Wal-Mart parking lot. But there was nothing going on.

"Let's go to my house," said Clint. "My parents are out of town for the weekend."

Clint lived in Indian Oaks. His house was a two-story brick colonial with white pillars. In his basement, we watched MTV. He'd given up on church a while back, he said, unable to sacrifice music and cigarettes himself. I shuffled through his record collection. He had the new Megadeth.

While I spun the platter with my head next to the speaker, Casey was getting restless. He suggested we try to get some beer.

"How are we gonna get beer?" Clint asked.

"Ask your brother."

"I'm not asking him. You ask him."

"I will if you come with."

"All three of us. Let's go."

We climbed the stairs and found Clint's brother sitting on the back patio with a friend.

"Hey, Scott," Casey said. "You still playing in that band?"

"You still giving handjobs out in the boy's room?" Before getting a response, he turned to me. "Who the fuck are you?"

"This is my friend Louis," Clint said. "He's from LA."

"Lower Alabama?"

"Uhm, no..."

"What the hell do you spazzoids want?"

Casey asked him about buying us beer.

"We got something better than beer." Scott held up a can of butane. "This stuff is killer. It'll mess y'all up good. Way more than a couple beers."

"Really?" Casey asked.

"Who wants to go for it?" Scott asked.

"I'll do it." I took the can, put my lips over the tip and pushed down on the nozzle. The can hissed and my mouth filled with ice cold gas. I didn't feel anything, but to amuse the others, I held out my hands like I was trying to maintain my balance and plopped down on a lawn chair herky-jerky. "Oh, man! I'm flying!"

Everybody laughed.

"Here, let me try." Clint took the canister and sprayed a shot into his mouth. "Hey, it's cold as hell." He smacked his lips. "Whoa, everything is melting."

"Okay, my turn." Casey huffed and passed it back to me.

We kept passing the canister around until we were rolling around on the porch.

"So what's the verdict?" asked Scott. "You guys high?"

"B-b-b-b-b-butane!" I stuttered in a sing-song howl.

"B-b-b-b-b-butane!" Casey and Clint shouted in unison.

And then we all chanted together. "B-b-b-b-b-butane!"

The next morning, I woke up with Joey standing next to my bed.

"What the fuck?"

"The door." Joey said. "It's for you."

I crawled out of bed, rubbing the sleep out of my eyes. When I opened the front door, I immediately stepped back, too stunned to muster more than a grunt in recognition.

"Wassamatter?" Missy asked. "Ain't you happy to see me?"

I quickly regained my composure and stepped outside. "What're you doing here?"

"I can't stay long. My friend Stacy's waiting for me. We're gonna lay out at her house." She giggled. "I convinced her to stop by to surprise you. You surprised?"

"I'm totally blown away." I looked over the crown of her head and saw the Chevy in my driveway, a girl behind the wheel applying makeup in the rearview.

"Hurry up and kiss me!"

At first, our lips met like strangers. Then I went in for a big one. It had been weeks since we'd gone to church together. I never thought I would see her again.

After a few minutes of making out against the front

door, she pulled away.

"I gotta go now."

I reached for her but she ran across the lawn. As the car pulled out of the driveway, she waved.

I went back inside not sure if the brief make-out session was a figment of my imagination or a side effect of the butane.

───────────

Over the next few days, Joey, Casey and I wandered from house to house looking for action. I carried a Metallica tape in my back pocket, hoping to commandeer somebody's stereo. One day, we explored this kid Sam's attic to spy on the chicks laying out at the pool with his sister. The next day we bike-surfed down Morrow Road with Bobby, a guy who lived behind Casey. After Bobby almost got run over by a semi, his mother wouldn't let him outside so we stopped by every once in a while to watch a movie on his VCR. One night Casey and I swiped a jar of his father's homemade muscatel, but we couldn't stomach more than a few sips.

Sometimes, while Joey ran around with kids his own age, Casey and I hung out in his treehouse talking about how great our lives would be if we weren't stuck in the armpit of the universe, though we usually just discussed the girls of Saks High: who had the best tits, the hottest ass, the cutest face and who was most likely to be a slut.

When we got bored, we wandered down to the Magic Mart parking lot and watched the world pass us by.

After a week and a half of freedom, I began to

worry that all the distractions would interfere with my plans. I'd blown most of my money on junk food and cigarettes. But I figured I might as well have some fun. Soon, I would either be on my way to Calgary Manor or on my way to French Camp. Even though the thought of being at French Camp filled me with dread, I couldn't really picture myself on the side of the interstate with my thumb out. There had to be another way...

When doubt encircled my enthusiasm like the arms of a deranged killer in a slasher flick, I thought about killing myself.

Sure. There was always suicide. Door number three. I thought about it all the time, how I could go out into the woods behind our house with one of Rick's razor-sharp buck knives, lean up against a tree and slash my wrists. I knew just how to do it to get the job done right, lengthwise, so the arteries were ripped open and I'd bleed out fast.

I filled pages in my notebooks, detailing the pros and cons of offing myself, psyching myself up for the final act. I must have listened to the song "Fade to Black" a hundred times.

"Growing darkness taking dawn... I was me but now he's gone..."

I wrote the lyrics down in my notebook multiple times, until the scrawl was perfect and the sharp letters dripped blood.

I held onto the idea of suicide like a warm blanket as I went to sleep each night, counting down the days, wondering if I'd have the guts to go through with it.

———

At night, Joey and I sat in the living room staring at the walls. I'd read every book in the house at least once and all my magazines more than a hundred times. There was nothing left to do besides sleep. But the time alone was too precious to waste unconscious. Complete boredom was still better than being under Rick's thumb. In a few days, he and the old man would be back. And then no more fun and games. No more running around the neighborhood. No more going to bed when we felt like it and waking up late. No more junk food for breakfast. No more nothing.

As if Joey were thinking the same thoughts, he said, "I wish Rick would stay away forever."

"It won't matter to me much longer," I said.

"Cause you're going to that place in Mississippi?"

"Nah, I ain't going to no French Camp."

"What do you mean?"

I wasn't sure if I could trust Joey with my real plans, in case he ratted me out. "Nothing. Forget it."

"What?"

"I'm not gonna let them lock me up in no Christian boy's home. That's all I'm saying."

"What are you gonna do?"

"What's with the fifty million questions?"

"I just wanna know."

Despite my hesitation, I felt the need to talk about it. "I'm taking off before they get back."

"Where you going?"

"I'm going to this place called the Calgary Manor. It's in Canada. I'm gonna go live with the punks."

When he heard my plans, Joey leapt to his feet. "You can't leave me here! You gotta take me with you!"

"Sorry, Charlie. No can do."

"Please! Please! Don't leave me here. I hate it here. I wanna go with you!"

"What the hell's your problem? I thought you liked hanging out with Rick."

"No, I don't. It sucks. I'd rather be with you."

"You're just a kid. It's too dangerous."

"But you hafta take me with you. You just hafta!"

"This is something I gotta do by myself. But hey... I'll come back for you later."

"No, you won't! You'll ditch me! Like you always do!"

I was surprised by his vehemence. "I don't know, man. I don't have any money and I don't know what's gonna happen out there."

"I can help. I'm good at panhandling. Remember?"

I sighed. I felt bad denying him a fantasy that had sustained me for the past month. "Okay, you can go. But you gotta do everything I say."

"I promise. Just don't leave me, please. I don't want to be here without you. Please."

"Alright! Enough already! I said you could go."

Joey beamed. "We're gonna go join the punks!"

"You'd look good with a mohawk," I said and slapped him on the back.

The rest of the night, we talked about hitchhiking and all the adventures we would have. "We'll be like the kids in *The Legend of Billie Jean*!"

———

The next morning, we woke up to banging at the front door. I sat up in panic, thinking Rick and the old man had come home early.

"There's someone at the door," Joey said.

"Who is it?"

"Mrs. Shelton."

"Well, talk to her. Find out what she wants."

"I don't wanna..." Joey stammered.

I groaned. "I gotta do everything around here!"

I opened the front door and the light of day blinded me. I squinted in the glare. "What's going on?"

"Can y'all come with me for a minute?"

"Is something wrong?"

"No. There are some folks who'd like to talk to y'all."

"Alright, give me a second." I went back inside and put on a shirt. Joey had barricaded himself in the bedroom. "Let's go next door. Something's up."

We followed Mrs. Shelton back to her house. In the kitchen, sitting at the table with cups of coffee, were the two ladies who had come by our school.

"Boys, you remember Clorise and Sandra?"

"Hey, what's up?"

"Go on and have a seat," Mrs. Shelton told us. "I'll let y'all talk." She walked out of the room.

"How are you boys doing?" Sandra asked warmly.

"Fine."

"Mrs. Shelton tells us that y'all home by yourselves."

"Yeah, but they're watching us. And feeding us... and uhm, I'm fifteen, you know."

"No, no, it's fine," Clorise said. "We're not worried about that. We just wanted to have a little chat."

I shrugged. "Sure."

"The last time we talked it seemed like there was something you wanted to tell us."

"There was?"

"Maybe you felt like you couldn't tell us the truth.

Maybe you felt pressure to keep certain things secret. And now that you're alone, perhaps you'll feel more comfortable revealing any problems you may be having at home."

"Like what?"

"You told us before that Rick's not really your brother, but you never explained why he's living with y'all."

I looked at Joey. "Uhm, he just does."

"Does he have some sort of power over y'all?"

"Power?" I laughed. "Like Superman? He wishes he had that kind of power."

The ladies smiled.

"He tries to boss me around…"

"Does that upset you?"

"Well, yeah. He's only four years older than me."

Clorise turned to Joey. "I'm going to ask you a question and I want you to be completely honest with me, okay? Will you promise me that?"

Joey looked at me and I gave him the go-ahead.

"Are you being held inside the house against your will?"

Joey turned away.

I quickly came to his defense. "What do you guys want, anyway?"

"We're worried about you two. We know you're in trouble and we want to help."

"Help us, how?" I eyed them suspiciously. "What can you do?"

"We can get you out of the situation you're in. We can put you somewhere safe."

Joey and I sat silently while the ladies presented their case. It was intriguing. A way out that didn't involve running away or suicide.

"Tell you what," I said. "Can you come back tomorrow? We might have something to tell you then."

"You don't want to talk now?"

"No, we need to go over some things, me and Joey."

"When does your father come back?"

"In three days."

"Okay," Clorise said after a few seconds of deliberation. "We'll see you tomorrow."

Back at the house, I sat down with Joey. "You wanna get out of here?"

"Yeah."

"Then let's give those ladies what they want."

"What do you mean?"

"I found these pictures in Dad's room..."

Joey started to cry.

"Why are you crying?"

"No. Not that."

"If we give them the pictures, they'd give us anything we want."

"I don't know..."

"C'mon. This is our chance."

I knew I had to sell him on the idea. He was scared.

"But I don't want anybody to think that I'm... *you know*."

"Fuck that. *Rick's* the fag. And that's why we're gonna make him pay."

"But Rick said if I ever told anybody he'd kill me and Dad and you and everybody."

"Rick won't be able to touch us anymore. He won't be able to find us."

"What about Dad?"

"Fuck Dad! It's time we started looking out for

ourselves."

"Why can't we just run away and go to that Calgary Mansion place?"

"Manor. It's Calgary Manor."

"Yeah. I wanna go there. I wanna be with the punks."

"And how are we going to get there? Don't be stupid. We got no money. We got no food. We got nothing. This is our way out."

"I thought you said we were gonna hitchhike. Or hotwire a car."

"We don't even know how to hitchhike. Or hotwire a car. What are you worried about anyway? Those ladies are gonna do what we want. They need us. Not the other way around. You saw them over there. They're dying to get some dirt. We can get anything we want out of them. They'll give us a reward for sure."

"I dunno…"

"Do you wanna stay here and be Rick's slave forever? Is that what you want?"

Joey started crying again.

"This is the only choice we have," I continued, pushing my case. "We can't run away. We don't have any money. This is our chance to get what we deserve. Our reward!"

Joey didn't say a word. Rivulets of tears lined his cheeks as he choked back another downpour.

"C'mon, do it for me. We'll be together. We'll be buds. Don't leave me hanging, man…"

"But… can't we wait for a while?"

"If we don't do this before Dad and Rick get back, it's all over. There'll be no point anymore."

"Where will we go?"

"Who knows? But anything's better than being here.

Right?"

"Do you think they'll send us to live in a house like the ones in Indian Oaks?"

"Fucking eh! They'll send us anywhere we want. They're gonna owe us, man. Big time! They'll buy us badass clothes and video games and all that shit. We'll get a free ride."

"And we'll be together?"

"Of course. They're not gonna split us up."

"You promise?"

"I promise." I mussed his hair, trying to mollify the hangdog pout. "Are we cool then?"

Joey nodded.

The next day, while the ladies sat at the Sheltons' kitchen table, I dropped the stack of Polaroids, the letters, the magazines—everything I'd found in the old man's dresser when I was searching for cigarette money—right in front of them and said, "Is that enough to get us outa here?"

As if I had to ask.

I could see the look on their faces.

"Okay, boys, we need to take these to a judge so we can get custody. We'll be back for you in the morning."

That night, we sat around the house, worrying what would happen next. Without a single distraction to take our minds off the uncertain future.

"You know what would be really cool right now?" I pondered aloud. "Some Super Mario Brothers."

"Yeah." Joey sighed.

"I mean, if we're gonna take off anyway," I said thoughtfully, "I don't see why we couldn't have a little fun before we go."

"What are you talking about?"

"Follow me." I walked to the bedroom he shared with Rick and pointed at the footlocker where Rick had stored the VCR, the cable boxes, the phone and the Nintendo along with his BB guns and knives. "I wonder what it would take to bust that lock?"

We contemplated the silver braided Master.

"Pick it?" Joey suggested.

"What do I look like, a fucking locksmith? Nah, there's only one way into that footlocker."

"Smash it?"

"Now you're thinking! Get the hammer!"

It only took one blow, but I gave the lock another for good measure. We hooked up the Nintendo and put a six-pack of Dr. Pepper in the freezer to get cold fast. We each ripped open our own bag of Doritos and shared a box of Russell Stover.

Once the sugar rush took hold, we grabbed Rick's BB guns and started taking pot shots at the crap on his dresser. I made a bull's-eye on the wall and we took turns practicing our aim until we ran out of BBs. Then we switched to the knives. After the bedroom walls were full of holes, we moved on to the rest of the house.

I stood at one end of the hallway and tried to see if I could hit the kitchen wall. I missed, but took out a lamp. Joey was a better shot. On his first throw, the blade pierced a cupboard door.

We howled with delight at the destruction. For hours, we went from one room to the next, leaving our mark. We emptied the kitchen cabinets onto the floor and smashed Rick's Nintendo into tiny fragments of plastic, wires and shards of motherboard.

It was a beautiful mess. As we surveyed our handiwork, we laughed until our sides hurt. I got a magic marker and scrawled "FEEL THE WRATH OF THE INNOCENTS!" in giant letters on the living room wall. I knew that would fuck with their heads.

Big time.

PART TWO
INSTITUTIONALIZED

NIC FIT

When Mrs. Gertie called us downstairs for dinner, the sun was still shining. As we followed the old woman through the house, our heads formed figure eights. The hallway was lined with snapshots of black people in assorted scenarios and beatific poses, some smiling, others visibly uncomfortable in front of the camera. In the kitchen, we sat at a oilcloth-covered table. Mrs. Gertie served us bologna sandwiches, cheese macaroni and glasses of milk.

I pushed the milk over to Joey's side and pulled the sandwich apart.

"Oh, great, mayonnaise," I mumbled. "What the fuck? Who ever heard of mayonnaise on a bologna sandwich?" I looked at Joey, chewing happily. I was inclined to skip the meal altogether but figured there was little chance of raiding the fridge later. Grudgingly, I lifted the sandwich to my mouth and went through the process of mastication with a scowl.

From an adjacent room, I heard the faint sound of a TV. The social workers had said the old woman had a husband. This must be where he spent his days, I thought randomly. While I was ruminating over the lackluster meal, I noticed the scent of cigarettes. It had been hours since my last smoke and my nic fit was driving me mad.

"Somebody's smoking," I whispered. This was my chance! I wracked my brain for an excuse to wander into the room and bum a cigarette. But before I could think of something, Mrs. Gertie sent us back upstairs.

That evening, as we watched sitcoms, the canned laughter on the screen did little to mitigate our sullen outlook.

"We need to call Mom," Joey said during a commercial.

"Yeah, right. Like she'd do anything for us."

"She has to. She's our mother."

"That don't mean shit."

I reminded Joey of the last time we'd seen our mother. During the custody hearing. She was screaming at us, her shrill voice echoing off the polished marble floors of the courthouse: "You ungrateful little brats! After all the sacrifices I've made you're going to turn your backs on your own mother?" Black trails of mascara ran down her cheeks. On opposite benches in the hallway outside the courtroom, Joey and I sat with the old man and his lawyer, caught in the middle of our parents' fierce negotiations. The lawyers walked back and forth between the two benches, hashing out the details until they finally asked us, "Who do you want to live with, your mother or your father?" When she heard our unified response, Mom flung more accusatory threats at us, then she went after the old man's lawyer, as well as her own. But the brunt of her vitriol was directed at her soon-to-be ex-husband: "You're a monster for turning my own children against me. They'll figure out one day what a horrible person you are..." She stared us down, her eyes filled with rage. "And when things get tough, don't come crying to me!"

Less than two years had passed and it didn't seem likely that now that the trouble she had predicted had come true, Mom would be running to our aid. But to shut him up, I told Joey that we'd give her a call eventually and let her know what was going on.

The next morning, I woke up in a rage. The sound of Saturday morning cartoons pierced my ears like darning needles. I lay on my bunk with a pillow over my head. I desperately needed my morning cigarette. The high-pitched chatter and exaggerated sound effects of the *Muppet Babies* in the background were grating my already serrated nerves. I was on the verge of homicide.

"Turn that shit off now!" I seethed.

"What's wrong?" Joey asked.

"I'm fucking dying for a cigarette and that shit is getting on my fucking nerves."

"Maybe they'll let us walk to the store?"

"Yeah and how much money do you have? Cause all I got is nineteen fucking cents. Lotta good that'll do me. I need a dollar, at least, just to get Basics. Where we gonna get that much money?"

As I lay prostrate on my bunk, Joey rifled through the contents in the Hefty bag.

"Do you have to make so much fucking racket!" I shouted. "Jesus fucking Christ!"

"Here." Joey stood next to my bed with his hand out.

I squinted at what he held between his fingers. Slowly, the folded greenback came into focus. "Is that a...? That's a dollar!" I leapt to my feet and snatched the bill. "Holy shit, dude! You fucking rule!" I sat down and spread it out on my knee, as if to verify its validity. "Now we just gotta get to the store."

During breakfast, I asked Mrs. Gertie if we could go for a walk to the Piggly Wiggly down the street. I'd noticed the store on the way to the house. The name always cracked me up. When the old man told us what they called grocery stores in the South, I thought he was full of shit. But there it was: the Piggly Wiggly.

"What y'all need?" she asked.

I hemmed and hawed. "Just stuff."

"Well, I don't think y'all should be leaving the house on your own. Not without permission from your case-workers."

"But it's Saturday," I protested. "You can't call them till Monday, and what I need, I need before then."

"You gonna tell me what it is? Cause I ain't no mind-reader."

"Cigarettes," I said, figuring I had nothing to lose. "I need cigarettes. My dad lets me smoke," I added. "And I'm almost sixteen."

Mrs. Gertie sized me up. "I ain't letting y'all leave the house, but Mr. Jackson smokes. You can ask him for one."

I looked at the doorway where the TV noise was coming from. Sheepishly, I walked into the room. The man was sitting with his back to me watching *Jeopardy*. On the arm of his recliner was a pack of Newports. Oh, great, I thought, menthols. Still, better than nothing.

I cleared my voice and said hello.

Mr. Jackson looked up and studied me with his yellow eyes. He looked ancient, his gaunt face cracked and beat-up like an old baseball mitt.

"Mrs. Gertie said I could ask you for a cigarette." I spoke quickly, to justify the intrusion.

Mr. Jackson hesitated before he picked up the Newports. In a snap maneuver, he tapped a cigarette out of a hole in the bottom of the pack.

I thanked him profusely. "I really appreciate this. I've been craving a smoke something fierce." I sat down on the couch and let out a stream with a sigh of relief. "Used to smoke menthols back in the day, when I first started. Benson & Hedges Menthol 100s. Those were my brand."

Mr. Jackson turned his head sluggishly in the direction of my voice. He barely seemed to register my presence, but I continued to chatter nervously.

"Used to buy them from a vending machine in a bowling alley by my house. Buck twenty-five. Which was expensive for cigarettes back then. Most places were ninety-five cents, but most places wouldn't always sell to us. After a while, I switched to Marlboros. Marlboro Reds... that's my brand now. Not much into menthols. I mean, I don't hate them. Sometimes I smoke my dad's Kools. He likes menthols too. He lets me smoke as long as I take it seriously and don't make a game out of it, like blowing smoke rings, or flipping cigarettes up and trying to catch them between my lips... things like that get on his nerves." I smoked the cigarette down until the filter collapsed. I laughed and stubbed the butt in an ashtray on the coffee table next to a worn Bible and two bottles of green medicated rubbing alcohol.

Even though I couldn't tell if he had heard a word I'd said, I pointed at his pack of Newports and asked, "You think I could have a couple more, for later? I have the money to buy my own pack, just got no way to get to the store."

Before I got a response, Mrs. Gertie came through the doorway. "You can go back to your room now."

I stood up and paused. Mr. Jackson made no motion towards the pack. I thought about repeating myself, but decided to wait for another opportunity.

"Thanks for the smoke."

Back in the room, Joey was in a panic. His face was red from crying.

"Where were you?" He wiped his tear-streaked cheeks.

"Smoking with the old man," I said. "What the hell's wrong with you?"

"I thought you took off," he said. Just as quickly as he was freaked out, he was calm again.

"Man, you're such a baby. Can't you just be cool for five minutes? Sheesh." I reclined on my bunk. "Turn on the TV."

That night, after a supper of frozen fish sticks, Mrs. Gertie handed me a pack of Marlboro Reds.

"Mr. Jackson got these for you," she said.

"Oh, wow! Thanks!" I turned the pack over in my palm and stroked the cellophane. "Do you want the money for them?" I reached into my pocket for the dollar. "I was gonna get generics—that's all I could afford. But I'll give you what I got."

Mrs. Gertie waved the money away. "Here's the rules: Ain't no smoking upstairs. Not in the room and not in the bathroom. I don't allow no smoking anywhere else in my house 'cept downstairs in the den or on the porch. Y'hear?"

"Sure thing," I said enthusiastically and flashed the scout's honor. "The porch works for me!" I shuffled out of the room smacking the top of the pack against my palm.

"I'm coming too!" Joey followed me out the front door.

On the porch, I smoked until I had a headrush. With the nicotine surging through my veins, I felt invincible. I thought about taking off, just running out into the night and leaving this whole nasty business behind. It was an enticing idea, but I lit another smoke and wondered aloud where we were.

"Somewhere in Alabama?" Joey offered.

"No shit, Sherlock. I meant where in Alabama."

I knew Anniston was surrounded by the foothills of Appalachia, accessible only by a four-lane highway that cut through a never-ending series of valleys and rolling mountains. I knew the closest metropolis was Birmingham to the southeast and Atlanta was a couple hours to the east. The geography was a no-brainer. But figuring out our current location in relation to the highway that led to the interstate was a mystery I needed more than a map to solve.

Somewhere in Alabama.

That's all I had to go on.

Might as well have been dropped off in the middle of nowhere...

The Adolescent Ward

After two weeks at the Jackson Home, we had the TV schedule down to a science. Joey got up every half-hour to change the channel based on the previous day's discoveries. When I went outside to smoke, I made sure he tagged along. Constantly on the verge of losing his shit, Joey kept thinking of any way out of the situation, talking about going back to Mom's house in Rosemead, running away to Calgary Manor and being punks... At one point he even suggested we tell the social workers we'd made the whole thing up.

"And then what?" I asked testily. "Go live with Rick and Dad again?"

"It's better than being here."

"Yeah, and what about the Polaroids? You forget about those, smart guy?"

One morning, during an episode of *The Price Is Right*, the ladies returned, all smiles and good cheer. Told us they were taking us to a place in Birmingham called Hillcrest, where we'd be with other kids our age.

"It'll be like camp," Clorise said. "You'll have fun."

I looked at Joey and he cracked a smile for the first

time since that last night at the house. This was what we'd been waiting for.

The audience cheered as we headed to the bonus round.

Birmingham!

The big city!

Things were finally looking up!

Before we hit the highway, the social workers made a few stops. First to their office at the Department of Human Resources, where Clorise told us the old man and Rick had been arrested.

"They're being charged with sodomy, child abuse and possession of child pornography," she said. "If convicted, they face life in prison."

I looked at Joey. "Life?"

They were giving us this information because I had wanted to be a part of the process. But when I learned the old man's fate, I wished I'd never asked to be kept in the loop. A life sentence? All I wanted was Rick out of our lives, convinced, for some stupid reason, that nothing really bad would happen to our father. A slap on the wrist, at worst. I never pictured him rotting in a jail cell for the rest of his life...

"What about Misty Two?" Joey asked.

"Oh, she's fine. Mr. Shelton has a friend who hunts and he's going to take her in."

"That's cool," I said. "She is a bird dog after all."

From the DHR offices, we drove to a medical center on the other side of town.

"What are we doing here?" I asked in the parking lot.

"Need to get y'all checked out," Sandra said. "Make sure you're healthy."

"We already had all our shots," I assured them. "We're cool."

"Don't worry. This is just normal procedure."

Normal procedure? I didn't like the sound of that. Neither did Joey. In the waiting room, he looked at me nervously. When we heard our names on the intercom, we went to our separate examination rooms. In mine, a young nurse with red hair handed me a blue gown, folded tight like a newspaper, and said, "Put this on."

I peeled off my jeans, wrapped the gown around me and sat on the table. Several minutes later, the door opened and a man in a white coat entered. He sat down on the stool and looked over my chart. "How you doing, champ?"

I tried to tell him that I was fine, that I'd just been to the Navy hospital in Long Beach before we left California, that I'd gotten all my shots for the new school and that I didn't want any more needles stuck in me.

"No needles," he said with a reassuring grin. "This time, we're looking for something different."

The exam started off like all the other exams I'd ever had, with the snap of translucent gloves. But there was no velcro strap around my arm for the big squeeze, no icy chrome disk on my chest, no popsicle stick on my tongue, no flashlights down the hatch and no rubber hammer on my knees. This exam consisted of only one test.

"Just go ahead and roll over on your side and relax," the doctor said. "Won't take but a second."

"Is this necessary?" I asked desperately as I began to comprehend what was about to happen.

"Don't worry. You might feel a slight discomfort..."

A slight discomfort? I clenched my eyes shut,

waiting for the excruciating pain that was about to shoot through my entire body. But just as I thought he was taking his sweet time about it, the doctor pulled off his gloves and said, "Okay, you can get dressed now."

From the medical center, we went to a drugstore where the ladies told us to get whatever we needed.

Lights started flashing and the audience erupted.

SHOPPING SPREE!

Joey and I each grabbed a basket and ran wildly through the store collecting items. I ended up with two spiral notebooks, a packet of Bics, Chapstick, a bottle of Canoe and batteries for my Walkman. They even bought me a carton of cigarettes.

After stopping at McDonald's for lunch, we hit the highway. On the way to Birmingham, my excitement increased with each mile between Anniston and us. I listened to Black Flag on my headphones and stared out the window. There wasn't much to see as the van undulated through the rolling foothills. The scenery in Alabama never seemed to change. A wall of pine trees lined either side of the highway. An occasional ridge covered in kudzu. A long narrow field of switchgrass in the median.

When we got closer to the city, the dense vegetation gave way to rows of blank houses, gas stations and a Waffle House. In the distance, I spotted a shopping center and traces of vehicular congestion. The outskirts of Birmingham offered a semblance of an urban life I hadn't seen since we left LA. But just as I anticipated a view of the skyscrapers downtown, we took the Eastlake exit and drove through a neighborhood with brick houses and manicured lawns that looked exactly like Saks.

Hillcrest Hospital was at the top of a hill. Hence, the name. It wasn't obvious at first that we were at the funny farm, but as I watched Sandra fill out my forms, I figured it out. In the main office, we were processed. Joey was assigned to the Youth Ward and I was put in the Adolescent Ward. As soon as he realized we were getting split up, Joey started crying.

"You said we were gonna stay together!" he bellowed in the hallway, his voice bouncing off the walls.

Clorise and Sandra looked at me and I stepped forward to calm him down.

"It'll be cool." I socked him lightly in the arm. "This is just temporary. It won't be so bad." I didn't know what else to say. I was just as confused.

"You'll see your brother all the time," Clorise said as she led him away. "Don't worry."

Don't worry. Don't worry. They were like a broken record, telling us all the time not to worry. But as I followed Sandra through a set of double doors that separated the Youth Ward from the Adolescent Ward, I couldn't help but expect the worst.

I was led into a room where a woman separated my belongings into two piles: the things I could keep and the questionable stuff that was getting locked away. I groaned as my Walkman was added to the second pile. On the bright side, I got to keep my notebooks. But not the pens. How did that make any sense? I wanted to protest but bit my tongue. Then my carton of Marlboros went into the second pile and I couldn't hold back anymore.

"Smoking?" I asked.

The woman responded, "Not until you get to the second level."

"The second level? What's that?"

"You'll find all that out during your orientation tomorrow morning." She pointed at my jacket. "Do you want to take the pins off or turn the whole thing over?"

"What? This is my jacket." I bristled at the thought but forced a smile. "Okay. It's cool. You can have the jacket."

"The earrings too. And the bandana."

I pulled out the loops and studs that ran up the side of both my ears and set them on the countertop. Then I untied the bandana from around my ankle.

"Are those safety pins in your jeans?"

"Yeah."

"I'm going to need your shoelaces as well."

I heaved a sigh. I really tried to hate this lady. But she had a kind face. Her name was Rosie Fitzpatrick. According to the nameplate over her left tit she was a psych tech.

With a consoling smile, Rosie put the rest of my things back into the bag.

"This way and I'll show you to your room."

I picked up my bag, lighter now with half my meager possessions confiscated, and followed Rosie down the hall.

The room was like any other hospital room. Two bunks, one on either side and a small wardrobe in each far corner. The one on the right was congested with toiletries and books, so I set my bag on the unoccupied bed. I pulled the heavy dark curtains aside to reveal a scratched plexiglass window. Through the hieroglyphic claw marks, there wasn't much to see. Just trees and the occasional rooftop.

"Everybody is in the common area right now," Rosie

said. "Follow me."

As we walked down a hallway, I heard the chatter of multiple voices getting louder with each step. Rosie pushed open another double door and we entered a large room with about thirty teenagers gathered in clusters on chairs and couches. At the far end was a pool table.

I scanned the faces for potential threats and alliances. I noticed a guy with long hair wearing a Rush shirt at the pool table. My homemade anarchy shirt trumped his a million fold, but I wasn't feeling picky.

"Everybody, can I have your attention?" Rosie said loudly. "This is Louis."

I blushed at the lackluster ripple of garbled acknowledgments and raised my hand—the guilty one. I stood in the center of the room for what seemed like an hour. Without my paraphernalia, I felt naked under the scrutiny. A few seconds later, the faces returned to reading magazines, playing board games and interrupted conversations. I casually wandered over to the pool table. Besides the dude in the Rush shirt, there were two other guys watching the game.

"How you doing?" the guy in the Rush shirt said. "I'm Alex." He had a firm handshake. "I think we're gonna be roommates. I got the vacancy." From a distance he looked older, like he was in his early twenties, but up close his face was covered in acne and pockmarks that offset the thin patch of dark peach fuzz above his lip. "Where you from?"

"LA."

"They sent you here all the way from LA?"

"No." I laughed. "I've been living in Saks."

"You must be military."

"Yeah. How do you know?"

"Why else would you be in Saks? Fort McClellan, right? I'm from Huntsville. Half the people there are military too." Alex pointed at the pool table. "Say, you wanna play doubles after this game?"

Even though I'd never played pool before and only had a vague understanding of the rules, I agreed and kept my eye on the current game to pick up some pointers.

Alex's opponent played skillfully. As he lined up his shots he brushed the hair out of his face with the back of his hand. He wore a pink Izod, plaid shorts and top-siders without socks.

At the other end of the table, a guy in track shorts and a tank top stood silently.

"Your shot," the guy in the Izod yelled.

"Again?" Alex took the cue and perused his options. "I might just have a chance to beat your ass if you keep playing like that." He lined up the cue and the ball landed in the side pocket. "Sweet. Now watch me run the table." Alex moved to the next shot. He aimed and pulled the cue back, but the ball bounced off the edge of the pocket and clattered against the other balls in the center of the table. "Crap on a stick. I suck at this game. You any good?" he asked me.

"Not really."

The guy in the track shorts walked over. Alex made the introductions. "This is Scott."

I shook his hand.

"So what's it like in here?" I asked.

"Boring as all hell," Alex said. "Not much to do but play pool. There's some games and stuff like that." He nodded at some teenagers playing Risk and Monopoly.

"Oh man!" Alex turned back to the pool table quickly. "Well, that's game."

"I kind of feel bad humiliating you all the time," the victor said as he approached smiling. "But not that bad."

"Ryan, this is Louis. He comes to us from LA via Saks. Louis, Ryan. He's from Mountain Brook. Nobody can beat him at pool."

"Billiards is a game that descended from French nobility," Ryan proclaimed grandiosely.

"Good to know." Alex rolled his eyes. "So, man, you up for a game?" he asked me.

"Sure."

It was Alex and me against Ryan and Scott. Just as I thought, I was terrible at pool. It took me several attempts before I was able to even hit the cueball with the stick. Each time I tried to nail it, the end of the cue bounced off the side. Before I could get the hang of it, a heavyset black woman walked into the center of the room and announced in a roar that transcended all the other noise, "Supper time!"

"Coolness." Alex rubbed his hands together. "Time to feast!"

Ryan and Alex followed several other kids out the door.

"Where're they going?" I asked Scott, the remaining player.

"Cafeteria. They're second level." Scott had a square jaw. His black hair was close-cropped on the sides and spiked on the top. He moved with an athletic gait but his deep-set eyes were full of confusion, darting left to right but never straight ahead.

Two men in white coats pushed three carts into the

room and everybody gathered around them. On the carts were metal pans containing Salisbury steaks in a thick brown goop, soggy french fries, corn niblets and green beans.

"Hey, it's a TV dinner without the tray," I joked as I sat down next to Scott. "Where's the cobbler?"

"Only the people on second level get dessert."

"So what do you have to do to get on this second level?"

"Be perfect."

"What does that mean?"

He swallowed a mouthful of steak. "The point system is a game. But with all these twists. Just when you think you got it figured out, they pull a fast one and change it up."

I had no idea what he was talking about, but I nodded as if I did.

Around the long table, a flurry of conversation had erupted. Discussions intermingled with waves of laughter and the screeching of girls. I examined the faces as furtively as possible. Three girls hovered together at the far end giggling. A redhead with a constellation of freckles smiled at me.

After the meal, I said out loud, "Man, I could really use a cigarette."

"On the second level you can smoke before coming back to the ward," Scott said.

"How come you know so much about the second level?"

"I made it to the second level already, but now I'm back on the first."

"What happened?"

"Ah, you know, accusations were made... Lies, mostly...

Every time I try to do something good, it messes up. But it's not my fault."

"Hey man, I know what that's like."

"There are a lot of people here who want me to fail."

I pointed at the pool table to change the subject.

"Wanna play a game?"

Scott and I shared the cue. While we practiced shots, the redhead walked by the table and looked in our direction. She smiled.

"Hey, Louis. I'm Shirelle."

"Hiya." I smiled back.

When the second level returned from the cafeteria, Alex and Ryan joined us at the pool table.

"Who's up for another game of doubles?" Alex asked.

Ryan grabbed the cue. "Rack 'em!"

While we waited for our turns, Alex stood next to me. I could smell cigarette smoke on his clothes.

"You smoke?" I asked.

"Like a fiend," said Alex.

"I'm dying for a cigarette." I thought if I kept saying it, maybe somebody would eventually just hand me one.

"The second level is mandatory for a steady intake of nicotine," Alex said.

"So what's the deal?" I asked. "How do I get on the second level?"

Over the next game, the guys explained the level system to me. Everybody started off on the first level. To get to the second level, you collected points and when you had enough and had done everything by the book, they moved you up to the second level. I thought for sure that since I hadn't actually done anything to warrant being there, I'd be on the second level in no time.

"So what brings you to Hillcrest?" Alex asked.

"Evaluation, they say."

Ryan scoffed, "We're all in here for evaluations. That's just a word. It doesn't mean anything. All that matters is your diagnosis."

"My what?" I asked.

"It's what they treat you for," Alex clarified. "You know, what ails ya. Like depression. That's the most popular diagnosis. There's Bobby over there, that guy Paul, Muriel, Fred and Caroline... and I think Thomas too. According to their evaluations, they're all depressed."

"They don't seem that bummed out," I observed.

"Exactly." Ryan handed the cue to Alex. "Everybody's all perfectly cheerful when they don't have to deal with the bullshit at home and school. That's the joke. They come in here all messed up but within a few days they're cool and it's like they've been cured. And then they go home and the problems start all over again."

"It's a total racket," said Scott.

Alex missed his shot. "Besides depression, suicide's another popular one. There's four of 'em right now, including Ryan."

"Oh yeah?" I was curious about the pool shark.

"Ryan here is the suicidal prep." Alex referred to him as if he were on display. "Born poor, raised by a single mother who worked two jobs to afford their apartment in Mountain Brook so he could attend a good school with the rich kids. But as much as he tried to fit in, he couldn't handle the pressure. So one day, he snapped. Drank a bottle of vodka and made spaghetti dinner with his wrists."

"That's fucked up." I looked at Ryan's arms and

noticed the scars.

Alex pointed at three skinny girls sitting in a tight circle. "See those girls over there? The bulimic sisters. Everyday they're dressed like they're going to prom night in Ethiopia. If their weight drops, they get put on feeding tubes."

"Gnarly."

"Any time I look at their fingers, I can't stop thinking about how many times they've shoved them down their throats." Alex paused for several seconds and then shuddered. "The suicides and depressed are way more fun to be around."

"What's the deal with her?" I pointed at a girl with a large mane of blonde curly hair applying makeup on the couch.

"That's Cindy," Alex told me.

"Miss Fancy Pants," Scott said. "She's so stuck up it's like she's got a rake in her butt."

"Plus she's got the personality of a dishrag," Ryan added. "All she ever talks about is designer clothes, going on vacation, her father's Jaguar. Plus, she carries a BMW key around, but she's not even old enough to drive yet."

"What's her problem?" I asked.

"Besides the obvious? Nobody knows. It's a big mystery how she made it to the second level."

"She's a rich bitch," Scott said.

"Her parents have influence." Ryan took the cue from Alex.

"Must be nice."

"My parents are just influenced," Alex quipped.

"What about you?" I asked him. "What's your diagnosis?"

"Me? I'm still waiting for my evaluation to be over."

"So why are you here?"

"Shit, I got busted for selling pot. Even though I was the main distributor of weed in all of Huntsville, they got me on a lousy dimebag. Can you believe that?"

"They didn't put you in jail?"

"At first, yeah. But then my lawyer convinced the judge I was emotionally disturbed, which is why I was selling pot in the first place. So they sent me here for a psych review."

"How long ago was that?"

"Three months."

"Shit."

"Hey, it beats jail. I don't know what's gonna happen when I get in front of the judge again, but for now it's smooth sailing."

"What about you, Scott?" I asked.

"Have you talked to Scott?" Ryan guffawed. "He's got a new problem every day. He's the screw up."

"Man, whatever," Scott said. "It's my parents who are messed up."

"Oh yeah, that's just what a screw up would say." Ryan cracked up while Scott pouted. "So, you know who you gonna be yet?"

"It's not like that for me," I said. "My parents didn't send me here. I had my father arrested."

"That's awesome," said Scott. "I wish I could send my dad to jail."

"We just moved here and we don't have any family around... So there's just nowhere else for us to go. This is like a stop-off or something. I'll be out of here in no time." I saw their doubtful expressions. "Once I get evaluated..." I laughed nervously.

Alex reached for the cue. "Well, you better hope your evaluation doesn't take as long as mine."

Later that night, the black woman from earlier walked back into the middle of the room and barked, "Quiet time!" Her name was Vera. The guys had given me the rundown on the staff. Rosie was in charge and Vera was her second-in-command. There were several other psych techs, a whole army of them to keep tabs on us.

I followed Alex back to our room. I was glad we ended up roommates.

As we lounged on our bunks that evening, Alex told me, "I was worried when the last guy left, cause you never know who you're gonna get."

"You seen a lotta whackos in here?"

"No, not really. Just lamers."

I pointed at the portable stereo on the table between our beds. "What kind of music you listen to?"

"Here, check it out." Alex handed me a box of tapes.

I read off the titles. "Doors, Floyd, Zep. This is some good shit... I'm mostly into thrash and punk." I listed some of my favorite bands: Black Flag, Metallica, Anthrax, Sex Pistols.

"Punk's cool. But this is where it all comes from." He showed me a tape with a black cover.

I leaned in close to read the title. "Motörhead. Oh, man, I've been wanting to check them out!"

"Oh, we'll check 'em out alright. We're gonna be rocking some major tunage. For sure."

From the hallway came a bellowing command: "Lights out in five!"

"Jesus, does she just scream like that all the time?"

"Yeah. Vera's got a real set of pipes."

"She could front a hair metal band."

"No shit."

That night, I was out with the lights.

Group

I woke up the next morning and stared at the cottage cheese ceiling. If I squinted just right it could be the surface of the moon. The light in the room was dim through the tinted plexiglass. I leaned over. Alex was reclined on his bed with a tattered paperback. I read the title: *Breakfast of Champions*.

"What's up?" I asked. "You studying for the big test?"

"Check this out." He held the book open to a page with a drawing of a large asterisk. "It's an asshole."

I laughed and then coughed. "Man, I need a cigarette."

"I remember when I first got here and couldn't smoke. It was torture."

"So you got any tips on how I can get to the second level as fast as possible?"

Alex pondered the question before he replied.

"Talk." He paused to let me absorb his sage advice. "It doesn't matter what you say, just talk. That's the name of the game. And the best place to talk is group."

"Group?"

"Group's a breeze. Every day after breakfast we gather in a circle with this guy Ron and talk about our feelings and why we're here. It's all a bunch of bullshit, but if you wanna get to the second level, you gotta talk in group. So it's always good to have something to talk about. Otherwise you have to make something up on the spot, which seems easy, but it's not. Trust me. That guy Ron's no schlub. He'll make you sweat. The best thing to do is offer people advice. Add in a dash of insight from your own perspective—anything to be a part of the discussion. That's what they're looking for."

There was a knock on the door and Rosie walked in. "Time to line up for breakfast," she told Alex.

"Smoke one for me, dude."

I joined the rest of the first level in the common room. On the pushcarts were large pans of scrambled eggs, bacon, grits and biscuits. Arranged on the table were jugs of orange juice and milk. I piled some eggs, bacon and a few biscuits onto my plate and sat down next to Scott.

"I'm so sick of scrambled eggs." Scott stuck his fork into a pile of grits with a crater of melted butter on top.

"I know, they're all runny and gross. Bacon's alright though."

"In the cafeteria you can get omelets. And hash-browns. Pancakes. Waffles."

"Scott, all you do is complain." A guy sat down and introduced himself as he shoveled a forkful of eggs into his mouth. "Larry's the name, being crazy's the game." He laughed heartily and specks of food flew across the table. "Welcome to the Adolescent Ward."

"How long you been here?" I asked.

"Two weeks, but it feels like an eternity," Larry said. "Be a lot better when I'm on the second level though. Gonna get the bump any day now. All my ducks are in a row."

"I guess if you're on the second level it's not so bad here, huh?"

"Oh, sure. The doors are locked, the windows are thick plexiglass, we got video cameras aimed at us all the time and techs watching our every move... But yeah, as long as you can eat in the cafeteria, it's not so bad." His sarcasm was obvious without laughter, but he let out a snort to prove his point.

"So what're you in for?"

"I'm a Jew. In Alabama. Do the math." Larry glanced at me knowingly. "Not that being a Jew is reason enough to get locked up anymore. I'm here cause I beat somebody up. Actually, I almost killed this guy who used to always pick on me, making cracks about Nazis and all that stuff. One day I just snapped. When they finally pulled me off the guy I was bashing his head into a metal door. I didn't even know I was doing it. I'd totally blacked out. They sent me here to find out why it happened and if it's ever going to happen again. So uhm... watch out!" He laughed again.

After breakfast, everybody gathered in a circle on the couches and chairs. Alex waved me over to where he was seated. "Hey, I saved you a spot," he said cheerfully. "I forgot to tell you the most important part of group. You gotta get there early if you want a good seat."

"Why?"

Smiling wide, Alex leaned in close and whispered, "Cause, man, group's a total freak show."

When Ron entered, the collective roar of multiple conversations went quiet. Ron sat down in the empty chair reserved for him and asked, "How's everybody doing today?" He received a weak ripple of salutations.

"Let's see..." Ron scanned the faces and asked, "Who haven't we heard from lately... How about you, Jasper?"

A boy with brown curly hair perked up.

"Last time we heard from you I believe you were talking about feeling isolated from your family and your schoolmates. Have you gained any new perspectives on that?"

Jasper sighed. "Yeah. I've learned that I have a problem making friends because I expect too much out of people, and I never give anybody a chance." Jasper talked reluctantly, his tone forced and his words practiced.

"How do you feel about going home and dealing with your parents and school again?"

"I'm going to be more assertive and less defensive with my parents. Since they're just trying to help me. And I'm gonna try not to be so distrustful of people at school."

"Very good, Jasper. I'm glad to hear that. Who wants to go next?" Ron paused and scanned the group. "Gloria, why don't you tell us why you're here?"

Gloria heard her name and sat up straight. "Well, I'm at Hillcrest cause my mother doesn't want me dating a black boy. A few weeks ago, she was tidying up my room—you know, being a nosey Nelly—and found a stack of letters from my boyfriend that I'd hidden in the back of my closet. At first she was happy that I'd found somebody, but also hurt that I hadn't told her about it. She kept asking me about him and I kept putting her off, coming up with any excuse for why she couldn't meet him. But eventually I told her. Even though I knew what she would say. Shoot, I figured when I told her my boyfriend was black she'd have a cow. But she not only had a cow, she had a sheep, a pig, a chicken and a goat. And then she sent me here. Said I needed help to get it out of my system." Gloria shook her head. "I love my mother, but I think she's wrong about black folk."

"We don't always agree with our parents," Ron said.

"It don't matter none. Soon as I leave here, I'm gonna get right back together with Quentin. It's nobody's business who I date."

"Let's hope that you and your mother can both learn to respect each other's differences and find some common ground."

The room was quiet for several seconds, in honor of the star-crossed lovers. Then Ron cleared his throat and said, "Shirelle, why don't you go next?"

"I'm here cause I'm broken," Shirelle said, matter-of-factly. "And they still haven't figured out how to fix me."

"We've talked before about this, Shirelle. Why do you feel the need to label yourself?"

"Cause everybody thinks I'm crazy. People always say, 'I want some of what you're on.' But I try to tell 'em that I'm just doing my thang, you know? People say, 'That girl's not right in the head.' But I just say, 'Y'all can suck my ass!'" She chortled loudly.

"Is it really important what other people think?"

"It ain't. I'm just telling you what they say. I don't give two hoots. They call me crazy when I'm doing my thang, but when I'm quiet and just thinking to myself, they say I'm depressed. Everybody thinks one thing or another... I got a list."

"Is skank on the top of your list?" asked Cindy.

"Suck my ass!" Shirelle snapped. "You think you so

special, acting all highfaluting. But you from Leeds and Leeds ain't no *Lifestyles of the Rich and Famous*."

"Least I'm not a skank."

"Let's try to be civil," Ron said. "Shirelle, what is it about Cindy's attitude that bothers you?"

"I just don't like these girls who think they're so high and mighty, putting on airs like they're better'n everybody else. Cindy's just a bitch in a pretty dress. And that don't make her special."

"As if you could even afford a dress that wasn't made out of an Alpo bag."

"Ah, hell no!" Shirelle stood up and raised her fists.

The group oohed and ahhed.

Ron tried to restore order. "Shirelle! You know where that kind of behavior will get you."

"Yeah, you're not being very assertive," Cindy said with a snicker as she leaned back in her chair.

"Don't aggravate her, Cindy," Ron said. "Shirelle, I'm asking you to please take your seat."

Shirelle sat down and pointed her finger at Cindy. "If we weren't in here, I'd turn your ass inside out. Then take a picture and mail it to your grandma."

"In your dreams, potty mouth."

"Girls!" Ron raised his voice. "This is not acceptable."

Rosie emerged from the nurses' station. "Do we have a problem in here?" Her voice carried such commanding resonance, she didn't even have to yell.

"No, ma'am," Shirelle and Cindy said meekly in unison.

"Then I suggest you settle down."

"Let's try to stay focused on constructive comments only," Ron said. "Now, Cindy, if you have a problem with the way Shirelle is acting you should try to be more courteous in your approach. Maybe you can help each other. It's important to learn from your peers and express yourself without fear of ridicule. That's what group is for. This is your forum, but we can't have this name calling and insults." Ron let us soak up his words for a few minutes. "Now, does anybody have something constructive they'd like to share?"

"I have a question," Alex said.

"Yes, Alex."

"What would a chair look like if our legs bent the other way?"

Everybody cracked up.

"Settle down, people. Alright, thank you, Alex, for that insightful contribution." Ron kept a straight face. "That's all the time we have today."

On the way back to our room, Alex told me, "And that was group. Best way to spend an hour when you got nothing else to keep you entertained."

MISTER NICE GUY

Later that day, in a small conference room, I met a portly, middle-aged man. Dave. My therapist.

"In this room you are free to say whatever's on your mind," he said. "You can ask questions you think are too personal to bring up in group. And if you feel the need to use expletives, that's fine too. I understand how kids talk these days. If it helps you express yourself, go for it."

Dave had an unfinished face. As I sat there listening to him talk, I imagined him with a different look. He needed something, a beard or a moustache. Maybe a goatee. Dave the beatnik. An accessory wouldn't hurt either. A pair of glasses or a monocle. That's it! A goatee and a monocle. Maybe a top hat, like the guy on the Monopoly box. I smiled as I rearranged Dave's face.

"Do you have any questions?" he asked.

"Just when I'm getting to the second level."

"That will be determined as you participate in the program."

"But isn't my situation different?"

"Every situation is different. The important thing is to follow the rules and take advantage of what we have to offer here."

"And what about my brother? They said I'd be able to see him. But if I can't go anywhere, how can I talk to him? He doesn't like to be alone."

"Your brother will be fine. Don't worry."

I sighed and straightened my legs. "So what are we supposed to talk about then?"

"We could talk about why you're here," Dave suggested.

"I don't know why I'm here. They didn't tell me."

"You must have some idea."

"Oh, you mean what happened with Rick, my dad and Joey?"

"Okay. Let's talk about that."

"What's to say? I found these pictures when I was snooping through my dad's stuff. They wouldn't let me smoke so I had to take matters into my own hands. After I found them, I gave them to the social workers." I paused. "That's it."

"How did you feel about the photographs?"

"I guess I would've rather have found some money or cigarettes, that's for sure." I laughed uncomfortably. "It sucks, you know? But what can you do?"

Dave grunted and made a note in his file.

"Anyway, I figure you guys know more about what's going on than I do," I added. "You have all the files. You've talked to my brother, right? And you've seen the photos. That pretty much sums up the whole story. With a feather in its cap."

Dave continued making notes as I blabbered on, almost against my will.

"I was just trying to do the right thing, you know? Now I'm starting to feel like I did something wrong."

"This program isn't about whether or not you've

done something wrong."

"You lock people up as a reward?"

"We're not trying to punish you. We're trying to help."

"Help me with what?"

"You don't feel like you have something to work through here?"

"Like what?"

"Like what happened with your father?"

"Nothing happened to me, if that's what you're thinking. I'm not in any of those pictures. So... nothing to worry about here." I smiled. "I'm fine."

Dave sat there looking at me without making a sound.

"Really, I'm fine." I felt like I had to say it multiple times to get him to believe me.

After a few minutes, Dave said, "I think we need to start getting serious." He reached into a briefcase and placed three spiral notebooks on the table with band names and logos scrawled onto the covers.

"Hey, my notebooks!" I'd forgotten them in the rush to get out the door when the social workers picked us up.

Dave spread them out on the table and flipped through the pages. "What were you trying to express in this song, 'Fade to Black'?"

"That's a Metallica song."

"Yes, I see you have that written underneath. You have a whole section devoted to what you call your favorite rockers: 'Mommy's Little Monster,' 'Suicide's an Alternative,' 'Annihilate This Week.' What is it about these songs that made you want to write them out in your notebook?"

"I wanna be a songwriter, so I write out lyrics as

practice. I study how the verses, bridges and choruses work together. Most of the songs in there I wrote."

"I see that..." Dave flipped through the pages. "This is one of yours: 'If telling you would kill you, to realize would be suicide.' What did you mean by that?"

"It just, you know, sounded cool."

Dave turned the page. "Here you have, 'One of these days when I have the guts, I'm gonna jump right in front of a pick-up truck.' Another one goes, 'Sometimes I just wanna blow it all away. Light a fuse and watch the world go up in flames.' That one you titled, 'Hate Bomb'."

"They're just songs," I said with an awkward chuckle. "They aren't supposed to mean anything."

"What kind of songwriter would you be if you wrote songs that had no meaning?"

"I mean, yeah, sure... they have some meaning. But you're reading them all wrong. I'm just trying to come up with songs that rock, you know?"

"You don't think this subject matter reflects your true feelings?"

"No. I'm not afraid to say what I want." I laughed to show how good-natured I was. "Look, you're totally judging these songs based on the words. But that's only part of it. My songs are about the music as much as the lyrics. These are just words on paper, so you have to imagine the rest of the song... the power of the music." I reached for one of the notebooks and flipped to a particular page. "Take this song right here, 'Prisoner of Time.' This one I just wrote. It starts out real mellow, almost a ballad—but once the verses start, it gets fast, but not too fast. It's still slowly building up to the bridge. Then it's like—" I replicated the sounds of the instruments with my mouth, blowing out air rapidly through pursed lips: "*Dun dundun! Dun dundun! Dun dundun! Dun dundun!* Then it goes back into the verses again. But after the second bridge it keeps building to the chorus where the guitars go, *Chuga chuga chuga chuga. Chuga chuga chuga chuga.* The double bass kicks in and it's getting faster..." I tapped my feet rapidly against the floor. "Then the lead guitar starts to wail." I pantomimed playing a guitar. "Right, and then it's like, 'I'm a prisoner! Prisoner! Prisoner of time! And the walls! The walls! They're all in my mind!'" I covered my mouth to replicate the background vocals. "Then it just goes totally insane, the drumbeat is all over the place as the bass follows the lead guitar: 'Prisoner! Prisoner! Break free!'" I leaned back in the chair and folded my arms across my chest. "So you see, that song's really about freedom, you know? I wasn't trying to be negative or anything."

Dave smiled at my performance. "I can see you are very enthusiastic about your music."

Just when I thought we were getting somewhere and Dave would realize I didn't need his help, he pushed the notebook with the plain green cover across the table. "What about this one?"

The green notebook was my journal. My mind raced as I tried to remember all the crazy stuff I'd written. I knew there were detailed descriptions of my trysts with Missy, commemorated so I didn't forget anything. But there were also death fantasies, the pros and cons of suicide versus running away, as well as my short autobiography, in case anybody ever wondered why I'd offed myself.

As Dave stared at me, I didn't know what to say. I

just sat there, trying to not look crazy.

"I think we need to start talking about why you're here," Dave finally said.

"I don't want to kill myself." I tried to be adamant but reassuring. "Honestly. I was just writing that stuff out. Half of it is bullshit... Just stories I was writing. You can't hold me to that."

Dave said nothing for several minutes while I squirmed in my chair, waiting for the verdict. I could sense my diagnosis was grim. The room was hot. I was sweating bricks.

"Okay, our time is up for today." Dave gathered all my notebooks into a stack with the file on top and directed me out the door. "You can join the others now."

Later that day I met Dr. Winscott.

"I just have a few questions for you." He clicked the end of his pen in and out as he alternated his gaze between me and my chart. "How have you been feeling?"

"Fine."

"Good. Are you sleeping alright?"

"Sure."

"Appetite normal?"

"Yeah."

"Good. Good. Good. Any recent thoughts about hurting yourself?"

"No," I said quickly. "I never wanted to hurt myself. If you're asking about that stuff in my notebooks, I was just making things up, you know, writing out loud, so to speak. I'm not suicidal." I laughed. Would somebody who wanted to kill themselves laugh? I wondered.

The doctor looked up from his chart. "Any allergies?"

"Nah, I'm cool like that."

That night, Vera called me to the counter and set two small white paper cups in front of me. One had two round pills on the bottom and the other was water.

"What's this?" I asked.

"Your medication."

"I'm not sick."

"Doctor's orders."

"What are they for?"

"Just take the pills."

I dropped the two pills into my mouth and drank the water.

"Now open wide and lift up your tongue."

Back in the room I told Alex, "Oh man, this sucks! I'm never gonna make it to the second level!"

"What happened?"

"They think I'm suicidal or something and put me on pills!"

"That's a drag."

"Man, they just don't get it."

"Yeah, well, welcome to the land of confusion, where everything is a misunderstanding."

THE DAILY THERAPY

After several days in lockdown, I was numb from the recycled air and the lack of nicotine. I couldn't tell if the meds were kicking in yet, but the days had coalesced into a blur of revolving faces and authority figures as I moved from one therapeutic activity to another.

Life at Hillcrest revolved around a tight schedule.

Every day after breakfast we gathered in the common room for group therapy. The spectrum of realities in the circle changed constantly as the participants cycled through the ward. It seemed like there were always new faces and others missing. Most usually kept quiet or mouthed off to get attention. Some talked of the trouble at home, the burden of expectations from their parents. Others discussed problems at school, the pressures of making the grade and fitting in, going with the flow and the constant fear of failure. Some were at odds with life in general, connecting their own malaise with the issues that plagued our generation: the threat of drugs, AIDS, the nuclear holocaust... It wasn't easy to make it in the world. It was enough to drive you insane. Some seemed apologetic or slightly embarrassed as they recited their confessions, and there were those who talked nonchalantly, as if they were relating the plot of a TV show they'd just watched the night before.

"I got in too many fights with my parents."

"I feel ugly inside. And yet everybody always says, 'You're so beautiful, what do you have to complain about?' But I don't feel that way. Inside, I'm a monster."

"I was depressed and swallowed a handful of my mother's sleeping pills."

"I don't wanna be fat."

"My dad's a fag and he raped my little brother. So I turned him in to the cops."

I must have said it so many times the words had lost their meaning. I related my story with bravado and pride, knowing that I wasn't at Hillcrest for any action of my own. An innocent bystander, a good Samaritan... anything to distinguish myself from the others.

After group therapy, Dave and I met in the small conference room for individual therapy. Then it was on to educational therapy, which is what they called school, held in a small classroom with one teacher. We all had our own lesson plans, but the work wasn't hard. Just reading parts of a textbook and answering multiple-choice questions.

Recreational therapy was on Mondays, Wednesdays and Fridays, when we left the ward and marched through a caged walkway to a small gymnasium on the other side of the hospital. Some guys played basketball, others lifted weights. I told the recreational therapist that I didn't believe in competitive sports, so he made me walk around the court with the girls. Which was fine by me.

On Tuesdays and Thursdays we went to occupational therapy, where we sat around tables doing arts and crafts projects. While we worked, we chattered mindlessly. It seemed like the kids in the Adolescent Ward were always in the midst of a conversation. Scott usually got the ball rolling with one of his inane questions. Like the day we were painting coffee mugs and he asked, "What's the most embarrassing thing that's ever happened to you?"

"Getting asked this question." I'd decorated my mug with an anarchy symbol and the Dead Kennedys logo.

"C'mon, I wanna know."

"Okay, I'll go first," Shirelle said. "My mom still laughs about the time me and my family drove to Florida and I saw the license plates and said, 'Oh, look, they have their own license plates.' My dad was like, 'Of course they do. Florida's a state.' It was so funny. I didn't know that Florida was a state. I just thought it was part of Alabama."

"Florida's a state?" Cindy asked with a sarcastic snap of her Juicy Fruit. "I didn't know that."

"Suck my ass."

"You're so rude."

"And you look like you just kissed a cat's asshole."

"I know what Cindy's most embarrassing moment is," Scott said. "Remember the other day when she fell asleep on the couch and she was sucking her thumb?"

Cindy snorted. "That's not the most embarrassing thing that's ever happened to me."

"Then what is it?" Scott asked.

"I'm not telling you, twerp."

"C'mon. Say."

"My most embarrassing moment would have to be getting sent here. And being around the likes of y'all."

"Whatever."

"Next."

"My whole family are Alabama fans," Wendy said quickly, before Shirelle had a chance to get too worked up. "But I secretly like Auburn."

"Yes!" somebody shouted. "War Eagle!"

"Roll Tide!" another countered.

"They should disown you."

"I got a good one," I said. "As a kid I used to watch WWF wrestling all the time."

"Were you a Hulkamaniac?" Alex asked me.

"No, I preferred Macho Man. He had the best manager. Anyway, I'd try out moves on my little brother. I'd put him in chokeholds and leglocks. I even pile-drived him once. But one day, he wasn't around, so I set up all the cushions from the couch on the living room floor, had them all laid out like a body resting against the ropes. I was about to do my finishing move—the Flying Crotch Shot. I ran across the entire length of the apartment and dove ass first into the pile of cushions. But I missed. Landed right on my tail bone."

"Wipeout!"

"Hurt so bad I saw white flashes and lost my breath. I was at home alone too, rolling around on the floor gasping for breath. I felt like such a dumbass. So now, my ass is broken."

"My ass is broken too," Larry said. "It's got a crack in it. Wanna see?"

"No one wants to see your ass, Larry."

"No, seriously, it's fucked up. It looks like this."

"Ewww, that's not right."

"I once ate dog kibble."

"Did it taste like chicken?" Scott asked.

"It was chicken flavored, so yeah."

"I used to stick keys in sockets as a kid," Alex said. "Did it all the time."

"Somehow that doesn't surprise me."

And on and on... until Nancy showed up to take us back to the ward.

During free time, when I wasn't hanging out with the guys at the pool table, I sat with Shirelle and talked about everything and nothing all at once. She reminded me of Missy, full of spunk and pushy as all hell. She wasn't the cutest girl in the ward, but I would have gone for it anyway. Except I didn't know how to make a move with all the constant supervision. Besides the techs at their station in the corner of the room, there were video cameras in each corner.

We always behaved with the awareness that we were being monitored. So one day I asked Ryan and Alex how to get with a girl on the ward.

Ryan said, "You can go through the ceiling."

I responded to his suggestion with a doubtful glance, wondering if I had made a mistake bringing my concerns to the pool table.

"It's easy," he swore. "You just push up the panels, use a chair to hoist yourself up and then walk along those metal bars. You kind of have to know where you're going though. Once this guy fell through and broke his arm."

"I don't know about climbing through the ceilings," I said. "That seems pretty extreme."

"There's the sauna in the gym?" Larry offered. "Ah, but you have to be on the second level to use the sauna."

"Why is everything better on the second level?" I asked.

"That's life in the ward, my friend." Alex slapped my back. "Newbies are second-class citizens."

"What do you guys do when..." Larry looked over his shoulder and made the universal gesture for jerking off. "You know?"

"I have no idea what you fools are talking about," Ryan said with indignation.

Alex laughed. "Man, you can't even service your own needs in here without them writing it down in your chart."

"The shower?" Larry suggested.

Ryan squinched his face. "I wouldn't want to use the shower after you've been in there... you know?"

"Well, you gotta do something to relieve the pressure or you start having wet dreams," Larry said, his voice low. "The pressure keeps building and building until you're all pissed off at the world."

"The man rag." Alex shook his head.

"The man rag," Larry echoed. "It's the worst."

We started cracking up just as Scott walked into the room.

"Were you guys talking about me?" he asked.

The worried look on his face made us laugh even harder.

Friday night was movie night. I sat next to Shirelle as Vera ceremoniously rolled a large TV on a metal stand into the common room.

"Tonight we're going to watch *Back to the Future*," she said as she inserted a tape into the VCR.

Shirelle smiled and tucked an unruly strand of red hair behind her ear. "You sure looked like you were having fun in the pool today," she told me.

I'd finally been allowed outside to go swimming that morning as part of recreational therapy. While Shirelle laid out with the other girls, I showed off my cannonball skills.

"You got a little sunburned," I pointed out. Her nose was red and her lips were flakey, coated with lip balm that glistened in the florescent light.

"I'm not supposed to be in the sun," she said. "I don't tan. I just freckle."

When Vera walked by, she looked at us sitting with our knees resting against each other. "Do I need to separate you two?"

"No, ma'am," Shirelle said weakly and moved her leg away.

Vera put her finger on my shoulder. "Where are your glasses? It says in your chart you're supposed to wear glasses. Do you have them in your room?"

"Yeah," I mumbled reluctantly. "But I can see fine."

"No. You need to go get them. If you want to watch the movie, you have to wear your glasses."

I hated wearing my glasses even though I couldn't see more than a few feet in front of my nose. I wasn't even sure why I'd brought them with me from the house when we were picked up. Of all the things I'd left behind and could've taken instead...

"Do I really hafta wear them?" I asked Vera.

"I'm not wasting my time telling ya to do something so I can just change my mind about it."

I looked in Vera's face for a trace of sympathy. The wrinkles in her face were deep set, as if she had worn the same expression her whole life.

I went to my room and fetched my glasses.

"Hey, four-eyes," Larry said gleefully when I returned.

"Don't listen to that stanken ass," Shirelle said. "You look real cute."

"Thanks," I said glumly.

When the lights went out, Shirelle relaxed her knee against my leg again. During the movie, I kissed her chapped lips. It was like kissing buttered toast.

───────────

Over the next week, Shirelle and I were inseparable. We made out two more times. Once in the laundry room and another time on the couch in the middle of the common room. It was a risky stunt, but we'd enlisted the help of several kids to form a barrier with their backs to us.

As I was beginning to anticipate spending my days with her on the second level, once I finally had enough points, Shirelle came back from her individual session one morning and announced that she was on her way home.

Just like that.

The following afternoon, we all gathered around and wished her luck, hugging her neck and promising to write.

After we'd said our goodbyes, I stood around the pool table, playing a game with little cheer.

"You know who's really in charge here?" Ryan asked and then answered his own question, "The insurance companies. They're the ones paying the hospital and everybody's paycheck. And believe me, they'd rather not spend their money. That's why when you start doing better, you go home. They figure you're cured and they cut off the payments. The parents aren't gonna pay out-of-pocket, so they take their kids home. But is anybody really cured? Hell, we all know everybody's faking it so they can go to the cafeteria and smoke cigarettes, right? The problem that brought them to Hillcrest in the first place isn't really solved, it's just hibernating. But hey, as long as the hospital gets paid, and the therapists get paid, and the psych techs—"

"We get it," Alex said. "The system is totally screwed. What else is new?"

I kept my mouth shut. As a military dependent, I had some of the best insurance around. Even one of the psych techs told me, "With Champus, you're not going anywhere anytime soon."

Playing the Part

Most adults didn't care what I had to say, but the therapists at Hillcrest were so captivated by my anecdotes, they made copious notes whenever I opened my mouth. I felt like I was on a stage, reciting my lines from memory, never deviating from the spiel I had practiced and perfected in my head. I reveled in bouts of wanton candor and filled the air with protean tales and random facts, casually embellishing the parts that didn't zing. I was more than happy to explore every crevasse of my subconscious, if that would get me to the second level. But no matter what I said, I was never any closer to that carton of cigarettes with my name on it in the cabinet behind the nurses' station.

At the beginning of each individual session, I made a point of appearing eager to get the ball rolling.

"So, what are we gonna talk about today?" I'd ask Dave. "You wanna hear about my dreams? Had this one last night where I was talking to a guy wearing a striped shirt and then, this morning, I went to the common room and there was a guy wearing a striped shirt. Weird, huh? You know, I think I might be psychic. Cause that's not the first time it's happened. A couple months ago I had a dream about bowling and the next day my friend invited me to go with his family to the bowling alley."

Dave smiled politely. I knew he didn't want to hear about my dreams. "Why are you so afraid to talk about what happened to you?"

"I'm not afraid of anything. I already told you, Joey's the one in the pictures. I'm just along for the ride. I don't know why you think something happened to me too."

"Did something happen to you?"

"No."

"Okay then."

I laughed. "But you don't believe me."

"Why do you feel that way?"

"Because I'm still on the first level."

"You still have work to do."

"But what am I supposed to work on?"

"That's what we're trying to figure out."

"Well, I think you're just wasting your time."

"How did you feel when you found the photographs?"

I thought about suggesting that I might be interested in discussing things if I had just one Marlboro, that cigarettes have a way of opening up new perspectives in my mind... *Nudge, nudge. Wink, wink.*

But I knew it wouldn't work.

I sighed.

"Was I surprised? No, not really. This wasn't the first time I'd found naked pictures. Before we left California, I discovered a stash while I was snooping through Rick's stuff. I even took one and put it in my mom's box of Frosted Mini-Wheats."

"Pictures of Rick and Joey?"

"No. They just of Rick and his friend Michael the Fly holding each other's dicks."

"What did your mother say?"

"Nothing. I always figured she knew what Rick was like and didn't care. She was just too busy with her own shit."

Dave made a bunch of notes in his files before he continued. "If you knew something was wrong, why did you stay with your father?"

"My dad was..."

I didn't know how to talk about my father anymore. It seemed weird to say anything in his defense. He was the bad guy. So how could I explain my desire to abandon my mother and live with a person who was so bad he deserved to spend the rest of his life in prison?

"My dad was..."

The old man made me feel special. When he picked me up for a visit to his apartment in Baldwin Park after he moved out of the house, we went on a shopping spree. Our first stop was Carl's Jr. Then Vons, where he let me fill the cart with all my favorite foods: Jell-O Pudding Pops, Brach's candy, French bread pizzas, chips, cookies, soda... all the junk food I could eat. And to top it off, his building had a pool. I was in paradise. The next day he dropped me off at the West Covina Mall with thirty dollars so I could get new clothes. He bought me shoes. All I had to do was ask for a tape and we were at Tower Records.

For the first time in my life, I was the center of attention. As one of five kids, spending time alone with my father was a luxury I had never known before. There had been hints, sure, during short excursions to the store, or when he drove us to Camp Pendleton the week of our birthdays to renew our military ID cards... but a whole weekend? Just the two of us? I was never happier, or more disappointed when he dropped me off at home Sunday afternoon and asked me to bring Joey the next weekend. I had a good thing going and I didn't want to share. Of course, Joey was thrilled beyond belief to partake in the bounty.

After a few weekends of the royal treatment, the old man asked if we wanted to live with him permanently.

We said yes.

Unequivocally.

That summer it was the three of us. Joey and I slept on Army cots in our own room. It was the best summer ever. We never had any money, but we went swimming every day. And there was a whole new neighborhood to explore. Some days we just started walking and didn't stop until it was almost dark. We'd panhandle a dime and call the old man to pick us up.

But then Rick came back from boot camp. As soon as he took up residence at the apartment, Joey began sleeping in the master bedroom with the old man and Rick. From the beginning, Rick asserted his dominance over the household.

The old man had always been laid back when it came to parenting, which Rick didn't like. He accused me of walking all over my father. Before we'd even left California, Rick started talking about how things were going to change when we got to Alabama, how we were going to be like a real family. I had no idea what he meant.

"So your father let Rick run the show?" asked Dave.

"Yeah, but I didn't need anybody telling me what to

do," I told him. "I've always been my own boss."

"You knew what was going on before you left California?"

I should have figured Dave would go back to that part of the story. But he didn't ask the questions I asked myself: What if the old man wasn't really a fag? What if Rick forced him into it, like how he forced us into it?

I always figured Rick was a fag. But I never thought of my father that way. Maybe it explained why he let Rick boss him around, why he hated Mom and why he never talked about women in his past. Just his "buddies." Still, when I found the photos, I was shocked.

Later that night, the old man and I were eating dinner at the table by ourselves. I couldn't even look him in the face. I just sat there while he talked, staring at my food, the images from the pictures polluting my brain. I wanted so badly to cleanse them from my mind, to wash my brain out with soap...

"Sometimes we have to accept things," Dave said. "Things that are difficult to... understand."

But there was more to it than that... there was always something else...

Peer Reviews

"How do you spell 'attitude'?" I asked Alex.

"A-S-S-W-I-P-E."

"Oh, that's what I thought, thanks."

Alex and I were completing our weekly peer reviews in the room. Metallica on the boombox.

"Who'd you get this week?" I asked.

"That new guy, Russell."

"I got Jill."

"Wanna trade?"

"Hell no."

The peer reviews were excruciating, but part of the program was evaluating each other, so we suffered through the task.

In just a short amount of time, most of the faces in the ward had changed. A few days after Shirelle left, Larry was discharged. Cindy was gone too. The new admissions were quickly indoctrinated and blended in almost seamlessly. Some we liked and hung out with, others we just ignored.

"I've gotten pretty good at writing these reviews," I said as I beat a rhythm with my pencil.

"Lucky you," Alex said sarcastically. "Suicides are a

snap. What am I supposed to say about this guy?"

"You know his story, just put that down."

"Let's see… Big ole black boy, local football star, out on a bender, breaks into a white woman's house and rapes her. The end."

"Man, I feel bad for the guy. He had all these colleges scouting him and everything."

"A first-class ticket to ride."

"And now he's fucked to the gills."

"Just a positive psych evaluation away from juvie, where they keep you locked up tight."

There was a knock at the door.

Rosie entered. "Louis, you have a telephone call."

"Hey, kiddo." It was Sandra. Her voice was like cotton candy. "How you holding up down there?"

"Everything's cool." I played along with her sunny disposition. "What's up?"

"Just want to touch bases, let you know what's going on with the trial. Your therapists at Hillcrest think you shouldn't have a problem serving as a witness. But how do you feel about it?"

"I guess that's alright. What about Joey? I haven't even seen him since we got here."

"That's the other thing I'm calling about. Joey is leaving Hillcrest. He's going to a place called the Big Oak Ranch."

"What's that? Another hospital?"

"No, it's a place for boys who need special attention and structure."

"A group home?"

"Not exactly. It's more like a community. There are several houses on the property where the boys live."

"Why's he going there?"

"Joey doesn't seem to be getting the help he needs at Hillcrest. He hasn't been cooperating with the program and they feel that the ranch is the best place for him right now, to get him the help that he needs."

"Why? What's wrong with him?"

"Louis, your brother has been through a lot. You both have. But for Joey, the ranch is a place where he can recover and grow. And he'll have fun there. They have lots of outdoor activities."

It sounded like she was reading from a brochure. I imagined the color snapshots of grassy fields with picture perfect houses and kids playing ball, all smiling like they were having the times of their lives. But I knew it was bullshit. I'd seen what they were selling with my own eyes. Except my brochure advertised French Camp.

"I thought we were supposed to stay together," I said. "They haven't even let me see Joey once since we've been here."

"I'll talk to them about that."

"I'm worried about him. He gets freaked out a lot."

"Well, once your evaluation is finished at Hillcrest, you can join him at the ranch. That way you'll be with your brother. You'd probably really enjoy it. There are other kids and horses, sports..."

Horses? I don't care about no stupid fucking horses! I wanted to shout into the receiver. We gave you guys everything you asked for! We did our part! Now give us our reward!

"But I'm going to stay here at Hillcrest for a little while longer, right?" I asked.

"Sure, for now. But eventually your insurance will run out. And the ranch is something to consider."

"Alright." I hung up and went back to my room.

"Hey, I got it!" Alex shouted in victory as I walked through the door. "His sense of judgment was temporarily impaired!"

"Awesome," I replied with faux gusto and fell onto my bed. I buried my face in my pillow and squeezed it against the side of my head.

Motherfuckers! I seethed into my feather death mask, trying to process the triple whammy Sandra had just laid on me: the trial, Joey sent to a group home, my future at the hospital in question... I wasn't sure how to make sense of all the developments. I squeezed the pillow tighter until I felt my temperature rise from the lack of oxygen and gasped for air.

"You alright?" Alex asked. "You need me to call somebody?"

"I'm cool," I croaked. "Everything's cool." The last thing I need is more interference from those... those... Motherfuckers!

I knew that if I didn't keep my shit together they were going to roast my ass. Just like Joey.

Motherfuckers!

I didn't want anything to do with the Big Oak Ranch. It sounded just like French Camp. After all the trouble I'd gone through to avoid going there, how could I just surrender and wind up at what was essentially the same place?

Fuck that!

And why were they sending Joey there anyway? French Camp was supposed to be my punishment and now it had been projected onto the one person who hadn't done anything wrong.

Motherfuckers!

I felt like an idiot for thinking that I was the one pulling the strings when I was the puppet! How could I be so stupid? I scolded myself for not realizing that they would eventually flip the whole scene. They already had Joey in their clutches and it was just a matter of time until they came for me. If I didn't think of something fast, I wouldn't stand a chance.

No More
Mister Nice Guy

Before he left for the ranch, Joey and I were allowed one short conversation at the double doors that
separated our wards. It was the first time we'd seen or
talked to each other since we'd been admitted.

"We're not gonna make it to the Calgary Manor, are
we?" Joey's head was like a deflated basketball.

"Man, you gotta forget about that place. Things have
changed and we need to go with the flow… see where this
new ride takes us." I tried to be enthusiastic about the
changes. "You know, we got the trial coming up and then
after that… we'll get something better. Trust me. Hey,
maybe this ranch place will be cool."

"We need to talk to Mom."

"What can she do?"

"She has to do something. She's our mother. I wanna
go back home." His eyes filled with tears.

"You just gotta wait a little bit longer. Everything's
gonna work out after the trial."

"I just don't wanna be alone. I wanna be with you."

"It's not like it'll be forever. I'll see you again soon.
C'mon. Be cool."

"You gotta ask them to send us back to Mom's house."

That's the last place I wanna be, I thought. But I promised him that I'd do my best. I didn't know what else to say. Joey began to tremble as he wept. I saw Rosie look in our direction.

"Everything's gonna be cool, okay? Trust me. I'll figure it out."

———————

During my next session with Dave, I sat with my arms tight across my chest. He wanted to know how I felt about my brother leaving.

"I'm fucking pissed," I said, thinking, You can take your mental manipulation and shove it up your ass! I'm so fucking sick and tired of going over the same fucking bullshit every fucking day! "We didn't even do anything wrong, and yet we keep getting the shaft. We made this huge sacrifice and what are we getting out of it? Nothing! Nada! Squat! It's like we're the ones getting punished! Where's the justice in that?"

"Why do you feel like you are being punished?"

Who do you think you are, fucking Socrates? "Cause I can't smoke. I can't have my Walkman. I can't eat in the cafeteria." I can't do shit!

Before Dave opened his mouth, I knew what he was going to say, because he always said the same thing. "Those are privileges for the second-level kids."

"So why can't I get on the second level already? I've done everything you guys asked. I turned in my father and Rick." Now just give me my reward!

"The level system isn't just some arbitrary torture."

It's not? Coulda fooled me. "But the level system shouldn't even apply to me. I'm not here because I did anything wrong."

"This isn't about whether you've done something wrong. It's about being a part of this program and trying to take advantage of what it has to offer."

"There's nothing for me to take advantage of! I'm not like the other people here. I shouldn't have to go through what they're going through."

"What makes you feel like you deserve special treatment?"

I got it coming. "Cause I'm owed." In spades.

"Do you feel like you're owed something because of what's happened to you and your brother?"

Hell yeah! "We turned in the bad guys, we did a good deed, we helped carry out justice. That's what you guys wanted, so that's what we gave you. And then you're gonna stab us in the back and have us locked up. I don't think that's very fair." If you ask me. "If you ask me."

"You don't feel like you have issues you can work on here, that you can benefit from this program?"

No. You guys don't get it... "Whether I do or I don't, all I know is that I'm locked up. You keep asking about my father and how I feel about what happened. I keep saying the same thing, but nobody believes me: I don't really care. I mean..." How do I say this? "I feel that it doesn't pertain to me on a deeper level." Is that better? Does that compute with your psychological mumbo jumbo?

"You're a smart kid. Look at it from our point of view. In our experience there are certain factors we see in adolescents who have experienced trauma. It has to be terribly painful for you to live with what's happened. It's normal to want to repress the emotions you feel are bad. But you have to work through them by acknowledging them. Does that make sense?"

But *this* is a traumatic experience, motherfucker. "So what you're saying is that I'm fucked up because of what somebody else did to another person? How is that possible? Why don't you think I'm telling the truth? Nothing happened to me. I just want to get to the second level. And it seems that the only way I can get to the second level is if I admit something that isn't true. Would it be better if I just made something up? Cause I can make something up, if you want me to." It would be my pleasure.

"Of course we don't want you to make anything up. We just want you to express your real feelings. Don't just keep everything bottled up like a tough guy all the time. Show us the real you. The real Louis."

I blanched. The real Louis? I knew who the real Louis was and I'd been running away from him since I first laid eyes on him. "I'm just trying…"

"Listen, the first thing you need to do is to start sharing some of these feelings with your peers."

"My peers?"

"You need to start sharing in group."

"I do. I share all the time."

"No, you make jokes and incite tangents."

"I'm doing the best I can." I tried to work on his sympathy. He had to have a heart in there somewhere. "I really am, but it's hard…"

"You need to come clean. Once and for all. Let go of all this baggage you've been carrying around with you and then you'll be on your way to the second level. That's all we're asking. If you do it for cigarettes and your Walkman, fine. If you do it to eat in the cafeteria, then that's your motivation. But you have to get with the program."

For the next several days, I thought about my options. Joey was in the jaws of the system. There was nothing I could do for him. Not until I got my head above water. I had to figure out a way to get to the second level so I could think straight again. I needed my cigarettes. I needed my music. Once I saved myself, then I could figure out how to save Joey. I'd gotten this far and if I let the system chew me up as well, we'd both be lost.

Motherfuckers.

Dave wanted me to come clean. But what was I supposed to say? That I'd always known Rick was a major perv? That from the moment he entered our lives, Rick had been a scourge upon my family? That, even though he came after us under the guise of friendship, once he learned our weaknesses, Rick absolutely wrecked our lives?

All of our lives.

Just thinking about it made me want to put a gun to my head and blow my brains out. That was the only way to exorcise all the horrible memories.

I wanted to fight against the memories, not embrace them.

Fuck you! I wanted to shout.

Fuck you, brain!

Fuck you, memories!

Fuck you, nightmares!

Fuck all of you!

But where would that leave me? Trapped in this

quagmire of what I could and couldn't face? I had to come clean. I had to tell them that over the years Rick had fondled, groped, molested—whatever you call it—every single one of us for the privilege of his company.

We did it for candy.

We let it happen for chips.

We went along for sodas.

We sucked it up for rides on his moped.

We took the pain because the rewards were so desirable.

It usually happened when Rick slept over at our house, which he did at least several times a month. We were always psyched when he spent the night. Nate, Joey and I would hang out with him in the pop-up trailer we used as a playhouse in the backyard. During these night-time hangouts, Rick talked about things like hard-ons and jacking off. We were old enough to know some of the facts of life, and what our parents hadn't explained to us, we'd picked up on the playground: to make a baby you put your penis in a woman's virginia. I was never sure why they named a state after a female body part, though I figured there had to be some connection. But Rick went into minute detail, particularly about dicks. He wanted to know if we jacked off yet and offered to show us all sorts of tricks, like how to use a vacuum cleaner so it felt like we were getting a really good blowjob.

I remember being confused more than anything. Going along with it and not knowing why he wanted to do something that felt so weird and… so *stupid*. It didn't make sense. But hey, as long as we got something out of it… you know? The trick was to just close your eyes and think about something else. It wasn't as bad as eating creamed corn or split pea soup, that's for sure.

Every once in a while Rick invited one of us to spend the night at his house. But only the best behaved, because sleeping over at Rick's place was a major privilege. He always made the occasion more special by stealing money from his older brothers and taking us to the corner store for junk food. And in the mornings, he'd help us with our baths, making sure all the nooks and crannies were squeaky clean. Because Rick only wanted the best for us. That's what he told us all the time.

But as I got older, I began to see Rick for who he really was: an asshole who got a kick out of inflicting pain on little kids. I learned to keep my distance and reject his advances. Then he moved on to Joey and I was relieved it wasn't happening to me as much. I figured that since Joey got all the special favors from Rick, he couldn't be too unhappy.

There were even times when I thought Joey had it made.

Sure, I knew it was a drag to be hogtied and get spanked and pinched, and those pinpricks—god damn, those hurt! And that smell—that acrid pungency, like a new bicycle tire. It seemed like everything Rick touched had that smell. I had to hold my breath whenever I went into his room.

But even though he had Joey to satisfy his needs, sometimes I'd wake up in the morning with my pants undone and my underwear all twisted around. I'd retrace my steps the night before, trying to figure out when Rick could have slipped me something. He always said, "The only reason you're here is because your father promised me a blonde ass." He called me a tease because I wouldn't play along.

A wet blanket.

A party pooper.

After a while, I started putting my dresser in front of the door at night.

But that didn't stop him.

And there was more to it.

There were the nightmares.

And there was the Beast.

For as long as I could remember, I'd had the same dream: I'm walking through a dark hallway. The walls are decrepit. The paint is peeling. The ground is littered with trash. Insects crawl among the debris. There is a fecundity in the air. I see pipes. In the distance, I hear a growl, summoning me. I have no choice but to follow. The sound of its guttural call beckons me down a flight of stairs… The growl becomes louder, echoing off the walls. As I move towards it, I wonder, Why do I keep going? Why don't I run away? Then I feel its presence. A million fingertips dance across my skin. I open the door to face it and I awake.

But I couldn't tell anybody about the Beast.

It was against the rules.

The Beast had told me that He would only make it worse for me if I ever talked about Him.

And besides, I couldn't admit any of that to a bunch of strangers. Fuck no. There was no doubt in my mind that I'd be locked up nice and tight for the rest of my life if I revealed the truth. Even a hint. Hell, if I thought about that stuff longer than a few minutes, I was ready to sign myself up for the straightjacket.

Still, I had to give them something…

They wanted dirt.

They wanted blood.

They wanted guts.

They wanted tears.
And they wouldn't be satisfied until they got it.
Motherfuckers.

Pyrrhic Victory

The next day in group, when Ron asked if anybody wanted to share, I raised my hand.

"I feel like I need to talk about why I'm really here." I heaved a sigh before I continued. "Since I first showed up I've been saying how everything that happened with my little brother and my dad had nothing to do with me. They say that's bullshit, and maybe they're right. They say I'm repressing my true feelings. Maybe I am. But why would I want to talk about all that horrible stuff? Hell, why would anybody even want to hear about that stuff? The way I look at it, I'm doing everybody a favor by not bringing it up. But it seems like I have no choice and I have to talk about my true feelings." I paused and studied a mole on my knee through the hole in my jeans. "My true feelings... How do I truly feel about what happened with my dad and my little brother? Well, I turned my father into the cops. I think that sums it up pretty much. What else is there to say? The rest is ancient history. Cause right now, I have more important things to worry about. You see, I just found out they put my brother in this place called the Big Oak Ranch. They say he's gonna be there for an undetermined time, which I guess means forever. They also said I could go to the ranch too. But I don't wanna go to a place like that. I don't wanna live with a bunch of guys and give up my music and my fashion and have Christianity shoved down my throat every day. That's not why I turned my father in to the cops. And how is it fair that they put Joey in a place like that? Where he's all alone. Yeah, sure, being at the ranch is probably better than what was going on before, but I thought maybe we could get something out of all our suffering. It looks like I was wrong. We all get screwed in the end. My dad's locked up in prison, Joey's locked up at the ranch, and I'm locked up in a mental hospital. Game over. Nobody wins.

"You see, here's the thing. They think I'm trying to buck the program, but there's nothing the system can do for me. What can anybody do? Pat me on the back, say, 'Hang in there, champ'? Come on, there are no solutions. So what if I feel like shit about my dad? Who gives a fuck about how I feel about what happened when there's all this other shit happening? I gotta save my brother. It's my only chance at making all this worth something. I shoulda done something sooner. But I didn't know what to do before. Now I do. Now I know what's gonna help my brother. And it ain't getting locked up in a group home with a bunch of rejects. I gotta save him from that life. They can either let me get to the second level so I can do something to help him before the next stop on this train to disaster, or keep me on the first level and maybe one day the meds will finally kick in. Cause sitting around talking about how I feel isn't gonna do shit for me or my brother. There's nothing else for me to figure out except how to make it through the jungle."

I started to cry. Even though I knew that's what they wanted to see, I covered my face to hide the tears. Wendy handed me a Kleenex. As I blew my nose into the tissue, I glanced askew at Ron. He was making a note in his chart.

The Second Level

"Never underestimate the power of a legal buzz," Alex said.

We were on our fourth cups of coffee.

"Man, I'm so jacked up right now it's like my face is melting," I said as I held the sugar canister upside down for a full minute, slowly stirring the brew into a caramel sludge. I exhaled the smoke from a Marlboro and the receptors in my brain singed from the overload of nicotine, sugar and caffeine. In the two days since I'd been on the second level I had smoked almost three packs of cigarettes. Making up for lost time.

When I was on the first level and thought about that inaugural cigarette, I pictured a slow intricate process that began with smacking the top of the pack against my palm, making sure the tobacco was nice and tight before I slipped my thumbnail under the tab in the cellophane and slowly pulled the strip. And then, as I folded back the top of the box, the smell of tobacco would get the juices flowing: Look out lungs, here it comes! Finally, I'd light the end and take a drag. Maybe blow a couple smoke rings for the dramatic effect. But on the morning of my first day on the second level, after Rosie pulled my carton out of the cabinet and handed me a pack, I ripped it open so fast I tore the hinge off the box. The moment I set foot in a designated smoking area, I lit up a cigarette and sucked it down until I was nauseous from the onslaught of nicotine. I got such a bad headrush, I had to sit down before continuing through the breakfast line.

The cafeteria was as glorious as I had expected. All the stories I'd heard were true. There was every type of food I could imagine: sandwiches, burgers, pizza. Even foods I'd only heard about on TV, like Beef Stroganoff and Veal Parmesan. There was a soda fountain with all the flavors of Coke. And for dessert, an array of cakes, pies and jello, as well as a tub of whipped cream and a bowl of cherries to top it all off.

I took full advantage of the influx of culinary delights.

"Y'all gonna make yourselves sick." Nancy shook her head in bemused resignation as Alex and I chased the coffee with chocolate cake.

"That's a risk I'm willing to take."

Alex and I laughed as we let out two simultaneous plumes that formed a murky cloud over the table. There were only three of us smoking, but our pleasure dictated the conversation.

"Smoking is such a disgusting habit." Emily waved the air in front of her face.

I sighed. "But I love it so."

"Why'd you start smoking?" asked Scott, who had made it back to the second level the same week as me.

"I wanted to be cool. Duh."

"Better luck next time."

"My mother smokes," said Alex. "After a while I

figured, if I'm gonna die from secondhand smoke, I might as well join in."

"My parents smoke too," Emily said. "But I think it's disgusting. I'd never smoke. I don't like the idea of being an addict."

"You're addicted to food," pointed out Scott.

"You can't be addicted to food, dummy. Everybody has to eat."

"What about meds?" I added. "They get us hooked on their pills." I had recently begun a campaign to get off the medication they were giving me, claiming it made my skin itch and flake off.

"They want everybody drugged up all the time to keep things flatline." Alex lit a new cigarette with the end of his old one. "They shove pills down our throat then tell us anything else that might make us feel better is wrong. Seems like a group of kids would be ready to start a riot if it weren't too much of a hassle."

I nodded. "It's hard to rebel when you're all drugged up."

"I myself try to avoid the manufactured reality of pharmaceuticals," Alex said. "But that's only cause they haven't offered me anything I want yet."

Rosie walked up to the table. "Louis, you have a phone call. It's long distance. They're holding the line so we have to go quickly."

I stubbed out my cigarette and followed Rosie back to the ward.

"Hiya," I said cheerfully into the receiver, assuming it was Sandra with the latest news on Joey and the upcoming trial. "What's up?"

"Louis?"

"Yeah?"

"It's your mother."

"Oh." I thought the voice sounded familiar. "Where are you?"

"I'm at the house in Saks."

"What are you doing there?"

"Somebody had to sort out your father's mess."

Hysteria

"How long has it been since you last saw your mother?" When he found out she was coming for a visit, Dave wanted to know how I felt about it.

"Nine months."

"You must miss her."

I shrugged.

"What was your childhood like?" Dave asked to break the silence.

"There were happy moments, I guess. Used to have pictures to prove it too, until my brother Nate and I took all the photos of us out of the family albums and ripped them to shreds. We even cut ourselves out of group pictures."

"What motivated you to do that?"

"To remove ourselves from the life of these crazy people who had brought us into the world."

"Were you upset about your parents' separation?"

"No. Them splitting up made sense. What seemed crazy was how my mom reacted to it. As much as she seemed to hate him when he was around, as soon as my dad left, she was desperate to get him back. She even tried to kill herself by swallowing a bottle of aspirin and slitting her wrists with a dull steak knife."

"That must have been very difficult for you?"

"Not really. While she was in the hospital, Nate and I threw a My Mom Tried to Kill Herself party." I laughed alone.

"She recovered obviously," Dave said after making a note.

"Yeah. But afterwards, she started crying all the time. She did it right in front of us, getting down on her knees and putting her head on our laps, asking us what she should do. It was embarrassing. Nate and I would look at each other and just cringe. We had no clue what she expected from us.

"At night, she'd come into my room, telling me she was gonna kill herself. She'd go into detail, how she would drive to the Union 76 and get a tank of gas, then run the garden hose from the exhaust pipe through a crack in the window. Every night for several weeks she came into my room and talked about it. After a while I just pretended to be asleep, hoping she'd leave me alone. Some nights she'd say the car was all gassed up and ready to go. She'd tell me goodbye and that she loved me, but she just couldn't go on living... I wouldn't say a word. I'd just lay there, frozen still. I'd wake up in the mornings wondering if she'd be alive or dead. Then one day, she just disappeared. During the day she was working, but at night she went to these Parents Without Partners meetings, where single people with kids got together at various nightclubs around town. She started bringing strange men home. We'd wake up and there'd be some random dude in the kitchen drinking coffee. A couple guys hung around for a while. This one dude named Eddie, he was cool. We liked him.

After Eddie, there was an old bald guy who drove a Porsche. This other guy lived with us for a few months. He used to sit around the house all the time watching TV or reading library books. Had an extra toe on each foot. One day, he stole Mom's car. Just drove off and left her high and dry. A few weeks later, the police tracked him down in Texas."

"How do you feel about all that?" Dave asked.

I laughed. "My mother's got lousy taste in men."

The next day, I was waiting in my room when I heard familiar voices. I looked out the door and saw my mother walking down the hallway next to Sandra. She was carrying Rick's boombox.

"I've been so worried about you." She squeezed me tight. Then she began to cry and pulled out a tissue to dab the mascara in the corner of her eyes.

I set the boombox on my counter, resisting the urge to focus on it rather than my mother.

"She brought you something else." Sandra handed me two bags. Inside one was an éclair. The other had the new Def Leppard tape, *Hysteria*.

I took a bite of the éclair.

She turned to Sandra. "He's always had such a sweet tooth. His grandmother encouraged it when he was a baby by putting sugar in his food. But that only increased his yearning for sweets. As a child he threw tantrums over what was on his plate, tossed bowls and spoons onto the floor, staged hunger strikes."

Sandra laughed politely.

"Do you like the new tape I got you?" Mom asked. "I can't believe how expensive tapes are these days. I forgot the list you sent me at home when I went to the store, but the salesman suggested this one after I told him you liked heavy metal."

Yeah, five years ago, I thought about saying. On the phone I had asked for a Sex Pistols tape. But I thanked her anyway. At least I had the most important item I'd requested, Rick's double-cassette-deck stereo. One of his prized possessions that I'd always been prohibited from even breathing on. But he wouldn't need it anymore. I knelt down and fiddled with the knobs to make sure all the decks worked. I was glad I hadn't smashed it with the rest of his stuff.

"He's always loved music," Mom told Sandra. "As a baby he crawled around whistling all the time. When he got older he used to dance like… what's his name, the singer with the big lips?"

"Mick Jagger."

"Yes. You loved that band, the Rolling Stone."

"Stones. The Rolling Stones."

"He wanted all the attention. Oh, and here, I almost forgot this." Mom held out a envelope. "This girl Missy came by the house. She wanted me to give this to you."

"Really?" I snatched the envelope and tore it open. It was a card. On the front was a bunny with a rainbow over its head and "Get Well" spelled out in the arch. It was from Missy's church. The whole youth group had signed it with little personalized notes:

"You're a cool guy. I wish we could have talked more."

"Be strong. Jesus loves you."

"May the Lord keep you strong."

Missy signed it, "I'm praying for you."

She's praying for me? What the fuck does that mean? I had been hoping for a letter promising a visit and major make-out session. Oh well... She was probably back with Waylon.

Cynthia, one of the staff psychologists who looked like Rosanna Arquette, led us down the hall to the classroom where four desks were arranged in a circle. Cynthia and Sandra remained in the room to monitor our conversation. I could tell Mom was nervous under their scrutiny.

"Am I going home with you?" I asked.

"I want you both to come home with me." She looked at Sandra.

"We're not sure what's going to happen yet," Sandra said.

"But after the trial we can go home?" I asked.

"We're still working on that. Right now you just need to concentrate on your treatment here at Hillcrest."

"What's gonna happen to Joey?" I asked. "How long does he have to stay at the ranch?"

Mom started to say something but stopped short. It was obvious they didn't want her to tell me something.

"A friend of yours, Casey, came over and talked to me," she said. "He seems like a nice boy. He wanted to know how you were doing. He said to tell you hello. And these girls came by the house asking about Joey. I had all this stuff from inside the house on the back porch, trying to sort what was trash and what to keep. The girls saw his photos from school and they each wanted one."

"Did you give it to them?"

"Sure, why not?"

"What'd you do with the rest of our stuff?"

"I had a yard sale."

"You didn't sell my guitar?"

"No, it's packed."

"And my amp?"

"It's in the car. Don't worry. I kept what belonged to you and your brother. Everything else I had to get rid of. But I can only take what fits in the car."

"You're driving Dad's Cadillac back to California?"

"At least I get something out of the marriage." She turned to the other women. "He was so proud of that car. I don't know how I'm supposed to pay for it. I'm barely scraping by as it is, with Avon and working at JC Penny. I'm already risking a foreclosure on the house by taking this much time off…" Mom complained about her finances and the struggle of raising three kids on her own without child support until they said our time was up.

Her entire visit lasted about an hour.

GABBY THE CUTTER

"I feel like a bug under somebody's shoe." The new girl was spread out on a chair, the scars on her arms like chaotic spider webs. When Ron called her out in group she made no attempt to hide her contempt for him, Hillcrest and the rest of us.

"Why do you feel that way?" Ron asked calmly.

"Why do you think?" She spit the words out, her ferocity like an unhinged shutter in a windstorm.

"Who are you angry with?"

"Everybody! Y'all think you can judge me, but you don't even know who I am. So, FUCK YOU!" She stood up and kicked a table.

Those nearest moved out of her way.

Ron leapt to his feet. "This behavior is unacceptable."

"Fuck you!" She screamed as she ran her fingers through her blonde hair, clenched her fists and pulled out two wads.

Rosie ran into the room. She and Ron grabbed the girl's shoulders. She struggled violently in their grasp, throwing punches at Ron and clawing at Rosie's face as they carried her down the hallway. She kicked her feet and gnashed her teeth like a feral beast. We listened to her screams until the door of the Time Out Room slammed shut. After that her wail was muffled, like the ominous screech of an owl in the distance.

I looked at Alex in awe. This girl was the most exciting thing to hit the ward since Justin, the Bible eater. We were both impressed. Not only was she a total mental case, she was gorgeous.

She'd showed up two days before. We were coming back from occupational therapy. Alex and I were charging up the stairs doing our usual routine: him growling in his best James Hetfield, "Back to the ward!" while I responded with a guttural snarl, "You will do! What I say!" And then in unison, "Back to the ward!" As we smashed through the door, we stopped in our tracks. There she was, in a Mötley Crüe shirt, standing at the nurses' station with her head down. When she looked up through matted strands of hair, her face was feline. Alex broke the spell. "Rock and roll," he said in his bad English accent.

On the ward, she kept to herself. In the common room she sat alone, barely registering anybody's presence. During group she scowled and refused to participate. She marched along reluctantly through the various daily activities, never smiling or showing any reaction beyond a deathray gaze.

"She's so fucking cool," I enthused to Alex and the other guys. "What do you think she's in for?"

"Murder?" Ryan suggested.

"You think so? That would be awesome."

After her episode in group, she spent a day in the Time Out Room. The next morning she was back in group. Ron wasn't taking it easy on her.

"Would you like to talk about what happened yesterday, Gabrielle?" he asked.

"Don't ever call me that. Nobody calls me that. I'm Gabby."

"Well, Gabby, I think it's important to discuss what's bothering you."

"Do I have a choice? You gonna lock me up again if I don't do what you say?"

"We're only trying to help."

"Coulda fooled me."

"What's upsetting you, Gabby? What are you feeling right now?"

"Right now?"

"Yes, this very moment."

"I'm sick of hearing everybody whine about their puny little problems. 'Wah, wah, wah, my parents don't love me.' 'Wah, wah, wah, mommy didn't put my math test on the fridge.' 'Oh, woe is me, daddy didn't come to my ballerina recital.' Boo. Fucking. Hoo. I'd like to see you hafta deal with a real problem."

"What do you consider a real problem?"

"I'm no expert."

"Do you have a real problem?"

"I got no complaints. Next."

Gabby seemed happy to be left alone, and everybody was more than willing to oblige. But I was desperate for any interaction with her. If our eyes just happened to meet for a split second, I tried to smile, though mostly I looked away quickly. Every conversation within her earshot was for her benefit. I spent hours thinking of witty things to say, hoping to break through her hardened façade.

After she'd been on the ward for about a week, Gabby sat down on the couch near the pool table while Alex and I were playing a game. She flipped through a tattered copy of *People* as we passed the cue back and forth to make our shots. I watched her in my periphery, racking my brain for a snappy comment.

When Alex sneezed, his whole body shuddered from the expulsion like he was having a fit. His convulsions usually came in triplets with a minute or so delay between each.

After the third outburst, I said, "Goddamn you!"

Gabby looked up as Alex stared at me in disbelief.

"Oh, man." His voice was anguished. "I can't believe you just said that to me. Now I'm going to Hell." He sobbed dramatically for effect.

I glanced in Gabby's direction and shrugged. "He was gonna burn in Hell anyway."

She went back to her magazine, but not before I noticed a faint smile.

The next day, during free time, I gathered all my courage and sat down next to Gabby.

"What's up?"

"Not much."

"Cool."

After a moment of awkward silence, she said, "I'm dying for a smoke."

"It sucks, I know. I was there myself. For three weeks. They told you about the second level and all that shit?"

"Yeah, but I ain't doing nothing for these assholes."

"I don't blame you. It seems like the worst thing in the world. I felt that way too, when I first got here. But you don't really hafta give them what they want.

All you gotta do is fake it. That's what I'm doing. We're all faking it. They think their system works, but it's all bullshit." I knew I was talking too much, but there was little I could do about it. I opened my mouth and the words just spilled out.

"These people are weirding me out," she said. "I wanna get the hell outa here."

It was hard to look her in the face. Her black eyes were like ink spots on parchment. There was a small mischievous sparkle in the onyx depths that transfixed me.

"Are you really from LA?"

"Yeah, my dad was transferred to Saks with the Army."

"Oh, I'm from Ohatchee."

"Really? Is Ohatchee close to Saks?"

"We're practically neighbors. I drive through Saks all the time."

"What a coincidence." I smiled as I stared at my sneakers.

Alex joined us.

"What's up?"

"I just took an IQ test." He winced. "My brain hurts."

"So now they're finally gonna be able to prove you're retarded?"

"I've killed enough brain cells over the years to qualify for the short bus."

"I've given myself whiplash, like, twenty times," I said. "That can't be good for the ole noggin."

As we laughed, Scott walked into the common room and made a beeline to where we were sitting. "What y'all talking about?" He plopped down on the couch.

I introduced him to Gabby.

"So who you for, Alabama or Auburn?" Scott asked her.

"What a stupid question."

"What? I ask everybody that question."

"I know. And it's stupid."

"I don't really care for football," Gabby told Scott nicely. "But my family's Auburn."

"Oh." Scott was disappointed. "I like Alabama."

"I haven't been interested in sports since I hit puberty," I pointed out with a nervous laugh. "By the time I was twelve, it was all about music."

"What kind of music you listen to?" Gabby asked me.

"I used to be into metal, but now I mostly listen to punk."

"I haven't heard much punk."

"I can make you some tapes," I said. "I have a stereo with a double cassette deck."

When Ryan showed up, he walked to the abandoned pool table and looked confused. He saw the four of us talking and slowly made his way to the couches.

"How was hypnotherapy?" I asked him.

"Relaxing, as always."

"What's hypnotherapy?" asked Gabby.

"Downstairs they got this room," I explained to her. "You sit in a La-Z-Boy chair and listen to tapes on headphones."

"What do they say?"

"Who knows? I always fall asleep."

"Me too," Ryan said. "I don't wake up until the tape ends. Those chairs are really comfortable. They must cost a mint."

"You can't remember what the voice says?" Gabby asked.

"Nope."

"They're definitely brainwashing us," Alex said.

We all laughed, including Gabby.

For the next few weeks, I followed Gabby around like a lovesick puppy. I sacrificed opportunities to smoke and eat in the cafeteria just to be near her. After a week of resisting the program, Gabby had learned to play along. She started sharing in group and participating in activities. She even began wearing dresses, to entertain her mother's wishes that she look more feminine. It was hard to imagine she was the same girl who had thrown such a fit when she was first admitted. But everybody got with the program eventually. There was no other way to the second level.

As we sat around the common room, discussing everything under the sun, I waited for the green light that never came. I convinced myself that our bond was deeper than what most guys and girls experienced. It was pure. I read the scars on her body and interpreted her razor vocabulary. She told me the blade was about perfection. When she ran the edge across her skin, it was like perfection.

"Who's Shane?" I asked one day. I had intentionally avoided the question despite the prominence of the name carved on her arm.

"He's this guy..."

"Your boyfriend?"

"It's complicated."

"Why'd you put his name on your arm?"

"Stupid, huh? I was in Florida with my parents. I didn't wanna go, but they forced me. I hate the sun. I hate the beach. I was bored and pissed. So I wrote his name in my arm. I don't regret it, even though I never showed him."

"Do they ever go away? The scars?"

"I hope not. In fifty years none of this will matter, you know? But I'll always remember what I went through because it's carved in my skin. I see them as mementos." She laughed. "Shit, if I had a razor, I'd probably make one to remember Hillcrest."

"What would you write?"

"I don't know..." She thought about it with a smile. "Maybe, 'I want out,' or something like that..."

"Oh." I didn't like to think about her leaving, but Gabby talked about getting out of Hillcrest all the time. She focused on her release more than anything else. That's how she justified her conformity. She did it to beat the program and go home.

"I don't think they're ever gonna let me out," I said. "But it's not that bad here. Being at Hillcrest is better than a group home or some other fucked up place. Plus, I never had anybody to talk to before who wasn't freaked out by the thoughts in my head. It's like I fit in, for the first time... in a mental hospital." I laughed.

"Eventually you'll leave, right? You can't stay here forever."

"I guess. I mean, my life is determined by a judge now."

"What about your brother?"

During group, I mostly talked about Joey, what he was going through and what the future held for the both of us. I knew he had to be on the verge of losing his shit at the ranch, all by himself. There were some in the group who thought I should go be with him, regardless of whether they made me cut my hair or took away my tapes. But I juggled the two rotten apples, hoping for a third that would sweeten the deal.

"I still don't know what's gonna happen yet," I said.

Gabby looked away. "I got a little brother too. I don't think I could just bail on him."

"What can I do?"

"You can't just leave him there."

"It's not up to me."

"Fuck that. Everything is up to you. As long as y'all are together, what does it matter?"

"You make it seem like I can just pretend I'm somebody else."

"All I'm saying is, don't let these motherfuckers think you don't have a say in your own life. They can take almost everything else away from you, but they can't take what's inside you."

"Yeah, well, I still don't know what's gonna happen. There's my father's trial and then after that..."

I didn't know what else to say. I wanted to tell her so much, about the prospect of going back to Rosemead and living with my mother, about what it was like before I left, the nightmares... the Beast. I was sure she'd understand. If anybody could understand, it was her. I wanted her to tell me that if I went back to Saks, we'd hang out all the time. I would have given anything to hear those words. But we just sat there until it was time for the next daily activity.

Olive Garden

I stood in the doorway of the bathroom as Alex filled both hands with mousse, fingered it through his curly hair and rubbed his head vigorously with a towel. He smiled at his reflection in the mirror as he sealed the mess of hair with Aquanet.

"We're gonna totally blow everybody's mind in that place."

After Alex finished his coiffure, I took his place in front of the mirror and molded my hair into a mohawk with gel and paste. Then we took turns applying eyeliner.

"Watch you don't poke your eye out," Alex told me.

"How do chicks do this?"

"They are mysterious creatures."

I caked on the eyeliner and smeared it with my fingers, just like the lead singer of Social Distortion.

When we walked into the hallway, Ryan was leaning against the wall in his usual attire, khaki slacks and a polo shirt. He shook his head. "You guys are out of your minds. Louis, you look like a psychotic raccoon."

Gabby and BJ walked out of their room.

"Crazy goddamn wow!" Alex whistled and slapped

his leg.

"My god." I walked up to Gabby. "You look amazing."

With her hair feathered Heather Locklear-style and her face lathered with makeup, Gabby had been transformed into a glamour girl.

"Who knew she could be so pretty!" BJ said as she pushed Gabby closer to me. "A little Maybelline and, voila!" BJ wore bedazzled bellbottoms with a pink feather boa around her neck.

"Hey!" Scott yelled as he stood in the hallway with his arms outstretched. "Nobody told me we were getting dressed up!"

"Oh, Scott." BJ ran back to her room and returned with a multi-colored scarf and a large floppy hat.

Scott danced a little jig and swung the scarf around dramatically. "How do I look?"

"Fabulous!"

"I can't believe I hafta be seen in public with you freaks," Ryan sneered.

As Nancy drove into the city, we all talked at once, excited to be away from the ward, if only for a few hours. Alex sat in the front seat and fiddled with the radio, looking for a rock station.

"This place has the best breadsticks," he shouted over the headrest.

"I already know what kind of spaghetti I'm gonna order," said BJ. "Fettuccini Alfredo."

"What's that?" Scott asked.

"I don't know, but it's good," BJ said.

BJ was from Oneonta. On her first day on the ward, she walked right up to the pool table area and introduced herself. "I'm Bobbi Jo. They call me BJ for short. Yeah, I know what it stands for." In group that day she came right out and told everybody why she was in Hillcrest. "I got caught making out with my friend. A girl. Now everybody thinks I'm a lesbian. But I was just kissing her. It's not like I was doing anything else. I'm not even sure what else we coulda been doing."

The restaurant was crowded with the after-church, Sunday-brunch crowd. We walked through the front door and every head in the place turned towards us in our motley outfits. The only sounds came from the pots and pans clinking in the kitchen.

"Rock and roll," Alex said.

Once we were seated with menus, everybody reached across the table for breadsticks at once. In the rush of hands, glasses of Coke and containers of parmesan were knocked over and silverware dropped on the floor. Nancy tried to keep us in line, though she could only do so much.

"Hey, those are my breadsticks!" Scott shouted when Alex snatched one off his plate.

"Tastes better if you steal them," Alex said with a mischievous smirk.

"Give it back."

"Hey! Not after they've been in your mouth."

"We need more breadsticks," said BJ.

"Garçon!" Alex snapped his fingers in the air. "More breadsticks!"

I sat next to Gabby. Under the table, I held her hand. Any day, she would be going home. We both knew it and the awareness filled me with so much dread it was hard to appreciate what little time we had left.

Once our food had arrived and we dug into our plates of pasta, Scott announced, "Okay. I have a question!"

"Here we go again!"

"What's the most disgusting thing you've ever done?"

"Oh, talk dirty to me, baby," BJ said lasciviously.

"I think I can win this one." Alex leaned back in his chair. "I once made out with my dog."

"No! Don't say that!" BJ roared with laughter.

"Let's try to reel it in a little," Nancy whispered as she glanced over her shoulders at the other diners.

"I don't think that's something you really want to admit." Ryan ate his noodles with precision, using both his fork and his spoon.

"I mean, I didn't, like, start it. Maggie came up to me, looking so seductive, with her tongue hanging out and all her eight nipples exposed."

"Did you make sweet, sweet love to your dog?" I asked.

"Wait." BJ tried to catch her breath. "Why are we talking about bestiality again?"

"That's enough!" Nancy seethed. "Really!"

"What about you, Scott?" Gabby asked. "You always ask the questions, but you never answer them."

Scott thought for a moment. "Do you think it's normal that I piss myself?"

"What?" Alex gasped and a wad of half-chewed bread flew across the table.

"Oh my god!"

"Children!"

"No, it's not normal," BJ said, her brow furrowed in concern. "Why are you peeing yourself?"

"I can't control it. I think it's from my medication."

"Scott the screw up," Ryan said. "Can't even pee right."

"Do y'all have to talk about this while we're eating?"

Nancy asked desperately, though nobody seemed to hear.

"I'd have that checked out if I were you," I told him.

"This is disgusting," Ryan said as he tried to seem respectable, slurping on his Coke. "Can I get my crazy on the side please?"

"I'm just joking." Scott was suddenly defensive.

"Scott needs a diaper," I said.

"He definitely needs to be swaddled," Alex said.

"Swaddle me," I intoned.

"I can just see it now," BJ said, holding back laughter. "Scott walking around in his jeans, his butt all puffed out from his pull-ups."

Alex and I made squishing sounds and laughed uproariously.

"I'm a big boy now!"

"Children!" Nancy seethed across the table.

"I was just joking." Scott was red in the face. "I wasn't serious."

"Children, for the love of god," Nancy pleaded. "Please, let's try to not make a scene?"

"It's too late for that," said Ryan.

"Oh, god. I feel dizzy."

"This discussion is beginning to display a distinct tendency towards the silly," Alex said in his fake English accent.

"My brain hurts!" I shouted.

By the time we were ready for the check the table was littered with napkins, spilled soda and marinara sauce. The floor around Scott's chair was covered with small pieces of bread.

"Here comes the waitress."

"Look at this mess."

"Y'all a bunch of pigs."

"Will y'all be ordering anything else?" the waitress asked.

"No, I think they've done enough damage for today," Nancy told her and chuckled.

The waitress tried to be friendly. "Y'all from a drama club or something?"

"We're from Hillcrest," I told her.

"Is that a high school?" she asked innocently.

"Sort of."

"It's a special school," Alex said. "For special needs."

"Who's special?" I asked.

Scott raised his arm high. "Me! I'm special!"

"Scott, you're an idiot," Ryan mumbled.

The waitress seemed frozen in her Clinics.

BJ leaned in close and told her in all seriousness, "We're from the funny farm."

We all looked at each other and cracked up.

"Children!" Nancy bellowed across the battle zone we'd left on the table.

"I prefer the term 'loony bin,'" Alex said.

"I'm partial to the 'nut factory,'" I said.

"I-I-I-I," Scott stuttered. "I'm cuckoo for the 'cuckoo's nest!'"

As we laughed and banged our hands on the table, the waitress smiled. She set the tray with the ticket in it on the table. "I'll just leave this here for when y'all ready." She crept away from the table without another word.

Nancy implored us to get in the van as quickly and orderly as possible. "If this is how you act in public I'm never taking y'all anywhere again."

"What did you expect?" Alex asked her. "You keep us locked up like animals, this is what happens when you set us free."

End of the Heyday

Three days after Gabby was discharged, I sat on my bed watching Alex pull things out of his closet and throw them into a suitcase. Conversation was stunted. Alex was all nerves, apprehensive about the upcoming court hearing.

I'd never seen him so stressed. But I couldn't blame him. In a couple hours, he would either be on his way home or off to juvie.

Once his bags were packed he looked over the drawings on the wall. "You can keep these if you want."

I thanked him. "It's gonna be so weird with you gone. I thought for sure you'd outlast us all."

"Yeah, well…"

"Send me a letter, let me know what happens. You know where to find me."

Alex held out his hand. "Take 'er sleazy."

I walked him out to the hallway. He said goodbye to BJ. Then Rosie led him through the double doors.

PART THREE

A LOST CAUSE

The Mutants

"Hey, Louis, did you know that Gayle steals clothes from the laundry room?" Daneesha's cackle made me shudder. She had a mouth like a picket fence.

Gayle overheard the comment and squealed, "Shut up, Daneesha! That ain't true!"

"Is so," Daneesha said haughtily. "You told me yourself."

"I did not. You lie!" Gayle was Daneesha's roommate. Cross-eyed and fat, she had humongous lips that hung open all the time.

"You the liar," Daneesha snarled. "You did tell me so. You'se a thief and a liar. Tsk tsk tsk. You gonna burn in Hell for your sins."

"Shut up, Daneesha."

Cliff giggled as he watched the quarrel, moving his head back and forth to follow the bickering, a wide grin spread across his face. He scooted his chair closer, half-standing in the process like he was walking with his pants around his ankle. "Wha-wha-what did she take?" Cliff was my roommate. He looked like an iguana with an Alfalfa haircut.

"Shut up, Cliff!" Gayle snapped at him. "It's none of

your beeswax."

"I'll tell ya," Daneesha said, leaning forward.

"Shut up, Daneesha!"

"I know just what she stole."

"Daneesha! Shut! Up!"

"She stole panties!" Daneesha screamed gleefully and exploded with laughter.

"Lies! Lies! Lies!"

"Ooop," Cliff bleated with delight, shaking in his chair and clapping his hands.

"I swear, Daneesha!" Gayle was on the verge of hysterics, her face beet red, wringing her hands and shaking like an epileptic.

"Girl, I talked to this lady and she says all her panties done gone missing. You best be giving that lady back her panties."

"SHUT UP!" Gayle screamed.

"And I bet you got them panties all nastified too, with all your nasty pussy juices."

"SHUT UP! SHUT UP! SHUT UP!"

"Cause I know you got a nasty pussy. It's all crusty from playing with yourself all the time. You think I's asleep, but I seen what you be doing to yourself. I bet you wearing 'em right now. All your pussy snot collecting in 'em."

Cliff bounced in his seat and clapped his hands. "Howie, did you hear that?" he asked Howard, who just sat there, staring at the TV screen and drooling onto his shirt.

Howard was a total coma case and had to be medicated 24/7 or he freaked out. Most of the time he barely said a word, his eyes perpetually glazed over.

As the tiff between Daneesha and Gayle reached a

crescendo, they suddenly went mum. Calvin, the night tech, was standing in the doorway, his face a disgusted grimace.

"This is all kinds of inappropriate!" he said. "Both you girls need to stop talking that raunch."

"She's the one talking nasty!" Gayle cried.

"Talking nasty's one thang," Daneesha said smugly. "Being nasty's a whole nutha thang."

"Alright!" Calvin shouted. "Everybody out! Now! Go on, get to your damn rooms. You pissed me off. No more TV tonight."

"You shouldn't be cussing us," Cliff said.

"Y'all forcing me to talk this way. Now, go on, get!"

Slowly, they filed out of the room, but I remained seated.

Calvin pointed his finger at me. "You too."

I held up my hands. "Moi?"

"Yeah, you. Did I stutter? I said, 'Everybody out' and 'everybody' means you too."

"Hey, I'm just an innocent bystander. I didn't come in here to get traumatized. And now I'm gonna be mentally scarred for life. Extensive therapy won't be able to remove those horrible, disgusting images from my mind…"

"Alright, alright!" Calvin dismissed me with a wave of his hands. "You're fixing to give me a goddamn heart attack."

"You? What about me? I have to live with them. At least you get to leave. I'm stuck here day and night."

"Ah, you ain't got it that bad."

"Yeah right." Fully aware that there was little anybody could do about the situation, I disguised my grievances as hyperbolic jest.

"Stop being so dramatical."

"I just don't know if I can make it here with these mutants."

"You could try to be civil once in a while. They aren't mutants, they're people. And they have names."

"C'mon. You don't like them either."

"I never said that. You're putting words in my mouth. And besides, it's not my job to like them."

"Yeah, but…"

"Look, you need to start showing respect to your fellow residents."

"Please don't call me a resident. It makes me feel icky."

"What makes you so special?"

"I'm ambiguous." I used one of the words I'd recently learned from the vocab builder in an old *Reader's Digest*.

"What the hell does that mean?"

"I'm not clearly defined."

"Oh, you are easily defined. A troublemaker, that's what you are. You have to follow the rules, just like everybody else. I don't know how UN-ambiguous I can be."

"C'mon. I got rights!"

"You got the same rights as everybody else."

"But you know I'm not like them. C'mon. Gimme a break."

"You really don't give up, do you?" Calvin shook his head. He didn't know how else to respond. I knew I was wearing him down.

"No."

"Just… just… ah, forget it!" Calvin exclaimed and left the room.

I grabbed the remote and changed the channel to

MTV.

Calvin and I got into these good-natured squabbles all the time. I gave him a lot of lip. He knew I didn't belong in the Residential Treatment Ward. But after my insurance ran out, this was my only choice if I wanted to stay at Hillcrest. It was either the RTW or a foster home.

At first, I was psyched, because I didn't want to leave the comfort of the hospital, but the RTW was where they put the kids who were too fucked up to make it anywhere else. They were the rejects of group homes and adolescent wards. The Mutants.

I did everything I could to distinguish myself from the other "residents."

The Diagnosis

After a week in the Residential Treatment Ward, I had perfected the mope of resignation. I walked around as if there were a bowling ball tied around my neck. In the mornings, I sulked from my room to the cafeteria to the schoolhouse, where I spent the time learning to type by transcribing song lyrics. Then I dragged heel back to my room. I avoided the Mutants as much as possible, hanging out on my bed, listening to my Walkman and reading magazines.

I missed the Adolescent Ward desperately. I had immortalized my old wardmates in a collage of snapshots, letters, song lyrics, drawings, intake bracelets and other talismans on the wall of my side of the room, convinced that nothing could ever compare to the past three months.

Sometimes one of my old counselors from the Adolescent Ward walked through the RTW. They always stopped to ask me how I was doing. I'd say, "Alright," because I didn't want to bother them with my problems. It wasn't their job to talk to me anymore. Even though I acted casual, I wanted them to feel sorry for me. I wanted so badly to exclaim, "I made a mistake! This wasn't what

I wanted after all!" But I knew it was hopeless. What other choice did I have? I concentrated on the only way out: going back to my mother's house in Rosemead.

Every week or so, Mom called. She sent me the occasional care package with batteries for my Walkman, notepads, pens, books and sometimes a fiver, which helped keep me in cigarettes, although I usually ran out before my next installment.

While I was in the Adolescent Ward, communication with my mother was limited. But without the therapists and psych techs monitoring my every move, she was free to fill me in on what was going on with the old man's case.

I had lots of questions, like why we had to testify at all. Didn't the Polaroids prove the case? That's when Mom told me that the family court judge who was presiding over our custody hearings had destroyed the pictures.

Apparently, some of the arresting officers had been taking other cops into his office and looking at the Polaroids for a good laugh. It got so bad, the judge took them all into the alley behind the courthouse and torched them in a dumpster. He claimed not to have known that the pictures were going to be used as evidence in the criminal trial, thinking the social workers had only presented them as part of the original custody hearing and, with Joey and me safely in the care of the state, they were no longer needed.

The burning of the photos raised a big stink and the judge was relieved of presiding over juvenile cases. The local newspaper even wrote an article about it.

There were a few articles about our case in the Anniston *Star*. Mom sent me photocopies of the clippings. The title of the first piece was: "Soldiers Accused of Raping Youth." They called it one of the worst sexual abuse cases to reach the courts in years. I was relieved, somewhat, that it didn't mention Joey or me by name. But they printed the old man's name. And it's not like there was more than one Baudrey in the phonebook.

"Without the Polaroids, they obviously need you and Joey to testify," Mom said.

Okay. "But what about after the trial?"

"They said you can come back here, to my house."

"With Joey, right?"

"Just you. Not Joey."

"Why not?"

"They say he has special needs." She went on to read me his evaluation from Hillcrest. According to the shrinks, if he didn't have extensive therapy, he would turn into a sexual abuser himself one day. After all the years of abuse, he wouldn't even be able to control it. Which was why they wanted him to be at the ranch. They said he could get the help he needed there.

"It makes so much sense," Mom said. "Why he was held back in kindergarten and the second grade. Why he was diagnosed with dyslexia in the third grade. Why he always seemed so distant."

I didn't know what to say. I didn't want to think about what his evaluation meant. "There's nothing you can do?"

"My hands are tied. You guys told the court you didn't want to live with me anymore. So your father had custody. When the state stepped in, they got custody from him. They say there are legal obstacles that have to be dealt with as far as transferring custody back to me again. I don't know..." She started to cry a little. "I don't trust those women at the DHR. They're up to something. I just feel it."

"You should get a lawyer," I said absently, wanting desperately to get off the phone with her.

"I can't afford a lawyer. I have too many bills as it is. I'm trying to sell enough Avon to make ends meet and go to school for nursing so I can get a better job. It's been rough since your father left me high and dry. Oh, why did this have to happen to me?" She began to cry louder. I sat on the phone with her until the weeping subsided and she complained about wasting the long distance minutes.

I hung up and made the doleful amble back to my room. Cliff was on his bed and tried to talk to me. I ignored him as I lay down. I hit rewind and then play on my Walkman.

At least I had the Sex Pistols...

The Point Store

Sometimes they took us to the mall. As soon as we got there, I ran off on my own so I wouldn't be seen with the Mutants. I spent most of my time at the bookstore and the record store. I never had any money, but I made a mental list of the tapes and books I wanted to buy. Now and then I'd meet people in the stores and we'd talk about music or books.

When it was time to go back to Hillcrest, I'd hear my name over the mall intercom, "Louis Baudrey, please report to the Information Booth." I didn't rush or anything. I was in no hurry to get back in the van with the Mutants. The ride to and from the hospital was like being in the cattle car.

One day at the Record Bar in the Galleria I found a copy of *Never Mind the Bollocks... Here's the Sex Pistols*. I couldn't believe it when I first spotted the tape in the rack. I'd never thought I'd find a genuine copy. Vic had made me a dupe from his dupe, which was a dupe from somebody else's dupe. The sound quality was horrible, full of hiss and talking in the background... I was desperate for a decent-sounding copy. But I had no money. So I asked Nina, one of the psych techs who talked to me about music all the time, if there was anyway I could get some cash to buy this tape. She told Julie, the ward director, and they made a deal. They'd buy it for the Point Store.

Instead of a level system like in the Adolescent Ward, the RTW had a Point Store. Every day, we collected points for doing the stupidest things like waking up without throwing a tantrum, eating meals in the cafeteria without causing a scene, doing our schoolwork and keeping our rooms clean. It was like they gave us points for just breathing. Once a week, we shopped at the "store," which was only a cabinet in the director's office. There were things like toothpaste, deodorant and other personal hygiene items, a few knick-knacks and stationery. Sometimes, if a resident wanted or needed a special item, they would buy it and put it in the store. Like when Cliff needed new socks, they put a pack of striped tube socks in the store. He only needed a few points to get them. They made it really easy for him. But he never got enough points.

None of the Mutants managed to get many points. I usually had as many as possible. I could have bought anything in the store. So, to prove a point, I bought Cliff's socks. I was going to start my own point system. At night, Cliff sang in his bed. Gwen, the night tech, had told him a million times to shut up, but he would just sing in a whisper instead. It annoyed the living crap out of me. After I bought his socks, I told him, "If you want your socks, you gotta stop singing." But that night, as always, Cliff burst into song. I said, "If you don't shut up, you're never getting your socks." But he wouldn't quit. The next day, in front of him, I dropped the package in the cafeteria trashcan with all the slop from people's plates. Cliff was actually surprised. "What did I tell you?" I asked him. He thought I'd give them back after awhile.

So when Cliff found out my tape was in the store he said, "I'm gonna get your tape."

"Like you'd ever get enough points," I told him.

But Cliff was convinced he could beat me. Since the shopping order was determined by the number of points accrued, it didn't matter how many points he actually got. He just had to get more than me.

I laughed it off. There was no way...

When the other residents heard about Cliff's challenge, they wanted in on the action too. All of a sudden, it was me against the Mutants, in a contest to see who could get enough points to buy the Sex Pistols tape. That whole week, everybody was playing it cool. Daneesha and Gayle were like the best of friends. Cliff did his homework and never talked back to Calvin. Howard... well, he didn't count. He just drooled on himself like always.

Every night before he went to bed, Cliff told me, "I'm gonna get your tape. I'm gonna get your tape and break it into a million little pieces."

He was getting all Charles Bronson on my ass. I just laughed and laughed.

After a while, the techs were talking about the tape challenge as well. To encourage the positive behavior, they began to suggest it was possible for any one of us to pull it off. Although they wouldn't say how many points any of us had, they acted like it was a close race. I knew they were just playing it up, convinced there was no way the Mutants could beat me. But secretly, I began to worry. I mean, anything could happen. This tape meant the world to me. To have it that close to my grasp was a dream come true... What if the unimaginable happened and one of them actually beat me? It would have to be a major fluke, but still...

Finally, after a week of near-perfect behavior, Nina and Calvin called us to the station and read off the points. Julie even came out of her office to watch the proceedings.

Howard was up first: Fifteen points.

Shocker.

Then Daneesha. She never got many points either, but this time she had fifty-two points, which was an all-time record for her. Julie said it was the best week she'd ever had on the ward. When she heard that, Daneesha beamed like she'd just won the Nobel Prize.

Next up was Gayle. She got sixty-seven points. Way above average. She was so excited, she almost lost a few points for her rabid outburst.

When they got to Cliff, they rode out the suspense until the tension was at a fever pitch.

Cliff writhed in his seat.

I feigned indifference, chuckling to myself.

After drawing the process out for several minutes, Calvin read the number:

Seventy-five.

"Seventy-five!" Cliffy raised his fists in the air and did a victory lap around the room.

Nina said that in all the time he'd been in the RTW, he'd never earned more than fifty points, his previous high score.

Julie said she was so proud of him.

Cliff looked at me and clapped his hands, practically foaming at the mouth, like the tape was already his.

Calvin made us wait even longer to hear my number, but when he finally got around to reading it aloud, I had ninety-seven points.

"Was there ever a doubt?" I said as I got up to retrieve my tape.

The Sex Pistols never sounded better.

THE COLUMBIA
STREET MAFIA

During the first week of October I turned sixteen. Mom called to wish me a happy birthday. After a few minutes of awkward conversation, she passed the phone off to my baby sister, Danielle. She was only four when I moved out of the house. I barely knew her.

"Do you remember me?" I asked.

"Yeah," Danielle said. "You're my Alabama brother."

I tried to explain that I wasn't actually born in Alabama, but had lived at the same house she lived in for most of my life.

Then I talked to Claudia, my younger sister. We had always gotten along. She filled me in on what was going on at the house and what to expect when I returned.

"What's up with Dad's Cadillac?" I was planning to get my driver's license as soon as possible so I could drive the car around Hollywood.

"It broke down right after Mom got back from Alabama," Claudia said. "Nate had tried to fix it, but he took it apart and couldn't put it back together again. Now it's just parked in the backyard."

Disappointed, I moved on to the next order of

business. "Where am I gonna sleep when I go back home? Is my old room still in the garage?"

Several years back, Nate and I had attempted to convert the garage into a two-bedroom apartment. We only finished one section before we gave up. But to get out of the house, I moved my bed in anyway.

"Nate moved in after you left, but Mrs. Garcia—you remember, our neighbor?" Claudia asked.

"How could I forget?" She was a real bitch. Used to steal our balls when they landed in her yard.

"She called the city."

There was a law about how a living structure had to be three feet from the property line. So Nate put the garage door back on and it had since been appropriated for storage. Mom needed more space to store her many Avon boxes full of old check stubs, receipts, our old baby clothes, toys, school papers... She was a major packrat.

"Who's Mom dating these days?" I asked.

"She's back with Robert."

I laughed. "That dude was such a loser."

Robert had been the most enthusiastic of the guys she brought home from Parents Without Partners. He was always trying to be friends with Nate and me. Told us a story once about this time he was driving on the freeway and a girl in another car threw a liquid substance onto his windshield. When he pulled over to clean it off, he discovered that it was cum. How or why this was possible boggled our young minds. After repeating the story to all the guys we knew, it was decided in the end that Robert was completely full of shit.

Claudia passed the phone off to Nate, who told me about the new high school I would be attending. Since

I'd been expelled from Mark Keppel, Mom was enrolling me at the continuation school where he went after he himself got kicked out of Keppel.

"Century's fucking cool, man," Nate told me. "They're so fucking laid back, you can get credit for fucking anything."

Nate was only a year older than me. We never got along. After the old man split the scene, we were at each other's throats nonstop to determine who would be the man of the house. There was really no other way around it. Somebody had to die for the other to reign supreme. But in the two years that I'd been away, he'd acquired the dominance he'd always wanted and could therefore afford a certain benevolence.

"It's gonna be fucking cool when you get back," he said. "We got our own fucking gang now. The Columbia Street Mafia. We made up hand signs and everything."

"Who all's in this gang?" I asked.

"Javier's the drugs. Oscar's the money. Cesar's got the gun. And Ben is the muscle. Our house is the chop shop. At night we go into Monterey Park and get bikes, bring them back here, strip them and put them back together."

"And then you sell them?"

"Nah. We just ride them around. We thought about listing some in the *Recycler*, but never got around to it."

"What do you do for money?" I asked.

"Collect cans. Odd jobs. I painted Andy's garage a while back. And if I'm really desperate, I'll snag some of Mom's food stamps and buy a banana and use the change to buy cigarettes or beer." Nate laughed. "We party all the time, man. You'll see... It's gonna be so rad when you get back."

Despite Nate's claims that everything was going to be a blast when I got back, I had my doubts. Rosemead was still a part of who I was. But after a year in Alabama, I knew I was different.

Homesick

"As a kid, I was constantly running away from home," I told Nina. "I ran away so much, when my mother called the police to report me missing, the cops stopped taking her seriously. I came home once and found my fifth grade picture on the ground next to the front door. On the back were my statistics. The cops had obviously tossed it, thinking she was crazy or something."

"Why did you want to leave home so badly?" Nina asked.

When Nina and I were alone, I talked to her about going back to Rosemead. That's all that really mattered anymore. In the RTW, they didn't care how I felt about things. My past. The pictures. The old man. There were no programs, no levels... We were just there, in a coma-like existence. Without Nina to talk to, I would have been completely alone with my jumbled thoughts.

"I was just sick of being at the house," I told her. "I figured everybody would be more than happy not to have me around anymore."

"Why do you say that?" Nina was in her early thirties. Mousy hair framed her plain features. Every day she wore the same casual attire and sensible footwear.

I'd always wanted a mother like Nina and often fanta-sized about being a part of her family. She had men-tioned in the past that her three year old daughter only fell asleep at night by listening to reggae music and that her husband was a plumbing contractor who lived on junk food, coffee and cigarettes. I was madly in love with her and wanted to make her happy.

"My mother didn't like me," I said. "Used to tell me all the time that she'd wished I'd never been born. She never seemed to have time for me. It was almost impossible to get any attention without setting some-thing on fire or getting a ride home from the cops. So that's what I did. I got in trouble all the time so she'd pay attention to me."

"Did it work?"

"No." I laughed. "That's why I split."

Nina smiled politely. "I can't help but feel that there's something else…" she said slowly. "Something about the house that brings back memories… or un-pleasant thoughts…"

I wasn't sure what she was getting at. I thought about the hypnotherapy sessions and wondered if I'd revealed something while I was under and that she knew about the nightmares. But why hadn't anybody else brought them up before? Whether I got her drift or not, I tried to control the discussion with my own narrative: "Sure. I hated that house, the street, the kids, the whole place… I remember when we visited other parts of the city, like Pasadena or Mission Viejo, where my uncle lived, I'd ask why we couldn't live in places like that. But Mom said we couldn't afford to move. She complained all the time about the two mortgages, how hard they struggled to pay the bills on an Army sergeant's pay and the weak profits from her fledgling Avon sales... I knew we were poor... Still are poor... I guess even poorer now."

"But there's more to it than being poor, isn't there?" Nina was pushing me and I felt the pressure welling up inside me.

I wanted so badly to tell her about the nightmares and the Beast that lived under my mother's house, in the crawlspace, where, as kids, we were always afraid to go. I remembered the earth beneath me, in my face, my nose in the dirt and the pipes over my head...

But instead, I told Nina that, after I'd spent so much time trying to get away from that house and that neighborhood, it seemed like the ultimate failure to go back.

Rehab Star

From the moment I set foot in the RTW, I campaigned relentlessly that since I'd already made it to the second level on the Adolescent Ward, those privileges should be transferred to the new ward, and I should be exempt from certain restrictions. Like the no smoking rule.

I pitched my case to Calvin because he was the most likely to bend the rules. It took some convincing, but he eventually let me sneak off the ward to smoke in the woods next to the building. He just looked the other way when I slipped out a side door.

I kept my pack stashed in a log. It seemed like a safe enough place since I'd never seen anybody in those woods. Until the day I was heading down the path and a guy walked past me going the other way. I didn't think anything of it at the time, but when I reached into the log, my cigarettes were gone.

I panicked. It was my only pack and I didn't have the money to buy another. Could that guy have taken them? I wondered. I didn't know for sure, but I took off after him.

"Hey, dude!" I yelled, as I ran down the path.

When I caught up with him the guy looked terrified.

"Hey, man, did you come across a pack of smokes back there in the log?" I asked, out of breath.

"I uh..." The guy reached into his pocket and held out the pack. His hands were shaking. "I uhh... I found them."

"Oh, man," I said with a major sigh of relief. "That's cool." I offered him a cigarette but he shook his head. "You live around here?" I asked, to make small talk.

"Uh, I gotta go." He ran away down the path.

It was only a matter of time before Julie found out that I was sneaking outside to smoke. Shortly after my run-in with the local kid, she posted a notice that stated all residents had to follow the same rules.

"No exceptions." Calvin read the last part twice. "Any idea who she's talking about there?"

I laughed it off, but I had to figure out a new tactic to maintain a steady intake of nicotine. Down the hallway from the RTW was the Rehab Ward. They had their own common room, a pool table, a bunch of couches, a television and even a piano. I was already sneaking in there occasionally to snag butts out of the ashtrays. Once they said I couldn't go outside anymore, I began to spend more time with the rehabbers.

I hung around the pool table and kept my mouth shut, listening to them discuss how they ended up at Hillcrest. I was worried that I'd get thrown out for violating their sanctity, though nobody seemed to mind my presence. After a week of lurking in the corner, I got to talking with this guy Josh. He was only a few years older than me. Speed freak. He played guitar. But he was into lame stuff like ELO and the Eagles.

One day Josh asked me why he never saw me at

meetings. I'd picked up enough rehabber lingo to know he was talking about Alcoholics Anonymous.

"Oh, I'd like to go," I said earnestly, "but I don't think I'm allowed."

"They can't stop you from going to meetings. Meetings are open to anybody who wants to attend. It's in the bylaws."

I explained that I was in another ward, thinking I was about to get kicked out. But he didn't seem to understand what I was telling him and said he'd look into it for me.

At first, I thought, Oh great. Now I've really stepped in it. Why would I want to attend a bunch of boring meetings and listen to these fucked up old people talk about how bad drugs are? Then it occurred to me that all the rehabbers did was talk. And while they were talking, they were also smoking. Talking and smoking, smoking and talking. It seemed to be part of their recovery or something. So if they were in these meetings all day long, doing all this talking, they must be doing just as much smoking.

All of a sudden, AA meetings seemed like the perfect place for me.

In order to attend meetings, I had to fill out a form. On it, there was a space labeled, "Drug of choice." I wasn't sure what to write. I made a mental inventory of the drugs I'd come across back in Rosemead. Weed was everywhere, but it didn't have the right panache. I needed something that would make an impression with the hardened drug users in rehab. Besides pot, I had smoked PCP twice and snorted cocaine several times. PCP seemed too extreme. So I split the difference and put down cocaine.

When Julie got the paperwork for my request, she called me into her office.

"It says here you have a narcotic dependency? I didn't see that in your chart before."

I told her that I did a lot of drugs back in LA and, since I was going home soon, I was worried that I might be tempted to take up old habits.

"Ah, a preemptive measure," she said. "Very well then."

A preemptive measure? I didn't even know what that meant, but it worked. Like a charm. From that day on, the psych tech on duty had to walk me to my meetings and pick me up afterwards. Calvin almost flipped out when he got the memo. "What kind of scheme is this?" he demanded. But I insisted that it was a preemptive measure and I couldn't miss a meeting. He just shook his head with bemused resignation.

I went to as many meetings as I could. There was a booklet that listed where and when the meetings were held. All I had to do was plot out my daily schedule of smoke breaks. Besides the AA meetings in the evenings, there were Cocaine Anonymous meetings on Friday and Saturday nights, Narcotics Anonymous every afternoon, and Al-Anon on Tuesday and Thursday mornings.

I usually got to the room at least half an hour early so I could start smoking right away. Sometimes there were free donuts with the coffee.

Each meeting began with everybody in the room introducing themselves. Then people went around the circle telling their stories. It was just like group in the Adolescent Ward, except each story ended with, "And that's when I hit bottom."

The stories were always tragic, but never boring.

When they got to me, I just said, "My name is Louis and I'm happy to be here." Even though I didn't claim to be an addict, it was a little nerve-wracking being a fraud and manipulating them over their misfortune. I knew I had no business pretending to be in their league. These people had real problems. Their lives were falling apart because of a disease. They knew suffering. And there I was, some pissant kid, running a scam so I could smoke. But, I was happy to be there. That was no lie.

Because I was the only kid in the rooms, when the meetings were over, people often came up to me and congratulated me. They'd say things like, "You're so brave." And, "You're an inspiration."

I had the perfect racket. Things were going great. As long as I kept my trap shut, I assumed I'd be able to maintain my subterfuge indefinitely. But a few weeks later, this guy named Phil called me out in the common room as I was smoking and watching the guys shoot pool. Phil was a one-man pity party. He'd lost it all. His wife, his kids, his high-paying job, his expensive car... everything. Even his self-respect. When he hit bottom he was living in a motel room on Lee Highway outside Sylacauga. He always had to be the star of the down and out. Any time somebody told a sob story, he'd try to one-up their tale of woe by saying, "You think that's bad. Well, listen to this..." I'd heard the other rehabbers talking shit behind his back.

"What are you doing here anyway?" he asked me. "Shouldn't you be at home with your parents?"

I didn't know if he was joking or if I really did have to defend myself. I tried to shrug it off. International man of mystery. That was me.

But he wasn't letting up. "What'd you do, stay out too late one night and get a whuppin'?"

There was a whole group of rehabbers looking at me. Should I admit that I was just hanging around to smoke? Even if they weren't totally offended by my deplorable actions, they'd no doubt put the kibosh on my whole scheme. So I told them about what happened with my father and my little brother. Surprisingly, once I started talking, I couldn't seem to stop. I told them about my brother at the ranch and the pending court appearance.

"And now I hafta testify against my father..."

After I finished talking, they told me how sorry they were about my circumstances.

"Bless your heart," Mama Teri told me. She was hooked on painkillers. Said she was thirty-nine, but she looked fifty-four. "Even if you're not ready to talk, eventually you need to let it out."

I was quick to brush off their concern. "It's no big deal. I just prefer not to talk about it. Don't wanna bum anybody out."

"Part of working the steps is sharing your story," Josh said.

"It's really good that you're trying to get your shit together so young," said Gordon, the alcoholic toilet paper salesman. "I wish I had the smarts to do it when I was your age. I'd be a lot better off today."

Even Phil came up and apologized. "If there's anything I can ever do for you, just let me know."

The Courthouse

In the van with Sandra, on our way to Anniston, I stared out the window. The trees were aflame with autumn colors, a nuclear explosion of orange, yellow and red. The last time I was on this highway, four months earlier, the flowers were blooming and all the trees were green. I'd spent the entire summer indoors with little indication that the season had changed besides what I saw through the plexiglass windows.

"Are you nervous about talking to the district attorney?" Sandra asked.

"Not really. This is just a formality, right?"

"They just want to make sure you boys are comfortable in the courtroom and know what to expect during the trial. She's a nice lady. You have nothing to worry about."

"I'm not worried." I kept thinking about what my mother told me about the judge destroying the Polaroids. Sandra had never mentioned it to me. I decided to force her hand. "Why do we hafta testify anyway? Can't we just make a statement or something?"

"I wish there was another way around it..." she said. "We're especially worried about Joey. We need your help, to make sure he understands just how important his testimony is."

"Oh, sure." I promised to talk to him.

When we got to the courthouse, Joey was already there, waiting with Clorise. Joey and I sat on a bench across from the social workers.

Joey looked like he was going to cry. His whole face was clenched like a fist, holding back the waterworks. My instinct was to give him a mean charley horse so he'd have a reason to be a crybaby, but I thought about his diagnosis and what Sandra had told me, that he was injured, wounded, fragile... Now that everything had changed, I didn't know how to act around him anymore. So I just sat there uncomfortably, waiting for the district attorney.

When Sandra reached down to adjust the stirrup on her pants, I whispered in Joey's ear, "She's a home-run hitter."

He snickered uncomfortably.

Sandra smiled. "What are you boys laughing about?"

"We used to have socks like that when we played Little League."

Sandra looked down at her ankles. "It's a lot of work to be fashionable these days."

Just then, a woman in a dress suit approached us.

"Boys, this is Mrs. Morgan," Clorise said. "She's handling the case against your father and Rick."

"Nice to meet y'all," Mrs. Morgan said enthusiastically as she shook our hands. "Call me Carolyn. I wanted to meet so we can go over what to expect at the trial. Does that sound alright?"

Joey and I nodded.

"Let's take a little tour." Carolyn ushered us through

a large wooden door into the courtroom.

"Swanky." I whistled. The walls, the banisters, the tables, the judge's stand—the whole room was polished mahogany. A row of massive oil paintings lined the walls. There were flags in each corner and thick velvet curtains over the windows.

"Why don't you boys take turns sitting in the witness stand," Carolyn told us, "so you can get a feel for it."

While Joey took the stand, I walked around to the judge's bench and picked up the gavel. "Can I?"

Carolyn laughed. "Sure."

I smacked the round block with the wooden hammer. The sound echoed off the walls.

"Hear ye! Hear ye!" I hollered, my voice resonating in the empty chamber. "I now sentence you to seven years in the Spanish Inquisition!"

This made Joey laugh. "Oh, let me!"

I handed him the gavel and he gave it a whack.

"Now back to the gallows!"

Mrs. Morgan stood with her arms crossed, amused at our antics.

"So how do you boys feel about testifying?" she asked.

We shrugged. "Alright."

"Have you ever been in a court before?"

"I've been to court twice," I said.

"Really?"

"Once when our parents got divorced and another time when this guy that lived up the street from us back in LA held me up with a knife and stole my bag of candy."

"They took him to court over a bag of stolen candy?"

"There was more to it than that. First, he killed one

of our cats. Smashed its head and then gutted it and threw it in the street. Everybody knew it was him, but nobody could prove it. The cops said since it was a cat there was nothing they could do."

"Goodness. Was he a Satanist?"

"No, I think he just hated cats... Anyway, since they couldn't bust him for killing the cat, they went after him for stealing my candy. There was a trial and everything. I had to get on the witness stand and testify. He got off in the end though."

"Well..." Mrs. Morgan cleared her throat. "When you were on the witness stand, what kind of questions did the judge ask you?"

"He asked my name, when I was born, where I went to school. Then he asked me to tell them what happened."

"The judge will ask you both the same questions. He'll start with simple things, like your age and where you went to school. Just to make sure you are comfortable and relaxed answering questions."

"Are Dad and Rick gonna be there?" Joey asked.

"Yes. Do you think you'll be able to deal with that?"

"I guess," he murmured and went quiet again.

After we left the courthouse, the social workers drove us to McDonald's. While I smoked in the playground area with Joey, I told him about the judge destroying the Polaroids.

"So there's no more proof?"

"Nah. That's why we gotta go to court."

"What if we say Dad had nothing to do with it? That it was all Rick? If they don't have the pictures anymore, we can say that Dad is innocent."

"I dunno, man. We might get busted for lying. It's kinda too late to back out now."

"I just want outa the ranch. I wanna go home." Joey's eyes welled up.

The ladies walked outside.

"What's going on?" Sandra asked, her face furrowed in concern. "Are you okay?"

"Oh, we're just messing around." I put my hand on his shoulder. "Right, Joey?"

Halloween

Halloween approached with little cheer on the RTW, one more aspect of the normal world filtered out of the Hillcrest experience. Some staffers embellished their uniforms with subtle ornamentation, but the rehabbers remained in their pajamas and robes and went about their normal activities, one day at a time, like any other day. The Mutants, however, in their constant pursuit of distraction, wanted to celebrate the holiday. After some deliberation with Julie, Nina drove Cliff and Daneesha to Kmart so they could purchase a few simple decorations.

Later that day, Cliff stood in front of the bathroom mirror smearing fake blood on his face. He'd been carrying the tube around with him since he got back from the store, occasionally stroking the smooth plastic and showing it to Howard. When he was finished rubbing it into his cheeks like rouge, Cliff asked me, "How does it look?"

"How does what look?"

"The blood!"

"What blood?"

"On my face!"

"I don't see anything."

Cliff grunted and went back to the bathroom to add another layer. "What about now?"

"I still don't see anything."

Cliff checked himself in the mirror again. "You can't see the red stuff on my face?"

"I told you already, I can't see any difference. Are you sure that's not invisible blood?"

"Invisible blood?"

"Yeah, they have two kinds of fake blood. The regular kind and the kind that makes you invisible."

Cliff wrinkled his forehead. "Say, you messing around? I ain't heard of no invisible blood before."

"The tubes look the same. You have to be real careful when you buy fake blood at the store otherwise you can get the wrong kind."

"You lie."

"Fine, don't believe me. See if I care." I returned to my magazine.

Cliff went back into the bathroom and washed off the blood.

Later that afternoon, Cliff and Howard were in the TV room, deep in conversation. Over the past week, Howard had become less catatonic, like he'd just woken up from a nap.

"Those two are up to something in there," I told Calvin.

"I really don't have time for this..." Calvin said as he walked into the room. "Alright, what's going on in here?"

"They got fake blood," Daneesha said. "Cliffy stole it from the store."

"I did not," Cliff swore. "I had some money saved up

and when you weren't looking I bought it. It's mine."

"He stole it. I saw him put it in his pocket!"

"It's mine," Cliff whimpered.

"Hand it over," Calvin said firmly.

Cliff held out the tube of blood and Calvin set it on the desk behind the nurses' station.

That evening, Daneesha ran into the hallway.

"Calvin!" she bellowed. "Them idjits is up to no good!"

Cliff and Howard emerged from the TV room and charged down the hallway. They had sheets tied around their shoulders like capes.

"Alright, you two!" Calvin shouted. "It's time to set-tle down."

"You can't make us!" Cliff let out a battle cry and rushed the nurses' station. He grabbed the tube of blood off the desk.

"What the fuck!" I exclaimed as the two marauders sped past me towards the rehabbers' common room. I leaned against the wall to give them plenty of leeway.

Calvin followed at a steady pace.

"They went that-a-way." I pointed.

Daneesha and Gayle turned the corner smiling glee-fully.

"Y'all get back to your rooms!" Calvin hissed.

In the rehabbers' common room, Cliff and Howard charged the exit that led outside, but the door was locked. They bounced off and fell to the floor on top of each other. As they struggled to regain their feet, I joined the rehabbers who had gathered to watch the slapstick.

Cliff and Howard ran around the pool table. They tried to run back the way they'd come, but Calvin was blocking the hallway.

"There's nowhere to go," he said. "Just give it up."

"You can't touch us!" Cliff shrieked. "We have super powers!"

Howard looked confused but stuck close to his partner. They charged the door again. Cliff pumped the handle furiously.

"Where do y'all think you're going?" Calvin asked.

"We're getting outa here! And you can't stop us!"

"You two best be settling down. Don't make me put you in the Time Out Room."

"You can't tell us what to do no more," Howard shouted.

Gayle laughed. "I ain't never heard that boy speak three words in a row and now he's calling the shots?"

Calvin ignored Howard and focused on subduing Cliff. "Now, come on! You know this isn't how you're supposed to behave. Just settle down and you can keep the tube." As Calvin slowly approached, Cliff kept his distance. Howard gnashed his teeth.

"You gonna need a rabies shot if you ain't careful!" Daneesha shouted and clapped her hands.

"Y'all want out?" Calvin unlocked the door and swung it open. "Here, be my guest." He walked back into the hallway to give them a clear escape route. "Go ahead, where you gonna go?"

The door led to the patio area, which was enclosed by a wooden fence eight feet tall.

Cliff was suspicious at first, but he eventually skulked towards the door with Howard shuffling along-side. In the threshold, they glanced furtively around the room and then dashed outside.

"See how long you last out there," Calvin said.

"Supposed to be in the low forties tonight. You'll be begging to come back inside soon enough."

We all rushed to the window for a view of the action on the patio. Cliff and Howard were standing at the far wall.

"Them fools are fixin' to climb the fence," Daneesha bellowed.

"There's no way," I said. "It's too high."

"And Howie's too fat," Gayle added.

"Cliff ain't no stick himself," Daneesha pointed out.

"Look at 'em go," a rehabber said.

Cliff formed a stirrup with his fingers and hoisted Howard to the top of the fence.

"That fat boy can really move his tail," Gayle squealed.

We all watched as Howard straddled the wooden slats of the fence, held his hand down for Cliff and helped him amble up the planks. A second later, they were on the other side.

"They're gone," Gayle said.

"Betcha didn't see that coming," Daneesha told Calvin.

Calvin looked alarmed but tried to remain calm. "Okay, show's over," he said. "Everybody get to your rooms."

For the rest of the night, I retold the story of the Great Mutant Escape to all the rehabbers who had missed the spectacle.

In the morning, Nina was doing paperwork at the nurses' station.

"Are the Freak Brothers still AWOL?" I asked.

"No, the police picked them up on the side of

Route 17. They'd built a campfire to stay warm and a sheriff happened to drive by and spot their campsite. Their faces were caked with that fake blood."

I laughed but Nina did not share my amusement.

"Howard was in the middle of a severe psychotic episode," she said. "It seems he had stopped taking his meds. He said Cliff told him the fake blood was supposed to make them invisible."

"Invisible?" I grimaced to hold back my laughter. "That's bizarre. I wonder where they got that idea?"

"They'll be in lockdown until their meds are regulated."

"At least we'll have some peace and quiet for a little while."

For the next week, I had the room to myself. When Cliff returned, he was emotionless and withdrawn. I figured they'd knocked him up with some serious meds. He lay on his bunk most of the time. I felt bad for him. All his usual vitality was drained away. Over the past few months, I had grown accustomed to his shenanigans. Even though he annoyed the living crap out of me, I felt bad for him in his comatose state, a giant slab of meat taking up space.

Twenty Years

During the first week of November, I got a phone call from Sandra. I had been expecting to hear about the trial, which was rapidly approaching.

"Turns out y'all don't have to testify after all," she said cheerfully.

"What do you mean?"

"Your father pleaded guilty to all the charges."

"He pleaded guilty?"

"Yeah. They offered him a plea bargain for less time and he took it."

"How many years did he end up getting?"

"Twenty. No chance of parole."

"Twenty years? That's a lot!"

"They were looking at life. So it's a good deal."

"What about Rick?"

"You father's plea bargain implicated Rick as well."

"What happens now?" I asked. "What happens to me and Joey?"

She said some more stuff, something about a custody hearing—the same mumbo jumbo as always.

The next day, I called my mother.

"What happened?" I asked.

"He said they told him if he didn't take the deal, they wouldn't let you and Joey see each other during Thanksgiving. He said he didn't want to drag you guys into court. He said he was tired. So he just gave up."

"But twenty years is such a long time."

"I know."

"Didn't they take his Army record into account? Like, give him time off since he served his country for so long and fought in the war?"

"Doubtful they'd do that. Your father was just an accountant. I think they only do things like that for real soldiers."

"But Dad fought in Vietnam. He was a door gunner on a Huey."

Mom laughed. "Louis, your father was just pulling your leg with all that talk."

"Really?"

"He kept track of who got paid and managed bank accounts. Accounting. That's what he's always done. Eventually you will come to realize, just like me, that your father told many lies. He was a fantastic liar."

I hung up and walked to my room. Put on my headphones. The emotions in my head were like a bar brawl.

I was relieved that I didn't have to testify against the old man, but I had bigger things to worry about now. Since the social workers no longer needed me, I had to be wise to their machinations or I would end up in a foster home, or someplace worse...

THE BIG OAK RANCH

On the way to the Big Oak Ranch, I sat in the passenger seat of the van and tried to make idle chitchat with Mr. Wagoner, Joey's house parent. But he was reticent, so after a while, I gave up and stared out the window.

Two days before, Sandra had driven me back to Saks to stay with the Sheltons. They had made a special point of inviting me. While I was in town, the ranch sent a van to pick me up for my visit with Joey. I assumed my brother would be along for the ride, but when Mr. Wagoner showed up, he was alone.

I had the sneaking suspicion this visit was a test, to see how I fit in at the ranch. Knowing it would make everybody's life easier if I agreed to live there, I was determined to prove it was impossible.

When Mr. Wagoner turned off the main highway, we drove over hills and through forests of barren, skeletal remains, shrouded in the mist of low-lying clouds like menacing dandelions. The heavily wooded landscape eventually opened up into a wide glen where the red brick houses of the ranch were surrounded by grassy fields and the occasional oak tree.

Mr. Wagoner pulled up to a house where several

boys stood on the turf tossing a football. Joey was among them. With my feet on the ground, I took a deep breath and looked around. There was a volleyball net strung up in the center of a field. In the distance was a stable. The air smelled like horseshit.

Joey ran up to me. "Hey."

"What's up?"

We stood facing each other awkwardly. I didn't know what to say. When two guys approached us, Joey introduced me to Dan and Leslie, his roommates.

A few minutes later, a woman called out the back door of the house, "Suppertime!"

The guys raced inside.

I sat next to my brother. The table was crowded with serving bowls full of food, a heaping mound of mashed potatoes, a stack of corncobs. The centerpiece was a massive turkey, browned and succulent.

Besides Joey and me, there were five teenage boys, who wiggled uncomfortably in their chairs.

"Who wants to say grace tonight?" Mrs. Wagoner asked and scanned the faces for a volunteer. "How about you, Joey? Would you do the honor?"

"Yes, ma'am."

Everybody put their heads down and folded their hands over the plates.

Joey cleared his throat and began to pray. "Lord, thank You for the food we are about to eat, for all that You provide us and please give us the strength to live in Your image. Amen."

"Amen!" the other boys shouted and reached for the serving bowls. As they dug into the meal and filled their plates, the boys chatted and laughed with full mouths. The parents directed the conversation, hushing any loud outbursts and keeping the talk wholesome and appropriate. Joey sat slowly forking the food into his mouth and sneaking furtive glances at me. I ate silently.

After the remnants of the meal had been cleared off the table, Mr. Wagoner invited me to join them in the family room for devotional. There was a slight lilt in his voice at the end of the sentence, but it sounded more like a demand than a request.

During the prayer, I kept my head raised and stared straight ahead. I'd only been there an hour or so and they'd already squeezed in two amens. As they read the Gospels and discussed the passages, Mr. Wagoner tried to engage me in the discussion. I begged off but he kept pushing me to talk about my faith. So I let him have it.

"I'm an atheist. So none of this concerns me."

"How do you know you're an atheist?"

"Why would I believe in the Christian God when he doesn't believe in me? According to the Bible I'll never reach the Kingdom of Heaven because I was conceived out of wedlock. My parents were married in June and I was born in October. Do the math. Not to mention all that 'Sins of the Father' stuff. I don't think I need to go into the details of what that means for Joey and me."

"But that's from the Old Testament."

"Oh, and the New Testament is any better? I may not believe in God, but I'm no stranger to the Bible."

"You're not afraid of burning in Hell?"

"Why does everybody keep asking me that? I've never heard so much talk about Hell before I came to Alabama. Hell is a creation of man. Heaven too. Both concepts are idealized extremes of morality. But why does it have to be so black and white? So what if I don't believe in God? Why must I be a Satanist? Why can't I just be free to think what I wanna think? I could be a Buddhist or a Hindu and yet, according to the Baptists, I'll still burn in Hell. How is that fair? I'll tell you what I do believe in… I believe in the possibility of rebirth, starting again. Most of what Jesus preached about was love and understanding and being kind to your fellow man. There's nothing wrong with that. But what I don't get is organized religion. Organized religion seems bent on dividing people rather than bringing them together. It's like the whole Alabama/Auburn thing. One religion versus another. It poisons people's minds with hate. It encourages people to attack and kill each other. And that's the opposite of what Jesus taught. All the suffering in the world is caused by the ignorance perpetuated by organized religion."

"You seem like a smart boy. But it's easy to get confused. Life is pretty simple, why make things harder for yourself?"

"I read somewhere that the unexamined life is not worth living. I truly believe that. I don't think you can reduce everything to its lowest common denominator."

I paused and looked around. I'd been so overwhelmed with proving my case for atheism that I hadn't noticed everybody was staring at me.

"Well, I think we've had enough of this discussion," Mrs. Wagoner said. "Joey, why don't you take your brother up to your room?"

I was grateful to get away. I followed Joey upstairs. For the first time since I arrived, we were alone. I looked around his bedroom, examining the amenities, which weren't as bad as the Jackson Home, but nowhere close to what we'd hoped to get out of the deal. He shared the room with three other guys.

"You heard they're gonna send me back to Mom's house?" I asked.

"Yeah."

"And that you gotta stay here?"

Joey nodded.

I thought about all the things I could say, but all I came up with was, "It's not that bad here, is it?"

"I hate it here!"

"C'mon, really?"

Joey listed off the indignities that he was forced to suffer at the ranch: "They make me pray all the time! I gotta call my house parents 'Mom' and 'Dad.' And they aren't even my real parents! I can't get my hair cut the way I want. I can't dress the way I want. They don't buy us any good clothes. Just donations! Everything here, even the food, is donated. This place sucks!"

"At least..." I couldn't even finish the thought.

"But that's not the worst of it... Somebody found out why I was here and spread the word around school. Now they call me 'Homo Joe.'"

I couldn't tell if he was lying. I wanted it to be a lie. "Did you tell your house parents?"

"They said I should pray for them."

"You understand why I can't come here to live, don't you? They'd squash me like a bug. They'd take everything I am and I'd have nothing left." I heard myself talk. I sounded like a vacuum salesman.

"But that's what they're doing to me! Why couldn't we just run away to that place, the Calgary Manor, and live with the punks?"

"I promise, as soon as I get things sorted out, I'll come back for you. I promise."

Even as the words came out, I knew they were

empty. I would have promised him anything, just to get away. It was all too much, the horror of being at the ranch and seeing my little brother reduced to a lap dog. All this "ma'am" and "sir" stuff, living with a bunch of strangers, the tyranny of religion… it was just as I'd imagined: a soulless prison.

Joey wiped his eyes.

I turned away. I couldn't acknowledge the obvious. We'd made a deal, and this wasn't it.

I was relieved when Dan and Leslie entered the room.

"What's up, guys?"

"What y'all doing?" Leslie asked.

"We were just talking about this funny story." I laughed and nudged my brother. "Hey, Joey, remember that time we were walking to the M&M market and passed the house where this Marmaduke dog was hanging out with a poodle? Then on the way back the poodle was gone and there was white fluff all over the grass. And you said, 'Oh, my god, he ate the little dog!'"

"Yeah," Joey said meekly.

"We totally freaked! And then, while we tried to figure out what to do, the poodle ran back into the yard from the side of the house. Turns out, it was a pillow that the Marmaduke dog had ripped up."

Leslie and Dan chuckled politely. It wasn't a very funny story.

"That was priceless what you said in prayer group tonight," Leslie told me. "The look on Mrs. Wagoner's face… whoa damn."

"So what do you guys do around here?" I asked.

Leslie gave me the rundown on life at the ranch. They went to a regular school, in Southside, which was the only time they were around kids who weren't at the ranch. To prolong their exposure to the outside world, they all played sports.

"Joey's one of our best players," Dan said. "He makes us all look good."

Leslie said that he hated sports, but it was better than being stuck at the ranch all the time. We talked about music. He was into metal.

"Can you listen to music at all here?"

"Nah," Leslie said glumly. "I got a friend at school and I can listen to his Walkman sometimes… long as the other guys from the ranch don't see me."

"Why, they'll rat you out?"

"Yeah!"

"That really sucks." I told him about the band I was going to start when I got back to LA.

"Man, you're so lucky," he enthused. "Here, check this out." He lifted up his mattress and pulled out a Memorex tape. One side was labeled "Anthrax" and the other side had the "Cro-Mags."

"Awesome, dude."

"I want you to have it," Leslie said.

"Man, I can't take your shit."

"No, I'm serious. It's yours. Take it to California and think of us trapped here when you're rocking out in Hollywood."

I thanked him profusely.

When it was time to leave, Joey said, "I'm never gonna see you again, am I?"

"You just gotta be patient, okay?" I gave him a clumsy hug. "I'll be back. I promise."

As I was walking out the door, Joey fell to his knees

and burst into a frenzy of tears. "You can't leave me here!" he shouted. "Please don't leave me here!"

I stood there, shocked at the outburst, and looked at Mr. Wagoner.

"Joey! You can't be acting like this, now." He reached down and grabbed Joey by his shoulders and lifted him to his feet. "A man doesn't cry like that."

Joey swayed like a drunk, his eyes streaming tears.

"Now act like a man and tell your brother goodbye."

In the van, I looked at Joey in the doorway of the house, watching us pull out of the driveway. I waved one last time. And then we were back in the woods.

THE RECORD BAR PUNK

At the Record Bar in the Oxford Mall, Clint and I shuffled through the racks of cassettes and whispered over the clicking of plastic. From the moment we entered the store, we were furtively eyeballing the vaguely punk-looking clerk behind the counter with a Clash button on his black employee vest.

"I swear, that's one of the guys I was telling you about," Clint said. "The band that played at the skating rink a couple weeks ago."

Before I went back to Birmingham, I was stuck at the Sheltons for a few more days, going out of my skull with boredom. I walked down to see if Casey was home, but he was out of town for the holidays. So I decided to give Clint a call. He was psyched to hear from me. His first response was, "b-b-b-b-b-butane!" We had a good laugh remembering the fun we'd had that summer. He suggested we drive down to Oxford and check out the music store at the mall. I had twenty dollars burning a hole in my pocket. All the way there, he told me about a punk band he'd seen perform at the skating rink. They were the most amazing band he had ever seen up close. "In between songs, the band members alternated positions," Clint said. "Switching from one instrument to the next."

Now that we were mere feet away from one of the members, I suggested we go talk to him.

Slowly, we crept up behind the guy and stood there for several seconds before Clint cleared his throat and said, "Hey."

The guy turned around nonchalantly.

"How y'all doing?"

"Didn't I see your band play at the Oxford skating rink?" Clint asked.

"Yeah, that was us. My name's Brian." He pointed at his nametag.

We introduced ourselves and shook hands.

"That was an awesome show, man."

"I can't believe they let you guys play punk."

"My friend Dave works at the skating rink," Brian said. "That's how we got in. But we were playing Dead Kennedys songs and insulting people, so Dave pulls me over to the side and says we gotta tone down the cussing. Well, the next song we play is 'Nazi Punks Fuck Off!'"

We all laughed.

"Man, after that, we were shut right the fuck down! The crowd was yelling, 'You suck!' We grabbed our shit and took off."

"That's so awesome!" Clint and I enthused.

"What's the name of your band?"

"That night we were The Whales. We change our name every time we play a show. Not that there are many places to play."

"I know. Nothing's going on in this shitass town."

"You guys always play punk?" I asked.

"We do a variety of tunes, some punk, some ska, a

little rockabilly. Sometimes all within the same song."

"Cool. I listen mostly to punk." I showed him the tapes I'd found, stoked beyond belief to finally have albums by Social Distortion and Minor Threat. I held them tightly in my hand like trophies. "I've been dying to find these," I told the guy. "Ever since I saw that movie *Another State of Mind*. Do you know that one?"

"Yeah. That's a cool flick. I just ordered those tapes a few weeks ago, hoping somebody cool would find them."

We talked about punk bands for a while. He recommended some albums, making me swear I'd check out *Plastic Surgery Disasters* by Dead Kennedys as soon as I had the money. He said it was their most musical album. A classic. I memorized every word he said.

After we'd made our purchases, Clint and I walked down to the Orange Julius. He wanted to know what it was like being in a mental hospital.

"Being locked up... man, it's all a big joke. They didn't know what else to do with me, and I guess if they don't know what to do with you, they lock you up."

"When my dad found out what happened to y'all, he was rearing to go beat your dad up and that other guy. I ain't never seen my dad so pissed off."

"Everybody knows about it now, huh?"

"Well, yeah. It was in the paper."

"Crazy."

"So are you coming back to Anniston before you leave for LA?"

"Maybe for Christmas. I don't know what's happening yet, where I'm going to end up..."

"We should hang out if you're in town. And hey, man... tell your brother..." Clint paused. "Tell him I said what's up."

A Fake Mohawk

Back at Hillcrest, I counted down the days until my departure. Sandra said I would be out of the hospital some time before Christmas. To commemorate my inevitable discharge, I requested a trip to Supercuts so I could get a mohawk. "It'll be my Christmas present," I told Calvin. "I got the cash. Just need somebody to take me to get it done."

As I was leaving the Sheltons' house, Mrs. Shelton slipped a bill into my pocket. "In case you need anything down there..." In Sandra's van, I unfolded it and smiled at Benjamin Franklin's smirk. One hundred smackeroos!

"You'll look like a fool with a haircut like that!" Calvin scoffed when I showed him the picture of the hairstyle I wanted. "I'd let you do it just to see how dumb you'll look afterwards, but I'm not that cruel."

"What do you know? It'll be tough."

After a few days of persistent cajoling, Calvin went to Julie, who decided that I needed to get permission for such an extreme hairstyle.

"From who?" I asked. "My mother'd let me do it."

"Your caseworker."

"Oh."

I was vaguely optimistic when I picked up the phone, but Sandra was ambivalent.

"I don't know... that sounds a little drastic."

"It's not a real mohawk," I protested. "I just want to shave the sides, that way if I want, most of the time my hair'll just fall over the side, or I could part it down the middle and nobody would be able to tell."

After she relented, Nina drove me to Supercuts, where the hairstylist wrinkled her brow when I described the haircut I wanted.

"I don't think that's gonna look very good."

I was persistent. But she refused to shave my sides to the skin. Instead she left an inch of hair that she slicked back with gel. So it was almost like a real mohawk.

With the last of my money, I bought a pair of combat boots from the Army/Navy store.

That evening, I was smoking in the rehabbers' common room when Gordon approached me. "Hey, I like your hair," he said.

"Thanks."

"Here, I got you something." He handed me a card.

"Oh, cool."

"You think I can get a hug?"

I'd seen the rehabbers embrace each other in meetings all the time. I wasn't into the touchy-feely stuff, but Gordon had always been cool to me, giving me cigarettes when I was out. So I said, "Sure."

Gordon put his arms around me. "I feel such a strong connection to you," he whispered in my ear.

There was something creepy about his tone. I tried

to pull away but Gordon squeezed tighter.

"You've got something special and I only wish that there was some way I could show you just how special you are."

"Hey!" I managed to break free. "I think you got the wrong idea!"

"Do I?"

"Yeah! Sorry. I gotta go."

I ran down the hallway to my room.

All night I thought about what Gordon said. He even wrote it in the card: "You got something special. If you ever need anything, gimme a call." He included his phone number.

Does he think I'm gay? I wondered. The implication made me feel dirty. Then I realized he was picking up on my father, that since I'd been raised by a gay man, some of his gayness must have rubbed off on me.

I threw the card in the trash and, even though it was painful not to smoke, I avoided the rehabbers' common room for the rest of the time I was at Hillcrest.

PART FOUR

A Welfare Case

The Tucker House

As the year ended, I thought about all the places I'd slept since I left California. Starting with the backseat of the old man's Cimarron, I was up to eight: the motel in Dallas, the house in Saks, the Jackson Home, the Adolescent Ward and Residential Treatment Ward at Hillcrest, the Sheltons' for Thanksgiving and Christmas and then the Tuckers', a foster home in Anniston.

A week before Christmas, I got a phone call from Sandra. She said the judge had agreed to let me go back home to California on a temporary basis.

"There's just some red tape we have to work through first," she told me. "And we need to transition you out of Hillcrest."

That's how she brought up the foster home.

"I know you don't want to be in a foster home, but it'll just be for a few weeks. The Tuckers are nice folks. You'll like them. And there's only one girl living there right now. Their niece, Katie. She's the same age as you."

I was reluctant at first. But my steadfast resistance to being in a foster home was more out of principle by this point. After six months in the hospital, I was desperate for a change of scenery. "As long as it's just for a few weeks, I guess it's okay."

Even though they said I would be back in California soon, until my plane touched down at LAX, I wouldn't be convinced.

Meanwhile, I waited in a small bedroom at the Tuckers' house, listening to my Walkman and reading the Stephen King books my mother sent me for Christmas. The Tuckers were nice enough. They let me smoke in my room. When it was time to eat, Rachel Tucker knocked on my door. We usually ate delivery pizza or drive-thru burgers. Every once in a while she cooked at home. I was surprised people could afford to eat fast food on such a regular basis.

Heavy set and jovial, Rachel laughed with little provocation. She cleaned office buildings at night and slept late in the mornings. Her husband, Glen, was a backhoe operator. He came home in the evenings and sat in his recliner watching television and drinking beer. By the time the news came on he was in a boozy confrontational mood.

"Used to be a truck driver," Glen told me one night. "I've hauled cargo cross the country and back more times than I've taken a crap." He snorted. "Been out to California many times. Got to say, boy, the place you come from—pardon my French—but it's just a shithole that ain't Alabama." Glen laughed. "Sorry, but I know it from experience. I've driven damn near all the lower forty-eight. Twice!" Glen took a swig of beer. "I once got stuck in LA. Place called Pacoima. You know where Pacoima is?"

I didn't know much about the City of Los Angeles besides my corner of the San Gabriel Valley, but I said,

"I've heard of it before, yeah."

"Well, it's a crap town. I can tell you that for sure. I was there during winter and the Grapevine was closed on account of snow in the mountains. Snow in LA! Who woulda thunk it. I was trapped in a crap motel for three days. Worst three days of my life, stranded in LA!"

I didn't know what to say. Glen seemed to be holding me responsible for his unpleasant experience in LA and all I could think to do was apologize.

Although I preferred the company of my books and tapes, I began to creep out of my room late at night while the house was quiet and turn on the television with the volume down low.

One night Katie came home later than usual. She worked the evening shift at the Jack's drive-thru in Oxford. When she saw me in the living room she sat down and asked, "Whatcha watching?"

"MTV."

"Oh, cool. I like watching videos too."

I wasn't sure what kind of girl Katie would be. All I knew was that she attended Saks High. We got to talking about potential mutual acquaintances. I asked about Missy, Casey, Brett and Vic, but she didn't know any of them.

"I mostly keep to myself," she told me.

After that night, when she got home from work, we'd watch TV together, chatting about nonsense. She wasn't very smart, but she was sweet and friendly. And once I got past the botched perm job and the caked-on makeup, she was kind of cute.

During my third week at the Tucker House, Sandra called.

"It's all set," she said as optimistically as ever. "I got a ticket in my hand with your name on it. In a week you'll be flying the friendly skies back to California."

That evening, during dinner, Rachel asked me, "Are you happy to go back home?"

"Sure. Of course. That was my plan all along."

"Because you don't seem that happy. Does he, Glen?"

"Rachel, leave the boy alone." Glen's voice was mired in his usual good-natured condescension. "Let him do what he's gotta do. He'll wise up and realize what a shithole California is eventually."

"Going back to LA is the only choice I have."

"You could stay here," Rachel said.

"And do what?" I asked. "I can't go back to school at Saks. Not after everything that's happened. It was in the newspaper."

"Forget about high school!" Glen took a slug of beer. "You can take your GED."

"But I'm only sixteen."

"You're old enough to take the GED," Rachel pointed out. "We both got our GEDs when we were your age."

"Ain't no shame in a GED," Glen said.

"You'd be better off just getting high school out of the way so you can go to college," said Rachel. "You could really do something with yourself. Right, Glen?"

"You're a smart kid, I'll give you that. You got book sense, just not a lick of common sense."

"How would I afford college?" I asked.

"The state'll pay for it. You'll get grants. As a ward of the state, you'd get a free ride."

"Don't get carried away, now," Glen told his wife.

"No, I'm serious. You could go from a high school drop-out to a doctor. All you do is read books anyway, might as well put all that reading to good use."

"I dunno…" I was taken aback. "I don't think I'm going to college."

"Why not?" Rachel demanded. "What else you gonna do with your life?"

"Why… I… uhm…" I tried to come up with a valid justification. "I guess I just never thought about it before. Besides, my grades… and I've missed so much school, with the transfer to Alabama… and then being at Hillcrest. And once they send me back to California…"

"I'm not saying you shouldn't go back to California," Rachel said. "But think of it as a visit. See how you like it. If you want to come back, I'm sure they'll buy you a return ticket. And you'll always be welcome here."

"You watch," Glen said. "In a month, you'll be begging to come back to Alabama."

I laughed. "Yeah, right…"

Even though I had never considered the possibility of college before, nobody had ever suggested that I had a chance at higher education either. It was flattering. I didn't know what was going to happen to me when I got back to California, but I doubted I would be on a fast track to higher learning. The new high school I was supposed to attend sounded like a stepping stone to trade school at best. Not that I intended to take advantage of any programs they had to offer. My plan was to get to Hollywood and find the punk scene.

That night, as I lay in bed waiting for sleep, my guts twisting and my heart racing, I kept repeating what I'd said to myself since I made the decision to go back to Rosemead: Something had to be worth all the trouble. I'd thrown my father to the wolves, and even though the social workers, the lawyers, the judge and the therapists all said he deserved it, he was still my father.

And what about Joey? I thought about him at the ranch, alone and surrounded by strangers he had to pretend were his real family. I was abandoning my little brother, reneging on so many promises not to ditch him.

But this is what I have to do, I told myself.

And then I just tried not to think about it anymore.

Flight 541

On Friday morning, Sandra arrived at the Tucker House to drive me to the airport. My bags were already packed. I was dressed and ready, but I took one last look in the mirror. My hair was combed over to one side and secured in place with a combination of gel and hairspray. All my earrings were dangling. My new Metallica t-shirt with the dagger sticking out of a toilet. My jean jacket covered with buttons and safety pins. The legs of my pants were pinned and tucked into my new combat boots.

I was ready to rock.

Katie was still in the process of getting ready for school. "I really wish you weren't going away so soon," she said as she hugged my neck.

Rachel was up before her normal time to say good-bye. "It was nice getting to know you these past few weeks."

"I'll keep y'all updated on his progress," Sandra told them as we walked out the door.

On the interstate I watched the landscape outside the window.

"I think I've just about got this highway memorized," I said. "I've been on it so many times over the past six months..."

At the airport, we sat in the waiting area.

"Have you ever flown before?" Sandra asked.

"Supposedly, when I was only a few months old, my parents took me to San Francisco to visit my aunt and uncle. I don't remember it, so I don't think that counts."

"Flying's fun. You'll like it. Just sit back and relax."

When they announced that my plane was about to begin boarding, I extended my hand to Sandra.

"Thanks for everything."

"We'll be in touch," Sandra said as I walked away. "I'll call you tomorrow to make sure you're settled in at your mother's."

"Okay." Somehow, that was a relief. To know I'd hear her voice again soon.

I had a window seat and looked out the small portal at the glass walls of the terminal. Sandra was watching the plane. I waved but I couldn't tell if she saw me.

A few minutes later, after the other passengers had taken their seats and our seatbelts were fastened, the plane barreled down the runway, shaking like crazy. I put my headphones on and clicked play. Social Distortion pumped into my eardrums as the floorboards rumbled beneath my feet. Then we were airborne.

I looked out the window at the patchwork land below. The buildings were getting smaller. The cars were like insects in a hive. I tried to keep track of where we were geographically. I mistook every narrow body of water for the Mississippi, but when we finally went over the river I knew why they called it the Mighty

Mississippi.

Above Texas, the land below looked as barren from the sky as it did from the car. We were flying over the same territory I had traversed just a year ago, but this time, in the opposite direction, at forty thousand feet.

Kelly Dessaint was born and raised in Los Angeles, where he lives with his wife, the artist Irina Dessaint. Graduate of the welfare system and University of Alabama, he has lived and traveled all over America since he left home at fifteen. A veteran of the small press, he currently publishes the zine *Piltdownlad*.

Read more at kellydessaint.com.

Printed in Great Britain
by Amazon